# In
# HAVOC
# LAYS
# Chaos

3

*memento mori*

## Samantha Barrett

J
memento mori
J

# Author Note

This book contains violence, explicit sexual acts, and language that may offend. Kidnapping and many other triggers such as torture, death and gruesome scenes.
If those are triggers for you then I recommend closing this book and moving on to another amazing read.
But, if you are down with the get down and want to get fucked hard and have your heart shattered and ripped out of your fucking chest then this is the book for you babes.
Welcome to the *Next Generation* of Murdochs that fuck harder and play dirtier than the OG's.

*Lizz,*

*Thank you for taking a chance on this unknown author and helping me with the Murdoch Mafia. Without you, I wouldn't have the OG's, bully series, Beast or the next gen, you my friend are amazing and I cannot thank you enough.*
*I love and appreciate you so much xxx*

# Memento Mori

*(Latin for 'remember that you [have to] die' ) is **an artistic or symbolic trope acting as a reminder of the inevitability of death.***

# Who Are They?

When the card is dropped, you are marked.
There is no escaping *them*, they come for their prey and will hunt
until your blood soaks the ground beneath your cold lifeless body.
They are the new generation and they have something to prove.
They are hungry to show the OG's that they are ready to lead,
except, the chaos is shrouded in darkness. The Jack of Spades is
being scattered as he lays waste to those who stole the Havoc
from him.
*The Ace of Diamonds is no more.*

The King of Clubs belongs to the heir.
The princess owns the Queen of Hearts.
Jack of Spades represents the coming Chaos.
Ace of Diamonds is for the Havoc.

Once marked, the kill is final or punishment will be inflicted.
A loved one can never be marked.
A royal flush is to be unanimous.
The caller is the one to kill.
If one shall fall their card will lay in rest.

# Prologue

## CHAOS

*Have you ever felt so empty inside to the point you wonder how the fuck you are still breathing?*

I wonder that every goddamn fucking day, why did I live and he didn't?

Why did the good twin have to die?

I know those are questions people have been asking themselves, can't blame the fuckers. I think it myself; it should have been me that died, not Havoc. The bottle of Jack dangles between my fingers as I stagger toward Johnny and Ricardo Jr. They both sit there with fear in their eyes, the closer I get, the harder they strain to get free of their restraints.

"Ace, they are just boys." I spin around and launch the bottle of Jack at her. Thanks to my slight buzz I miss and it smashes beside her head. I chained both her arms to the far wall, her eyes spit hatred at me, good, because I feel the same fucking way about her.

"You don't fucking speak, you remain silent. Be seen and not heard, you washed up bitch," I sneer as I tear my gaze from her to stare back at the only two male heirs of the Dominico family. I walk around them, letting the tips of my fingers brush their shoulders. Johnny is the first to whimper in fear, and a second later I smell piss. Coming around the front of them I see the pussy motherfucker pissed his pants. "What a little bitch," I snarl.

Ricardo Jr tries to speak but it comes out a jumbled mess thanks to the cloth shoved in his mouth. I yank the cloth out of their mouths and cross my arms over my chest.

*3...2...1.*

"Do you have any idea who the fuck we are?" There it is, the threats I knew would spew the moment the gags were removed. They think because of who their father is that they are safe, they couldn't have been more fucking wrong.

"I know exactly who the fuck you are." My voice is strong and unwavering. The two little bitches exchange a loaded look before turning back to me. "I am going to give you both a choice, a choice that was never given to me–"

"Who the fuck are you?" Piss pants tries to sound firm but the way his bottom lip trembles, and the way his eyes keep darting to his older brother, gives him away. He's trying hard to put on a show of strength when everyone in this fucking basement knows he is full of shit and is seconds away from pissing himself again.

"I'm the motherfucking Reaper bitch, and you're here to meet your maker. Now, it's time to choose," I snarl.

"Choose what?" Ricardo shouts, the slight waiver in his tone gives away the fear he is trying to mask, I smell it in the air and fuck, it makes me hard watching these motherfuckers try to appear strong and powerful. The truth is, they are nothing but weak little pussies that hide behind their master's name.

"Which one of you dies first?" They both shout and scream while thrashing against their metal chairs to get free. It's no use. The chains that hold them in place will never break, nor will the metal that I dino-bolted to the concrete floor. I allow them to continue spewing threats for another minute before I pull my knife and plunge it into the top of Ricardo Jr's thigh. He throws his head back and screams out in pain. Johnny turns and pales as he darts his wide-eye stare at me, I can see the cogs in his mind turning as the need to survive kicks in.

"Him!" There it is, the moment you face anyone with the prospect of certain death their true colors shine through. That is when true loyalty is tested and above all else, that is the time when true brotherhood comes into play. Ricardo turns pain-filled eyes to his little brother who refuses to meet his gaze, shame coating the latter's features as he drops his chin to his chest and begins to shake with silent tears.

"For the display of weakness you have shown, the Jack of Spades chooses to enact its pound of flesh from you." Johnny's tear stained face snaps up and his mouth opens but I don't wait for his words, I yank the dagger from Ricardo's leg and plunge it directly into his brother's open mouth grinning when I feel the top of the blade pierce the back of his throat.

"You motherfucker!" his brother screams as he fights harder than before to get at me. His brother begins to choke on his own blood, and the sight of him slowly dying has giddiness washing over me. Fuck, this shit gets me hard.

I waste no time in turning to Ricardo, scalping him, taking out his kneecaps, breaking his elbows, then I slowly drag the knife across his throat as I stare into the lens of the camera set up across the room. I don't conceal my face, I want Ricardo Sr to know it's me coming after each member of his family. I'm saving that cunt for last, I want him to watch each of these recordings and feel the pain I feel daily. I want the loss of every person he has ever loved to echo inside him every waking moment as the loss of my brother does to me, every second of every fucking day.

*This is all for Havoc.*

Her quiet sobs have my blissful haze disappearing. I slowly lift my gaze to hers and glare down at the bitch. "They were just boys," she chokes out.

"And you were just an innocent reporter who happened to be

related to the wrong FBI agent and yet here you are. You will be last on my list to kill and believe me, Cassandra, I will make you fucking suffer for the life your brother took from me!"

# Chapter One

## CHAOS

### *Four weeks earlier...*

It's been seven weeks since my world was blown the fuck up!

My jaw clicks as I blow rings out of my mouth, this blunt is hitting the spot!

I needed something to take the edge off after having to deal with Lailani trying to kill me again! I thought taking her with me when I ditched Royal and Sin for some space was a good idea, you know, so I could fuck with her daily and remind her that she is a worthless piece of shit. But, the rabid bitch attempts to shank me every chance she gets, which is why I find myself sitting in my fucking car smoking a blunt while I stare up at Cassandra's apartment.

Her curtains wide open, I can see how her black pencil skirt hugs her tiny frame, the white blouse she wears is untucked and her unruly strawberry-blonde locks are loose. cascading down her back. I drop my gaze to the file in my lap.

*Cassandra Blake.*

Twenty-years old, fresh out of college and working as a reporter. Unlike most reporters who report on the weather and traffic, this bitch reports on crimes. She may appear to be a blue-collar bitch but I found her dirty little secret. She runs a blog that is dedicated to exposing corrupt government officials, police and all the others, but her real talent is exposing the kingpins behind organizations like the ones we run. I've been watching her every single night since we got back to Miami. Tonight is the night I plan to take her and shatter her perfect little world. I watch as her boyfriend comes up behind her and places a kiss on the back of her head.

She doesn't sink into him or even melt from the touch of his hands on her body, she just stands there like a pole waiting for him to leave her be so she can go back to reading those fucking papers. Dylan Cross may look like a GQ model but the fucking punk is crooked. He has a gambling addiction and unbeknownst to his girlfriend, he managed to get the name of a loan shark from her research and he now owes said shark over twenty grand. I take another hit from the blunt and inhale holding the sweet smoke inside me before slowly exhaling it. The knowledge that I am about to hunt my prey is making my cock hard.

It's nearly one in the morning before Cassandra finally shuts off the lights, closes her curtains and heads to bed. I lean over and grab my black gloves from the passenger seat, slip them on, then reach in the glove compartment for my gun, knife and cable ties. Stepping out of my new Lincoln Aviator that is blacked out and on black 22s—I needed a new car after I ditched Royal and Sin, those two mean well but they want in on what I have planned but I'm not down to share, I stand beside my car and stare up at her window. The only person I want with me is my brother. The closest I can get to him is the necklace and ring I wear with his ashes in them.

I pull my hood over the ball cap I wear and bring the brim lower to shield my face as I dart across the street and head around the back of the building. The fire exit is the easiest way to get in but I know the alarm is active, so I go through the staff entrance as the door is held open by a brick–great security, not. I nix the elevators and go through the service stairwell. Once I reach her floor, I pull my phone from my pocket and log into her building's security system and shut off the lights. I know I have roughly six minutes before maintenance fixes the lights, so I dart into the hall and head to the third door on the left.

Picking the lock takes me four seconds, the dumb bitch should get a deadbolt if she wants to keep intruders out. I've studied the layout of her apartment so I know exactly where I'm going. The best part is, the sneaky little witch doesn't sleep with her boyfriend. Her living room is scarce of furniture and her kitchen counters aren't cluttered, there is nothing personal in this apartment that gives you a clue as to who she really is. She has her own room on the other side of the apartment, her door ajar. I slowly nudge it open with my shoulder. She rolls over and I get an eye full of her ass cheeks, in a red thong and a gold tank top shirt thing that girls wear. I snag a sock off the top of her dresser on my way to her, then take two seconds to center myself before I strike. One hand on her throat, the other shoves the sock in her mouth the second she opens it to scream. She thrashes beneath my touch, but it's no use, Dylan is a heavy sleeper so he won't hear shit.

If she were a dude I would have knocked her ass out already, instead, I flip her over onto her stomach and straddle her back, forcing her to bear my weight. The moment I bend down and brush my lips against the shell of her ear she stills.

"The harder you fight, the harder *I* get." Her gasp is so loud it fills the room when I pluck the sock from her mouth.

"What the fuck do you want?" she spits.

"Your misery, your pain, your demise. I want every fucking thing you have to give until there is nothing left of you!" I snarl, then stare down at her and smirk when the idea strikes me out of nowhere. "Lock the doors, batten down the hatches and try to keep me out, Cass, but know this," she tenses at the sound of her name coming from my lips, "I'll get to you every single fucking night. Each night when you close your eyes, I will be here taking a part of you away. But, before I am done fucking with you, I am going to fuck you and you're going to fucking love every minute of it."

"Fuck you, get the fuck out of my house now, if you ever come back I'll call the police." Her voice trembles, giving away the fear she feels. Fuck, I love hearing how scared she is. I wonder how long it would take before you scare someone to death? I suck the shell of her ear into my mouth and bite down, hard. She whimpers but refuses to give me the satisfaction of crying out in pain, I release it and lick it better, loving the shiver of disgust that runs through her perfect little body.

"Call the po-po, Cass, I dare you," I taunt. "The moment you call them is the moment I disclose your true identity to the KP's of all the crime families that you like to write about in that little blog of yours." Before she can answer or form a reply, I cover her mouth and nose with my hand restricting her airways, and her fight or flight instincts kick in. She tries to buck her hips and throw her arms around but it's no use, she is too fucking weak to throw me off. I don't release my hold on her until her movements turn sluggish and the fight starts to drain from her.

I returned to the house I recently purchased under an alias so my cousins wouldn't be able to find me. I know they wish to be there for me and help in any way they can, but right now all I need is to have the blood of my enemies coating my hands. The hunger for their demise burns through me, it's the fuel that gets me out of bed every day. Without this purpose, I have nothing. Heading inside my house I pause in the dark entryway, my senses going into overdrive. A smirk tugs at the corner of my lips when I hear the creak on the floorboards come from my right, *give me all you got* I think to myself as she makes her move. All the years of training with my father come naturally, I don't even have to think, I just act. I grip her wrist to stop her from plunging whatever fucking weapon she has in one hand, I use the other to grip her throat and spin around until she crashes against the wall, a whimper escaping her from the force, but it doesn't deter me.

"Foyer lights on," I call out. The lights flicker to life. Yes, I am that fucker that has voice-controlled lighting throughout my house for situations exactly like this. I look to see her holding a butcher's knife in her hand. I flick my gaze back to her and snarl. "Haven't learned from the last dozen attempts that you won't take me down easily?" I taunt, her eyes begin to mist but I'm long past caring about how this bitch feels, she should have died years ago but it was the love of my brother that kept her breathing.

"Fuck you, Chaos," she seethes.

"I won't sink my cock into that dirty cunt ever again," I snarl.

"I hate you!" I bend until our noses are a sliver apart.

"The feeling is mutual. You are nothing to me, I fucking hate you with fiber of my being. The only reason you are still alive is because I've still yet to determine if you are a lying sack of shit or not!" Her eyes blaze.

"Why the fuck would I lie to you about that?" I growl before ripping the knife from her grasp and releasing her with a hard shove, she grunts but says nothing.

"It's what you do Lailani, you lied to the both of us," I murmur as I turn my back to her, the sight of her disgusts me. She rushes to stand in front of me, my upper lip pulls back in warning which she ignores, brown eyes stare up at me, begging me to see the truth.

"If you thought my claim to Havoc being Ryat's father was a lie, you would have killed me that night instead of shooting the tree beside my head. Hate me all you want, Chaos, but your nephew is innocent!" Heat surges inside me, not the good kind of heat when you know you're about to fuck but the kind that begs for death. I step into her. I give her credit, the bitch doesn't shrink away or cower under the pressure of my gaze or the sheer height difference between us.

"Why the fuck would I believe a thing you say? You're alive because I want you to watch as I murder every single fucking cunt you share DNA with before killing you, nothing else." Her gaze searches mine, for what I have no fucking clue.

"Kill them all, kill *me* but I am begging you Chaos, do not harm my son. I know we have a fucked up past and shit was bad between the three of us, but Ryat had nothing to do with it." She pounds her fists against my chest as tears begin to trek down her cheeks, I weather her hits and relish in her hatred. If she thought me being this disgusting and unworthy of her time a couple years back, I wouldn't be in the position that I'm in now. "You don't deserve him, he is better off not having someone like you in his life! Everything you touch turns rotten—" Grabbing her fists in a punishing hold I glide across the wooden floor until she smacks against the wall, a whimper escapes her but I don't dwell on it.

"You are a fucking disease, if you hadn't come into *his* life he would never have tried to run from me–"

"He didn't want to be like you!" she screams in my face.

"You know nothing!" I roar, she flinches as a sob crawls up her throat, shaking my head, I release her and turn away, stalking toward the stairs that will carry me to the attic where I choose to stay.

"I know that he wanted a different life for the both of you." I pause at her words, I keep my back to her and listen, her words will tear open new wounds but I need it, I need the pain to function. "He never wanted to become what he did. You and I turned him into the cold, heartless killer he became, all because you wanted something that didn't belong to you. If I had known you weren't *him,* I would have killed you that day you slipped between my sheets."

*I hear the truth in her words and I loath to admit it, but, I wish she had killed me, it would hurt less then feeling this constant pain.*

# Chapter Two

**CASSANDRA**

I'm a jittery mess.

Every noise or gust of wind has me tensing and reaching for the baseball bat I have hidden beside the sofa. All day I haven't been able to concentrate on a single fucking thing, my fear is overriding my senses and I can feel it slowly choking me. Dylan decided tonight of all nights would be a great time to go and get sloshed with his buddies. I asked—begged him to stay home with me and all the fucker could say was, *don't be a clinger*!

I spent the whole day cooped up in my bedroom trying to figure out who the fuck was in my room last night. His threats didn't fall on deaf ears, I knew my blog would cause some backlash but I never thought it would expose my identity. I have been *so* careful, I use the computers at the library and never use any personal logins or passwords, I keep nothing at the office or at my apartment, all the intel I have on these low-life scumbags is stored in a safety deposit box. I hear a noise outside my door and tense, when I hear it again I grip the baseball bat and leap to my feet—waiting.

*Come on motherfucker!*

My breaths come in harsh pants, my palms are clammy and my brows are pinched as fear begins to take hold. Don't get me wrong, I live for the thrill of exposing crooked fuckers that think they are above the law. My brother and I may have been estranged but I guess we had something in common, we both want justice to be served. Last night was a first for me, at first I thought it was Dylan wanting to role-play, but when I realized it wasn't him, it didn't stop my greedy pussy from soaking my panties. I may seek justice for those that are wronged at the hands of the evil that lives in the shadows of this city but it gets me fucking wet when I'm restrained and dominated by my fear. Like right now, I'm scared and want to curl into a ball but my body is at war with my brain, my pussy is throbbing and getting off on the fear pulsing inside me.

I stifle a scream when darkness encases the apartment, the hairs on the back of my neck rise. I spin around swinging the bat wildly, my bottom lip beginning to tremble as tears prick the backs of my eyes.

*This can't be happening!*

Just as the thought flees my mind, I'm attacked from behind, a hand clamping over my mouth while another grips my wrist with so much force that I cry out into his hand and drop the bat. I try to thrash and get free of his hold but the moment he drops my wrist and bands his arm around my front to anchor me to him, I freeze. The tears now slowly cascade down my cheeks, my chest rises and falls in rapid succession, and I can feel how big he is behind me. The top of my head doesn't even graze his chin, and his hand covering my mouth is so big it almost covers my entire face. I try to calm myself but it's futile.

"Did you really think a bat would keep me out?" He keeps his hand across my mouth, not allowing me to answer, then glides across the room until I'm pressed against the far wall. I turn my face to the side and try to get a look at him from the corner of my eye but it's useless, it's too dark in here to see a fucking thing! He drops his hand and I suck in lungfuls of air. He places his hands on either side of my head using his body to pin me in place, even if I wanted to move there is no way I would be able to escape him. His entire body shields mine, I have never and I mean never felt this small in my entire life. I close my eyes and send up a silent prayer that I'll wake up from this horrible dream. He runs his nose up the side of my neck and inhales greedily. When a small groan escapes him, a whimper leaves me without consent. "You dirty bitch," he purrs.

"Don't call me that!" I bite back.

"You like this, don't you?" I shake my head no as best as I can given my current position, denying his claim.

"If I had to take a guess, I'd say that this shit gets you off." My breath stutters as he calls me on my darker side. "You like the fear, it turns you the fuck on not knowing who I am." I try to shove away from the wall but his midsection pins me back, he presses against me and I gasp when I feel the hard outline of his cock pressed against my back. He leans down scraping his lips against the shell of my ear sending a shiver down my spine. I'm ashamed to admit that the shiver isn't from fear. "Your fear gets me hard, I haven't been this hard since I stole something that didn't belong to me." I hear the regret in his tone and that has me confused as hell, what the hell did he steal? Before I ponder that thought any longer, his hand comes up to cover my mouth and then wraps the other around my throat. I fight with everything I have but it's no use, he's too strong. Besides him and I both know that he could kill me if he wanted to, but something tells me that isn't what he wants. That's the last thought I have before everything goes black and I pass out from lack of oxygen.

I bolt upright and gasp, darting my gaze around trying to center myself. I look around my dimly lit room and slowly start to relax as my breathing evens out, then frown when memories of the night before assault me. He knocked me out but didn't leave me on the floor. He brought me into my bedroom and placed me on my bed and even closed my blinds. I run a hand through my tangled hair and cringe, I must look like death warmed over. I grab my phone off the side table and cringe, I'm gonna be late for work if I don't haul ass.

I rush through my shower and change quickly only applying a light layer of makeup before rushing out of the apartment and grabbing the first available cab. Thanks to the morning traffic, I arrive at the office fifteen minutes late. I look around for my boss and sigh in relief when I don't see him, I make quick work of stowing my bag in my bottom drawer and powering up my computer, I should be out in the field covering the recent death of the governor but the truth is, my mind is to occupied with thoughts of my... what the fuck would he be, my stalker? My panty destroyer? My secret?

I push all thoughts from my mind when Alex saunters in. The office is bustling with reporters making calls, typing, or interns rushing around obeying orders like good little lambs. Normally I can tune them all out but I've never been able to do that with Alex, the guy rubs me the wrong way but it's not like I can say much when he's my fucking boss! He stops in front of my desk and raps his knuckles against it. I grit my teeth and slowly lift my gaze to meet his stare. His eyes are the color of baby shit, and the suggestive look in them sends dread pooling inside me. Alex has made numerous passes at me and the fact I have a boyfriend doesn't even deter him, if anything I think he views it as a challenge.

"How are you doing this morning, sweetheart?" he asks.

*Oh, just fucking peachy, I've had a guy break into my apartment two nights in a row and destroy my panties.*

I say none of that. "Good, thanks. Got a lot of work to get to so better get back to it." I try to brush him off but he doesn't take the hint like normal people would. Instead, he perches on the edge of my desk. I can feel Tabby glaring holes into the side of my head. Tabby not only works alongside me but she is my best friend and knows that Alex gives me the creeps.

"We've been invited to a prestigious event and I want you to come with me." I cringe and try to mask it as I type in my password for my emails. "I know you missed out on the last gala but I want to rectify that and bring you along as my plus one for this event." I spy Tabby out of the corner of my eye shaking her head, she knows damn well that he is only offering me this because it's his way of being able to spend time alone with me since I always refuse to *work late*, which is code for he wants to fuck me.

I take a deep breath and steel my spine as I look up at my boss and prepare to let him down as gently as I can. "Alex, I would love to but–"

"I heard Royal Murdoch will be there along with his cousins, Chanel and Chaos." *Motherfucker*.

He knows he has me, ever since I started reporting I have always covered the Murdoch family. They may be based in New York but their reach is wide. I may not have been able to prove it yet but I know they are the ones running shit all around the country. We heard whispers that Royal, Chaos, Chanel and even Havoc Murdoch were all in Miami but no one knows exactly who they are because they erase every image of themselves and so they can hide in plain sight. For all we know, they could be in this office and none of us would be the wiser.

Alex may not know about my side blog or the fact I use the intel I gather from reporting to run it, but his infatuation with me has allowed me free reign to report on whatever I want, which of course is the gangs in the US. My brother was making headway in his case that he was building against these corrupt sons of bitches but he was killed. He and I may not have been close but that doesn't change the fact that he was my brother and that loss still stings like a bitch. I guess Chaos Murdoch and I might just have something in common seeing as he lost his twin the same day my brother was murdered.

I have no solid proof that the Murdoch's were involved. But, news of a new family that has taken up residents in Miami and leaves calling cards behind is my key suspect. A card was left on my brother's body, giving me the niggling suspicion that the baby Murdoch's are the ones behind these cards, there is no way Havoc and Quintin dying that same day is a coincidence. I just need to keep digging and when I find the proof I need, I'm going to bring these bastards down and get justice for my brother's death. Which is why I smile up at my boss and flutter my lashes. "How could I say no to that offer?" Alex's eyes spark with joy while Tabby groans from her desk beside mine.

"Perfect, the event is in three weeks, get yourself a dress and bill me for it," he says as he saunters back to his office with a swagger that has me fighting back a gag.

"You nasty bitch." I spin toward Tabby and frown, seeing my best friend pinning me with a scathing look.

"What?" I snap.

"He is going to expect to be paid in full for that dress and taking you as his date. Need I remind you that you have a man at home?" The reminder of Dylan has guilt gnawing inside me. Don't get me wrong, he is a good guy, but over the past couple months he and I have drifted so far apart I don't see us coming back together. He would rather go hang out with his friends than stay home and fuck me senseless. What type of guy passes up the opportunity to fuck his girl six ways to Sunday?

"I'm not spreading my legs for Alex. He can buy me whatever he likes but this is just work, Tabby." Her brows raise, mocking me without words.

"Right, well, I hope Dylan likes sharing because you, my dense friend, are going to have to put out or you're going to lose your job in three weeks' time." She ends the conversation by answering her phone when it rings. I slouch back in my chair and groan. I know she is right but this is the first time I will be able to get close enough to the baby Murdochs. This may be my only chance to put names to faces. Since they have arrived in the state, our governor has gone missing, my brother dies and then an FBI agent has managed to make it to the top of the most wanted list and has disappeared off the face of the planet.

On top of trying to crack this case, I know I have to deal with a crazy bastard breaking into my apartment every night. For some reason his threat of going to the police doesn't seem idle. I believe him when he says he will hurt me if I do that. A huge part of me wants to confide in Tabby about this but I also know that my best friend would lose her mind and move her ass into my apartment and put herself in harm's way to make sure I'm safe. I can't do that to her.

I get so lost in my research of the Murdoch children and trying to find out any information I can about the FBI agent, Kacey Vaughn, that I jump in my seat when Tabby shouts my name. I place my hand over my heart as I swivel around to glare at her, the smirk on her face has my eyes narrowing.

"What the hell, Tabby?" I snap.

"I called your name like three times, you didn't answer so I had to resort to drastic measures." When I bare my teeth, she throws her head back and laughs. She's such a bitch.

"What do you need?" I cut in, breaking off her laughter.

"It's an hour past knock off." I frown and check the time on my watch. Shit, she's right. It's after six and I didn't even realize. Tabby and I shut down our computers and chat about nothing as we do it. We say our goodbyes when Tabby snags the first cab and heads home while I hop into mine and head back home feeling utterly spent. I lean my head back and close my eyes trying to relax but that reality is shattered when my phone begins to ring in my purse. Sighing I pull it out and answer without checking the caller ID.

"Yello?"

"Cass, where are you?" The panic in Dylan's voice has me sitting up straighter.

"Dylan, what's wrong?"

"Cass, I need you to stay away from the apartment tonight."
A sick feeling washes over me.

"Why? Dylan, what the hell is going on?" I seethe.

"Just stay the hell away for the night, okay? It isn't safe here."

"What the hell do you mean it isn't safe?" I push.

"I'll explain everything tomorrow, just... Please, Cass, don't come home tonight. I promise I will explain everything tomorrow." He ends the call. I try to call him back immediately but he sends all my calls to voicemail. The rational side of my brain knows I should heed his warning, Dylan has never done anything like this before so I should do as I'm told. But, the reporter in me wants to get to the bottom of this and uncover the truth, which is why I don't tell the cab driver to change direction and keep heading home to get to the bottom of whatever the fuck is going on with Dylan.

# Chapter Three

## CHAOS

I've been parked across from her apartment for the past hour watching, the sun has set and darkness is creeping in, blanketing this fucked up world in black, the color that matches my insides. I watch as her and her sorry ass excuse of a boyfriend fight right in front of the windows. I can see how angry she is from the way she is throwing her arms around as she screams at him. I intercepted one of his messages today, he's late on his payment and they plan on coming to collect tonight. I give the pussy credit, he tried to do the right thing and warn the bitch to stay away but she ignored his warning and has unknowingly put herself in harm's way, which fucks with my plans.

I am the only one who gets to fuck with Cassandra Blake, which means I am going to have to get my hands dirty and switch up my plans for her. My phone vibrating in the console steals my attention. I debate sending Sin to voicemail again but I know the stubborn shit that she is, she will just keep calling now that she managed to get my new number. I'm still unsure how the fuck she managed to get it.

"Yeah?" I say in lieu of greeting.

"Where are you?" I grit my teeth and white knuckle the steering wheel of my car.

"Out."

"Chaos—" I cut her off before she can start her spiel. I'm tired of hearing her and Royal's shit. I know they just want to be there for me but I can't be around them and see the pity in their eyes. I know they loved my brother as much as me but I can't deal with their pain on top of my own, which is why I took off.

"I don't want to hear it, Sin. Unless this is Memento Mori business, I'm not having this conversation with you," I say in a tone that leaves no room for argument.

She sighs, I can picture her scrunching her eyes shut and trying to remain calm. "Fine, in three weeks' time we will have an event to attend–"

"I'm not going," I cut in but she ignores me and carries on.

"The Dominico family will be there." That grabs my attention, those bastards have gone underground since I started taking out their high ranking members daily and sending their bodies back to Ricardo with my card nailed to the foreheads of their dismembered bodies. No matter how many lives I take, it doesn't quiet down the beast inside me that hungers for the blood of Ricardo and all his children's blood to soak my hands. I'm saving Lailani and Cassandra for last.

"How do you know?" I force out.

"They are the ones hosting the prestigious event. Ricardo's company hosts it yearly and he has no choice but to come out of hiding. He and his sons will be there." A dark smile tugs at the corners of my lips, warmth surging inside me, as I allow myself to feel the excitement of finally being able to kill those cunts.

"I'll be there." I'm about to end the call but her words give me pause.

"Your mom and dad are flying in for the event, the whole family is actually." I tense. I haven't spoken to my parents since I returned to Miami, I can't. I know they blame me for my brother's death, they may not say it outright but I know they do and honestly, I can't blame them. I failed Havoc in life and I fucking refuse to fail him in death. I will avenge my brother even if it's the last thing I do. I grip the necklace that hangs around my neck with some of his ashes in it and close my eyes.

"I'll deal with it," I rasp out.

"Chaos?" I take a shuddering breath.

"Yeah?"

"Royal heard from one of our informants that Ricardo plans to bring his grandson to the event." Anger surges inside me, I sit up straight and glare at my phone.

"What?" I roar.

"Royal and I think that Ricardo is using Ryat as bait to lure Lailani out."

"Why the fuck would he do that?" I snarl.

"We have a hunch that Ricardo thinks Lailani ran to us for help after losing... after... Havoc went away."

"Say what the fuck it is that you aren't saying, Chanel." I know her and I know she is holding shit back from me.

"Royal seems to think that Ricardo suspects that Ryat is yours or Havoc's son and is going to use the boy to get to us." Anger like I haven't felt since the day I lost my soulmate fills me. I have tried to push the idea of Havoc having a son out of my mind and doing whatever I can to never think about it, but now it seems I have no choice. If there is a chance that this child is my brother's, then I will do whatever the fuck I have to do to protect him.

"I'll be by tomorrow to meet with you and Royal to go over a plan. No one is to touch that fucking boy until I know for sure if he is my brother's son or not," I say before I end the call. I try to calm myself but nothing works. I need to maim, hurt or kill some fucker! My silent plea is answered when two blacked out sedans pull up out front of her building. Anticipation thrums through me as I wait to see who steps out, then I spot Tana Lawson and smirk. I've heard about this prick. He loans money to anyone and makes sure that the interest is so high that no one is able to meet the repayment dates, which is why Dylan is now in this predicament. I wait for Tana and four of his guys to head inside before I place my ball cap on and pull my hood over my head before exiting the car and heading around the back. I give them time to ride the elevator up and get inside.

I wait ten minutes giving them enough time to rough Dylan up a bit before I cut the power, then move with ease through the stairwell, not making a sound. I reach the landing of her floor and pause when I hear voices discussing which one is going to check the breaker while the other goes back to help Tana. The stairwell door opens. I flatten myself against the wall and wait for him to close the door. The moment he does, I dart forward, pull my knife out and slit his throat. The fucker never saw it coming. I step over him and dart into the hall.

I sheath my knife once I reach her door and pull both of my Kimber 1911's out that, already have the silencers attached, and quietly push her door open and drop as I round the corner to the kitchen. I peak around the corner of the counter to see Tana standing in front of both Cass and Dylan, two guards stand behind them, the other fucker must still be out in the hall somewhere.

"You either pay me what I am owed or I'll have no other choice but to take other measures." The menace in Tana's tone makes me want to laugh, the asshole sounds like a nasally Eddie Murphy.

"I just need a couple more days, then—"

Tana cuts off Dylan's rambling. "I have given you more than enough time. You either pay me now or... I'll have my men take turns on your pretty friend here to recoup some costs." I don't wait to hear more as his words have something inside me thirsting for the need to break shit at the thought of these cunts touching my new toy. I fire one shot, the bullet goes through the first guards head only to travel through the next one's skull with ease. Tana raises his gun and shoots blindly in my direction. I pivot around and leap to the other side of the counter, slide along the tiled floor, and the second I pop out the other end, I fire two shots. Tana goes down like the sack of shit he is. Before I can take a breath, the door flies open. I roll over and fire another three shots, taking out the final guard as the door closes behind him.

The lights flicker on, I dart toward the body of the fallen guard and smear my hands through his blood and wipe it over my face and neck. I expected to be out of here before the lights came back on but it appears this cunt managed to get them back on quicker than I thought. The sound of whimpers hit my ears. I stand and slowly turn to face them expecting to find Dylan with his arms wrapped around his girlfriend as she cries in fear, but that isn't the sight that greets me. Cass has her arms wrapped around a bloodied Dylan as he sobs and mutters incoherent apologies. I pull my cap lower and watch as she sighs in annoyance, her gaze flicking toward me and I expect her to begin to tremble and offer me money or some shit if I just leave.

Instead, her eyes harden and her lips form a thin line as her brows draw in. "Fancy seeing you in the light," she grits out, the snark in her tone pisses me off. I stalk toward them and pause a foot away with my gun pointed at her. She doesn't cower, just stiffens and waits for me to pull the trigger.

*Death doesn't scare her.*

I turn the gun on her boyfriend and that's when she snaps. She releases him and leaps to her feet, using her body to shield him. Panic flares to life in her green eyes, her hair is a mess from where those cunts grabbed her and no doubt shoved her to her knees. Her blouse is torn, showing off her pink lace bra. The sight of a red handprint on her cheek has me gripping my gun tighter and my teeth clenching to the point my jaw aches.

"I'll remove whatever article I wrote, I'll say I lied." I frown and cock my head to the side confused. "He knows nothing about what I do, it's me you want, not him!"

"W-we c-can pay," the pussy sobs out as he wraps his arms around her legs and clings to her like she is a lifeline. The sight disgusts me. He calls himself a man and yet he hides behind his female like a dog.

"Just let him go and I swear I will retract what I wrote, you don't need to hurt *him*." Her bartering for his safety and not her own just serves to anger me further.

"You think they were here for *you*?" I grit out. Her brows bunch as she nibbles her bottom lip. The fact she isn't trembling in fear with the four bodies littering her floor says a lot about her character.

"Uh, yes?" I scoff, then point my gun toward the sorry ass excuse she is protecting. He whimpers and ducks behind her legs like a pathetic piece of shit.

"They were here for him." Her eyes widened at my declaration.

"What?" She yanks free of his vice-like grip on her legs and turns her back to *me* as she stares down at him. Stupid move on her part not keeping the real danger in her sights. "What the fuck is he talking about, Dylan?" She doesn't give him a chance to answer. "You told me that people were coming here tonight because of an article I wrote." I clench my teeth, trying to temper the urge to shoot the cunt for putting his fuck up on her.

He stares up at her with tears rolling down his cheeks, snot is dripping from his nose into his mouth. "I... I don't know what the fuck he is saying, baby. He just killed all these people. How could you think I would lie to you?" Fuck this. I shoot the cunt in the shin and relish in the scream that tears out of him. Cassandra whirls around to face me as she blocks her screaming bitch of a boyfriend from my sight again.

"Don't hurt him!" she shouts. I shift my gun to her, she tries to hide her fear but fails, her body tenses as it senses the danger she is in. "Please."

"Get rid of the trash, Cass," I grit out before turning on my heel and heading toward the exit. I step over the body blocking the door and grip the handle only to pause when she speaks.

"You said not to go to the police."

"Yeah?" I answer without looking back.

"What do I do about... them?" I growl low in my throat.

"A clean-up crew will be here within the hour, do not speak to them or get in their way," I snarl as I leave, not leaving my card behind as I don't want Cassandra to know who I am. I have a feeling she has been digging into the Memento Mori, my card would confirm her suspicion. I pull my phone out of my pocket and dial Marco as I dash into the stairwell and sneak out the back. He answers on the fifth ring.

"Chaos?"

"I have a clean-up. One in the stairwell, four in the apartment, two occupants are breathing. Clean it and leave. I'll send you the location. Do not speak to her." I warn.

"I'll have a crew on standby as we wait for the location." I end the call and text him the address when I make it back to my car. I gun the engine and floor it the whole way home, needing to get the fuck off the streets and get this blood off me.

The second I step through the front door, I'm on high alert waiting for Lailani to make her move. I'm too fucking tired to deal with her shit tonight. The idiot would have a better chance of catching me off guard if she didn't have all the lights in the house turned off and attacked me every time in the entry way, I mean for fuck's sake, at least switch shit up. It takes her three seconds tops to pounce on me when I round the corner heading for the stairs, this time the bitch does manage to get a hit in. Instead of a knife, she has a six-by-four and manages to land a hit to my side, drawing a groan of pain from me.

When she draws the timber back to go for a second hit, I charge her ass and tackle her to the ground, wrestling the fucking thing from her grasp. She fights with everything she has, screaming threats and promising me pain. I toss the wood to the side as I straddle her and pin her arms to her sides.

"Foyer lights on!" I call out and within a second we're bathed in light.

"You son of–" She cuts herself off, her jaw unhinging at the sight of me.

"You fucking done?" I snarl, the bitch got me good. I'll make sure to stay on my game from now on and not allow her to get the jump on me again.

Her eyes burn with hatred. "I wish I never met you," she mutters as I shove off her. She sits up and wraps her arms around her legs, resting her chin on her knees as tears slowly trek down her cheeks.

*Jesus Christ, why does everyone keep crying?*

"The feeling is mutual. If you were never born, my brother would still be breathing instead of you." A shudder rolls through her, I'm surprised when she screws her eyes closed and nods somberly.

"I would give anything to take back what happened to him." I clench my hands into fists at my sides as I scowl down at her.

"Well, you can't!" I scream down at her, and she flinches but doesn't comment for a minute. I take the time to try and compose myself. If my plan is to work, I need her to be on the same page as me and not fuck me over.

"You didn't even let me say goodbye to him." I tense and spin away from her, giving her my back. I slam my eyes closed and force the pain of his loss down so it doesn't cripple me. "He hated me because of you," she accuses.

"No, he hated you because I showed him that every bitch is a liar. You tried to take him away from me and I stopped you," I throw back at her as I rest back against the wall and fall to my ass, bringing one of my arms up to rest atop my knee as I rest my head back against the wall, feeling drained.

"Lie to yourself all you want, Chaos, but you tricked me into sleeping with you because your fear of being alone without your twin scared the shit out of you." I grind my teeth.

"You don't know shit," I force out through clenched teeth.

"He was happy with me. He knew I was the daughter of his enemy and he didn't care because he loved me, and loved who he got to be when he was around me."

"Shut the fuck up," I snarl, hating that she is voicing all my guilt and bringing to life the truth that I have tried to keep buried.

"Fuck you, I loved him!" she screams. "Havoc was my person and I was his. You ruined us because you were jealous of the fact he could be happy without you. You're just a sad little boy who wanted to make sure that he broke his own brother enough to keep him by your side."

"Fuck you!" I roar as I pull my gun and point it at her. She doesn't recoil in fear. Her eyes dare me to do it, which just pisses me off further.

"No. Everyone thought he couldn't function without you, but you and I both know that isn't the truth. He was thriving without you but you made sure you ruined him enough that everyone's thoughts about him not being able to be without you came to life. *You* destroyed your brother, not me."

# Chapter Four

## CASSANDRA

I wanted to call in sick to work but I was too scared in case *he* was watching me, as I didn't want to give him a reason to think that I was planning something against him and risk him coming back. Last night he kept his word, men turned up in cleaning uniforms, disposed of the bodies and you guessed it, another power outage happened as they transported the bodies out of my apartment. I stayed in my room and left the men to work, I may report on this type of shit but seeing it is a whole new level. I barely slept a wink. Dylan tried to talk to me after the clean-up crew left but I ignored him. I told him to pack his shit and get the fuck out, he lied to me and made me believe that my job was the reason that men were coming to our home to hurt him!

That little bastard had the nerve to ask me for money as he left this morning, I can't believe I never saw what a useless piece of shit he was sooner, I literally stood between him and a gun because I thought what happened was my fault! Anger begins to brew inside me again as I stomp toward my desk ignoring the hustle and bustle of the office, I couldn't give a damn what I looked like today and judging from the wide-eyed look on Tabby's face I must look like utter shit.

"Uh, do I even want to ask what happened to you?" she says as I drop into my seat with a dramatic flair. I lull my head to the side to stare at her, she scrunches her face in disgust, trust Tabby to keep me humble at a time like this. I open my mouth to answer her but clamp it closed when Alex makes his way toward me with a grim expression.

"Sweetheart, what are you doing here?" I frown and dart a quick look at Tabby who looks just as confused.

"Uh, it's a Thursday and I have work?" I hedge. His eyes hold a pitiful look but I can also see a hint of glee in his shit-colored eyes.

"Sweetheart." I fight the cringe from breaking free at his pet name for me, I'm way too exhausted to deal with Alex's shit today. "You should be at home grieving." I scrunch my face, Quintin died weeks ago and now he's finally offering me time off?

"Alex—" I try but he cuts me off.

"Take the rest of the week and next week off to make the funeral arrangements." I reel back in my chair.

"Funeral arrangements?" I am utterly confused.

"I'm so sorry for the loss of Dylan if there—" I dart forward and grip the edge of my desk.

"Dylan isn't dead, we just broke up." I ignore the gasp from Tabby. As I stare at our boss, he cocks his head to the side.

"You don't know?" he murmurs.

"Know what?" I snap, my patience gone.

"There was a car accident, Beth saw the whole thing on her way in this morning and reported on the incident..." The rest of his words fall on deaf ears as denial thrums through me. I just saw Dylan this morning. There is no way he could be dead, I just spoke to him hours ago when I kicked his lying ass out. My mind is reeling, my vision blurs as tears begin to cloud my sight, I feel hands on me but I can't hear what they are saying.

*Dylan is dead.*

I gasp when water splashes me in my face and soaks my shirt. I splutter and shake my head to clear the fog. Tabby is kneeling in front of me with and empty glass in her hand, Alex stands behind her with a blank look on his face.

"Cass, take a deep breath for me, babe." I do as Tabby instructs, by now we have gathered a crowd and I shrink back dropping my gaze to my lap. My best friend looks around and groans. "All of you piss off. Don't you have work to do?" she scolds the crowd, they all begin to disperse begrudgingly. "Cass?" I lift my gaze to Tabby's and sigh.

"I... Tabby," I choke out as the first tear escapes. She wastes no time hauling me to my feet, snagging both our bags and telling Alex she is taking the rest of the day with me. He doesn't argue, instead he just says to call him if I need anything. That will never happen. The entire way back to my apartment I say nothing, too lost in my own thoughts.

*How the fuck did this happen?*

*Was this my fault?*

Tabby uses the key I gave her to let us into my apartment, the sight of the living room has me stilling as memories of the previous night assault me. I begin to tremble. Tabby turns to face me and whatever she sees on my face has her rushing forward and wrapping her arms around me. I don't realize I'm crying until she pulls back and brushes the tears from my cheeks.

"Come on," she says as she grabs my hand and leads me toward my bedroom. She takes us into the bathroom and releases my hand as she begins to fill the tub, pouring some of my scented oils in. She helps me undress and offers me a hand as I get in the tub bringing my knees to my chest, wrapping my arms around them and resting my cheek on top of them. Silence ensues for a long time as I sit in the tub while my best friend sits beside me on the tiled floor scrolling through her phone. The sound of my phone ringing from the other room has Tabby climbing to her feet and dashing off to answer it. A couple minutes later she returns with my phone in her hand

and a somber look on her face. "Dylan's mother is on the phone."

Guilt gnaws at me as I tentatively hold my hand out for her to pass me my phone, smiling encouragingly as I bring the phone to my ear. I've met Dylan's parents a handful of times but it's not like they were close or around much so this conversation is no doubt going to be awkward.

"Hello?" I say.

"Cassandra?"

"Hi, Mrs. Cross." I hear her sniffle on the other end of the line, my eyes slam close as I try to reign in my own emotions.

"I'm sorry, dear. Calvin and I just got the call about... about... our baby." Her sobs come through the phone making me feel like utter trash. If I hadn't kicked Dylan out this morning, he might still be here with us. Guilt is an evil bitch, she has a funny way of making you feel like every bad thing that has ever happened is your fault. It takes her a few minutes to get herself under control, then tells me that her and Dylan's dad are getting on the next plane from Colorado and will be here as soon as they can to handle all the arrangements. They plan to return Dylan's body back to their family plot in Colorado. I don't argue or make a fuss, it's not like I would know where he would want to be buried or what his final wishes were. We were together for two years and it sounds like a long time but the truth is, we only lasted that long because it was convenient. When I end the call, Tabby takes the phone back and places it on the counter before reclaiming her seat on the floor.

"Talk to me, Cass," she whispers softly. A whoosh of air escapes me.

"I don't know what to say, Tab," I answer honestly.

"How about you start with why you and Dylan broke up? I know shit was rocky with you two but I didn't think he would break up with you."

"He didn't break up with me, *I* broke up with him." Her brows raise in surprise.

"Wow, I didn't see that coming." I shrug my shoulders in answer. "What happened, Cass?" The moment I open my mouth, nothing but lies come out. I tell her that Dylan and I were fighting a lot lately. I wanted to snort because in order to fight the two of us had to have a conversation and those were few and far between these days. I mean for fuck's sake, we were sleeping in separate bedrooms, if that doesn't tell you that we needed to break up than I don't know what does.

Tabby and I sit on the sofa watching reruns of *Gilmore Girls*. She ordered us takeout but I can't eat. She has been trying to comfort me as best she can but gave up an hour ago when I snapped at her that I was fine. I know I'm being a bitch but I just need her to stop pushing for a minute and let me deal with this news. I'm wrung out and exhausted from worrying to care about food, instead I let my mind get lost in the TV show until sleep claims me. I welcome it, needing an escape from my errant thoughts and the guilt that has been eating away at me since the news of Dylan's passing.

The feeling of being jostled rouses me from my sleep, I lazily blink my eyes open and stifle a gasp when I realize that my... watcher has me in his arms and is carrying me to my bedroom. I peer around his arm and sigh in relief when I see Tabby is fast asleep on the couch. He places me on my bed and takes a step back. I may not be able to see his face but I can feel his gaze on me.

"I didn't kill him." His words give me pause, I won't lie, the thought crossed my mind.

"Could you blame me for thinking it? I mean you did shoot his leg last night."

"It was a flesh wound, the pussy would have lived." I purse my lips.

"That's beside the point, they will do an autopsy and when

they see the bullet wound questions will be asked. How am I supposed to answer them?"

He doesn't miss a beat. "The coroner has been paid off and so has the funeral home, no questions will be asked."

"Oh." Is all I can muster to say, something about my watcher has my thirst for information climbing to new heights.

*Who is he?*

*What does he want?*

*How did he find me?*

"You have tonight to recover. Tomorrow I'll be back and I expect your friend to be gone. If she isn't—" I don't let him finish.

"Don't hurt her!" I snarl.

"Don't fucking tell me what to do. You are a conquest that I plan to end soon."

"If that was true, why the hell would you carry me to my bed?" I volley back.

"To make sure you stay in view of the camera." My mouth drops open in horror, he has cameras in my house? "Make no mistake, Cassandra, I'm not your friend and will never be. You are going to pay for the crimes of those that wronged my family." He leaves me mulling over his cryptic words as he stalks out of my apartment. It's starting to piss me off not being able to see his face but I won't lie, the mystery surrounding him is appealing. I facepalm myself. What the fuck is wrong with me? My boyfriend —ex boyfriend just died and here I am fantasizing about my watcher!

I make a vow to myself, I'll use the time I have off work to dig deeper and find out who the fuck this guy is. With the skill and precision he used last night to take the lives of the men after Dylan, that means there is no way he is just some random thug. He's trained, skilled and resourceful–clearly since he manages to cut the power every time he comes over. I plan to use every source I have and turn over every stone until I figure out who the hell he is. I can tell this is going to become my obsession.

# Chapter Five

## CHAOS

After leaving Cassandra, I headed to Royal's house. I was supposed to be here today but the dipshits death put a wrench in my plans. I lied to her, I may have cut his brakes but in my defense I didn't expect the fucker to die. I'm not mad about it and it's not like she was distraught or anything over his death, the bitch should be thanking me. I stare at the front door as it opens to reveal Royal. I sigh knowing I can't sit out here in my car all night. This house... it reminds me of *him* and what we were starting—we were finally starting something of our own with our cousins and then that dream was ripped away from us.

No, that's a lie. Havoc was starting something for himself while I ran back to UNLV to try to go pro and live a different life. Unlike my twin, I didn't relish the thought of taking a life, I never did any of the killing that was all Havoc. He said I needed to keep my hands clean so he would handle it. It's not that I wasn't capable of doing it, I just didn't want to.

"Fuck," I growl as I scrub a hand down my face then get out

of the car. I stare at Royal over the hood of my car for a minute before I finally muster the strength to head toward him. The moment he steps aside and lets me past, pain blasts me as memories of the night we brought *him* back crash into me. My mom screaming and crying out for her son, her not being able to look at me without seeing Havoc. Royal places a hand on my shoulder pulling me out of my downward spiral, then shoots me a knowing look as if he can tell where my thoughts had strayed.

"It's just a house, Chaos. If it helps, we can burn it down and start again." The fact he is willing to destroy the home his grandfather left him means more than he will ever fucking know. Royal loved his grandfather more than anything, so I know it would kill him to keep his promise, which is why I shake my head and make my way toward his office. I'm not surprised to find Sin, Kacey and Erika all in there waiting. Erika rushes toward me and wraps me in a hug. I stand here stiff and shoot Royal a look that says *what the fuck?* He just shrugs his shoulders and claims his seat behind his desk. When Erika doesn't let go I decide to placate her and return her embrace, she melts into me and I stiffen further.

"I'm not him, Rika," I grit out. She sniffles and pulls back staring up at me with glassy eyes.

"I know you're not, Chaos." My brows pinch. Her and I have never been particularly close but I know her and Havoc were tight, which is why it's hard to be around her as well as my cousins. Every time they look at me, I know they see my brother—it's fucking hard not to considering we're identical twins. "Just know that we are here for *you*, not because we want you around because you remind us of Hav, but because we love *you*." Fuck, I'll admit her words have me stunned.

Kacey shoots me an understanding look as Rika leaves me and claims a seat on Royal's lap. Chanel is an emotionless bitch so I'm not surprised when she glares at Kacey for giving her a gentle shove.

"We're here if you need us," she says, then shoots her man a look that promises pain. I fight the smirk from breaking free, Sin is a bad bitch there is no denying that. She is the only woman aside from my mom and aunts that I trust. Chanel is loyal as fuck.

"Want to fill us in on why you wanted this meeting?" Royal asks as he wraps his arms around Rika's waist and draws her back into him. I run a hand through my hair and sigh. I know this is just as awkward for them as it is for me. A few weeks ago, I took off, bought a house and took Lailani with me without saying a word.

"This gala that's coming up, I have a plan and I wouldn't ask if I didn't need the help—"

Chanel cuts me off. "You never have to ask, you know we are always here for you and will have your back no matter what." I nod my thanks but don't comment on what she has said.

"I have a plan," I state firmly.

"Care to fill us in on this plan?" Royal pushes.

Taking a deep breath, I steel my spine and hold his gaze. "I plan to use Lani's marriage to Halil as a foothold into the Albanian's inner circle and rule those fuckers through her. They will help us surround the venue and make sure we get Ryat out of there unscathed." The four of them stare at me like I have lost my fucking mind and hey, they may just be right but this is a solid fucking plan.

"You must have bumped your fucking head because there is no way I heard that shit right," Sin snarls. I face her so she can see the seriousness in my features.

"This is a solid plan," I grit out.

"How the fuck are you going to get the Albanians to agree to be led by a woman?" Sin pins Kacey with a look, so he quickly explains himself better before she rips his balls off. "Baby, the Albanians are old school and don't see women as equals, so I find it hard to believe that they will follow Lailani Dominico."

"Kacey's right, this plan won't work," Royal tacks on.

"It will. The Albanians will fight it at first, until I explain to them that Lani is only leading until her son is of age to take over." Again, the four of them stare at me like I am some foreign creature.

"Come again?" Rika chokes out.

"By marriage, Ryat is technically Halil's... son." Saying that shit hurts more than I care to admit. "Which means that Lani is within their laws to lead until her son is of age. From the intel we gathered on Halil, he has no other heirs which means that Ryat is it and those cunts have no choice but to honor their own laws."

"Okay, say this plan of yours works. What the fuck happens with Ricardo? We can't just walk in there and kidnap his grandson in front of hundreds of people." I smile evilly at Royal.

"*We* won't be doing shit where the boy is concerned. Lailani will do as she is told so she can be reunited with her son." Erika gasps.

"You're using her son to force her into line?" The outrage in her tone is clear but I don't have time to deal with her conscience.

"I'll do whatever the fuck I have to in order to get my hands on those fucking bastards!" I snarl. Rika's eyes widen at my tone. Royal shoots me a scathing look but says nothing. Chanel nods her head, agreeing with me—that girl doesn't have a single maternal bone in her body.

"Chaos, if this shit is going to work we need to plan it out thoroughly now because the event is in three weeks. I don't think that is enough time to get the Albanians into line," Kacey says. I ignore him as I look at both my cousins.

"I need the help of the Memento Mori. I need you both with me when I meet with the Albanians. If they see our faces then it shows them that we aren't hiding, we are ready to end them, if need be, we proved it that... day." Royal and Chanel both drop their gazes at the mention of that day, none of us want to think about it. The sound of the door opening has me spinning around, a sleepy-eyed London stands there. The moment she registers who is standing in front of her, she pales and her eyes widen. My breaths come in short rapid pants, my palms turning clammy at the sight of the child my brother died protecting.

"Uncle Chaos," she breathes out, the sound of her voice has me closing my eyes and trying to block the images that flash through my mind like a movie. Havoc jumped in front of her to save her. He loved London, there was no doubt about it but the sight of this child has hatred exploding inside me. I open my mouth to curse her but she beats me to speaking. "I screwed up, I never should have snuck into the car but I got scared that Uncle Havoc wouldn't come back. I came to try and protect him but I ruined everything!" she screams, tears leaking from her eyes like a broken faucet. I have never seen London cry and judging from the gasps and tense silence behind me, none of the others have seen the little monster cry either. "I killed him and I am so so so sorry," she chokes out before she turns and runs from the room, the sounds of her broken sobs trailing after her. Erika is quick to chase after her, calling her name, but London doesn't stop, she keeps running.

"She knows you blame her." At the sound of Royal's voice, I turn to face him. He stands behind his desk, leaving me with a warning look.

I pin him with a look of my own as I answer. "She is the reason he fucking died!" I seethe.

"She is a child," he snaps back.

"She is a fucking curse, that kid has done nothing but fuck everything up since she got here!" I roar, Royal's eyes blaze with contempt. I find it fucking comical how he can stand there and judge me for the way I feel about the kid when he was the one who hated her first.

"That's my fucking kid, Chaos." The deathly calm tone of his voice lets me know that he is hanging onto his rage by a thin string. "I don't give a fuck what you do or who you kill but you will *not* speak about my daughter like that again in my fucking presence. Am I clear?"

I take some deep breaths and try as hard as I can to temper

the beast inside me—it's not working. I'm itching to inflict pain and break some shit, so I need to get the fuck out of here. With that thought, I turn and stalk out of the room, ignoring Sin as she calls after me. I'm three feet from my car when Kacey darts in front of me, forcing me to a halt. I pin him with a scathing look.

"Get the fuck out of my way," I snarl.

"Take a fucking second to calm down–" I ignore the fucker and dart around him, rip the door of my car open and slide in. I glare at Kacey when he slips into the passenger side and closes the door behind himself.

"Get the fuck out!" I start the engine and wait for him to leave. Gripping the steering wheel in a vice like grip, I spy him out of the corner of my eye pulling his seatbelt on. "The fuck are you doing, Kacey?"

"Since you won't stay here and listen to what I have to say, I'll just come with you." My nostrils flare in agitation.

"You're not coming with me," I grit out.

"Then you're gonna have to shoot me and let's be real, you won't do it because you know my girlfriend would hunt your ass down and make you wish for death." I growl but don't comment because the bastard isn't wrong. If I hurt him, I'll have to deal with a pissed off Chanel and no one wants that crazy bitch coming after them—she is relentless and ruthless. I ignore his smug chuckle and peel out of there, heading toward the city where I know Ricardo's underboss, Philly, hangs out every Thursday at the local bar. After a while I get so lost in my own thoughts that I forget all about Kacey being with me until my phone rings. I send the call to voicemail when I see it's my dad calling. "You know they're all coming to the gala, right?"

"You gonna lecture me about Daddy issues when your own father hates you and your future father-in-law wants you dead?" The second the words leave my mouth, I feel like an utter fuck-up as Kacey deflates beside me. I open my mouth to try smooth things over but he beats me to it.

"You're right, my dad does hate me and Chanel's father can't stand the sight of me and made that clear when he shot me. Thing is, your father doesn't hate the sight of you and loves you. Don't take that shit for granted because there are some of us out there that would kill to have a parent that loves us."

"Fuck off, Kacey, you know nothing about my parents or me."

"I know that they are hurting just like you are. I also know that they just want to be there for you and share in the pain you are drowning in daily." His words hit a spot that I wish they didn't, because if I allow them to, they will crush me. I can't face my parents until I have avenged my brother's death, only then will I be able to look them in the eyes.

"Mind ya fucking business. You may be sleeping with my cousin but that doesn't make us friends."

"We may not be friends but I am the only person who can relate to how you are feeling, losing a sibling is like losing a piece of yourself." Hearing that shit has me snapping.

"He wasn't just my fucking sibling, he was my other half, my life, my fucking everything and he was ripped away from me and you can never understand that pain."

The remainder of the drive is spent in silence. We pull up at the back of Firemen's Arms, the bar Philly comes to every Thursday. I shut the engine off and wait. Philly is the last high-ranking member of Ricardo's men that I have left to take care of, once I deal with this fucker all I have left is the main family. I plan to go for his sons first, I want him to see them die and feel half of the pain I do before I finally come for him and end his miserable life. Then, and only then, will I deal with his cunt of a daughter. Kacey remains still and on high alert beside me. The guy may piss me the fuck me off but it goes without saying that he was a good agent.

"Your dad is a fuckwit," I say breaking the silence. Kacey doesn't pull his gaze from the window as he answers.

"Doesn't change the fact that I long for his approval when I know I won't get it." I flinch as that shit must fucking suck. A part of me does hurt for him, I honestly don't know how I would feel if my dad was a prick and didn't approve of what I do. Before I can ponder that shit any longer, the back door of the pub swings open. Philly stumbles down the stairs and staggers toward his car. Shaking my head I glare at the bastard, it's fuckers like this that drive drunk and kill a family with no remorse.

Kacey says nothing as I follow behind Philly, by now I'm sure he's put the pieces together and knows what's about to happen. He leans forward and opens the glove compartment grabbing the spare Glock I keep stashed in there. He pops the mag out and checks it's loaded before slamming it back into place and jamming the hammer back, leaning forward to stash the gun in the back of his waistband.

"Help yourself," I mutter.

"If we're about to kill that fucker I'm not going in there with my dick in my hand, I'm going in there armed so I don't get shot. I'd rather not have your cousin raging at me when I get home because I have a bullet wound... again." That has a smile cracking across my face. Kacey spits a big game but the fucker is just as terrified of Chanel as the rest of us. I carry on past Philly's house as he pulls into the drive, do a lap around the block before turning back and parking down the street where I can see his house. Kacey and I settle into our seats and wait. He lives in a suburban neighborhood so we need to be silent and stealthy or we risk one of these nosy Karens calling the pigs on us and I'm not in the mood to buy off cops tonight, too much hassle.

Forty minutes later, Kacey and I are climbing out of the car and jogging across the street toward Philly's house. We sneak around the back, then I make quick work of picking the lock and quietly opening the door. Kacey goes ahead of me and we clear the bottom floor. I meet Kacey at the bottom of the stairs, then signal for him to watch my back as I go first. We clear one end of the second floor, then turn to the other side where we can hear the sound of a porn film playing from the master bedroom. Kacey watches my six as I take point. The door is ajar so I peer in and cringe at the sight of the beer bellied fat fuck jacking his cock to the film. I had planned to torture the fucker and film it so I could send it to Ricardo but this shit is way better. I want that frustrated look on his face from not being able to come due to the amount of liquor he consumed to remain, so I lift my gun. I press the silencer through the crack in the door and aim for his head, I gently squeeze the trigger and smile wide at the sight of him.

"What the fuck?" Kacey hisses behind me. I shove the bedroom door open further and step aside so Kacey can see my handy work. Philly remains upright against his headboard naked with his dick in his hand and that frustrated look frozen on his face. I pull my card out of my back pocket and cross the room to where a photo frame hangs. I pay no attention to the picture as I yank the thing off the wall and drop it to the ground. I peel the nail out of the wall then stalk over to Philly, place my card on his face and line the nail I just acquired up against it, using the butt of my gun to hammer it into his forehead. "Jesus, Chaos." I flick my gaze to Kacey who stands on the opposite side of the bed with a disgusted look on his face.

"What?"

"The fucker has warts on his *chode*." I dart my gaze to his sorry-ass excuse for a cock and scrunch my face in disgust—Kacey's right, his cock is covered in gentile warts.

"That is fucking nasty!" I blurt as I jump back from the fucker not wanting to catch whatever the fuck it is he has. Kacey follows me out of the house. I make sure to wipe the door handle on the back door so my prints aren't on it as we leave. The second we're in the car and racing down the street Kacey speaks.

"What now?" I turn and smile darkly at him.

"Now, I go after the heirs of the Dominico family." Raw

hunger surges inside me. I hunger for their blood to soak my hands and the ground beneath my feet. "I sent each of Ricardo's two sons my card a week ago, they know they're next." The thought of them constantly checking over their shoulders and living in fear fills me with gratification.

# Chapter Six

## CASSANDRA

It took me half an hour this morning to convince Tabby that I wouldn't crumble and die if she went to work. I love her but she can be over the top sometimes. Right now, all I need is to be alone so I can research, which is why I am currently sitting on my living room floor with the contents of the safety deposit box that I use to hide my findings on the floor around me. What's the point of hiding now when one of them has already figured out who I am and where I live, I just need to figure out which *one* he is. Over the last two years, I have outed so many crooks and I know without a doubt if my watcher was to broadcast my identity, I would need to be placed into witness protection as I would have a shit load of people vying for my blood.

My eyes are beginning to burn from looking at my laptop and all these papers for hours. I decide to take a quick break and eat some of the leftovers from last night. My phone rings for the fiftieth time today. I send it to voicemail not wanting to deal with another person sending me their condolences. The funny thing about death is people you haven't spoken to for years suddenly pick up the phone and call. It's not to check on how you are coping, it's just to get the low down on what happened so they can go and spread gossip. I drop my phone on the counter as I rifle through the fridge for what I want. When I'm done, I place all the Chinese containers on the counter ready to dig in until my phone beeps with a text. Groaning I swipe it open and freeze.

UNKNOWN NUMBER

Doing some light research huh?

My breath hitches as I dart my gaze around the room trying to find the cameras, the shiver of dread that races down my spine tells me it's *him*. My phone beeps again scaring the shit out of me to the point I squeal and nearly drop the phone.

UNKNOWN NUMBER

You won't find what you're looking for, all that shit from your safety deposit box is outdated.

My stomach churns as awareness prickles the back of my neck, he's watching me and if he can see what I'm doing then that means he knows I lied to Tabby and has seen me naked! A shiver travels down my spine. Don't get me wrong, I'm not vanilla or anything like that, I do enjoy role-play in the bedroom but this is a whole new level of kinky and I'm disgusted within myself for being aroused right now.

ME

Do you get off watching me?

His reply comes almost instantly.

UNKNOWN NUMBER

I get hard thinking about your blood.

My brows jump to my hairline, the churning in my stomach intensifies because I know without a doubt he isn't joking.

ME

Why are you watching me?

ME

Because I want you to know that you are marked, your time is limited and running out fast.

ME

Are you going to hurt me?

UNKNOWN NUMBER

No.

I sigh in relief at his response until my phone beeps again with another message from him.

UNKNOWN NUMBER

I'm going to destroy you, tear you apart and then dump your corpse on top of your brother's grave, how's that for not hurting you? Don't fucking get caught up in the idea that you mean something to me, you are a pawn in this game of chess, never forget that.

My phone slips through my fingers and clatters along the tile floor. I stare at the thing like it will transform into Optimus Prime or something. For the first time I realized I'm in over my head and I have no idea how the hell to get myself out of this mess. I close my eyes and give myself a mental pep talk, if this is nothing but a game to him then I'm going to have to out play this fucker. I may not know the rules of the game but I'm also not a weak little bitch either.

The rest of the day is spent making calls and researching, I don't limit my search to the Murdoch's, but go back through all my old findings and look up where each of them is to rule them out as possible suspects. Right now it would be handy to have my brother. He would have access to files that I don't and would obviously be able to conduct a wider search, even though if he was around he wouldn't help me. We weren't close. Quinn chose his job over me and left me behind when he climbed the ranks of the FBI.

It's nearly midnight. I've closed all the blinds in the apartment except for Dylan's room, I can't bring myself to go in there yet. I've left the door unlocked and currently sit in the center of my bed, waiting. He thinks he is slick and can outsmart me but I have a plan of my own tonight. I spent all afternoon preparing myself for this moment, I refuse to hide from him and allow him to scare me. When his shadow fills the doorway of my bedroom, I suck in a ragged breath. Anticipation thrums through me as he slowly stalks toward the end of my bed. The hairs on the back of my neck stand up, gooseflesh erupts all over my body as he bends and places his hands flat on the bed.

"If you wanted to hurt me you wouldn't have saved me." I'm proud that my voice doesn't waiver and sounds strong. The deep chuckle that escapes him has me stifling a gasp, it's such a rich sound that I never would have thought it would come from him.

"I saved you so I could have the honor of killing you myself." He crawls up the bed as he continues to speak. "I would never allow anyone to take that pleasure from me, your demise will be the vengeance I need most." I'm forced to lay flat on my back as he looms above me using his knees to push my legs open wider to accommodate his size. My breathing is erratic as I stare up into the eyes of the man who just promised to kill me. I may not be able to see the color of his eyes but I can see the pain that resides deep inside him. His face is free of facial hair, my hand itches to reach up and touch him.

"What happened to you?" My whispered words give him pause, he tenses above me and his eyes narrow to slits. "I'm sorry,"

I blurt out. I have no idea why the hell I'm apologizing but the need to placate him overcame me.

"Some fucker destroyed the better half of me and now all that is left is what you see before you, a cold heartless fucker that lives only to seek revenge on those who broke him." His words are layered in anguish. I lose the battle and my hand raises on its own accord to cup his cheek. He jolts at the contact but doesn't pull away, his skin is smooth and warm to touch. "What the fuck do you think you're doing?" he snarls.

"I-I don't know," I answer honestly. Something is seriously fucking wrong with me, this man has done nothing but terrorize me and promised to kill me, yet here I am, offering the monster comfort in the only way I know how. "I hope you find the redemption you are looking for, whoever hurt you should suffer."

"Oh, they will suffer, by the time I'm done with them they will be begging me to end their sorry ass excuse of a life." Truth rings out in his words. Feeling bold, I trail my fingers along his jawline. He doesn't wear a ball cap tonight, just his hood. He doesn't stop me as I slowly reach up and push his hood back exposing his thick hair. I run my fingers through it, relishing in the feel of his silky strands between my fingers, his eyes slowly drifting closed as I continue to explore his face and play with his hair. My confidence grows and I trail my fingers along his jaw, slowly working my way down the sides of his neck, but before I can get too far his eyes snap open, then he's gripping my wrists and pinning them above my head. My eyes are wide in fright, his body weight presses me into mattress but that isn't the part that robs me of air, it's the fact that I can feel he's hard for me.

Our eyes collide, shock ripples through me but the dark look in his gaze tells me he isn't happy with the fact I touched him in a place I shouldn't have, and the fact his cock is rock hard for me clearly has annoyed him as well. I dart my tongue out to moisten my suddenly dry lips. His eyes track the movement. Before my mind can conjure up a coherent sentence to break this awkward moment, his lips mesh against mine, drawing a shocked gasp from me. This gives him the access he needs to plunge his hot tongue in my mouth and a wanton moan escapes me when his taste assaults my senses. Fuck, the way he takes control of the kiss and doesn't ask permission, but demands it, has my body taking over. My hips rise on their own accord seeking some type of friction, the moment I grind against his hard cock he breaks the kiss and leaps off me. I remain where I am panting, confused and horny as hell.

"Fuck!" he snarls before storming out of the room without a backward glance.

*What the fuck just happened?*

It takes me a good five minutes to get my wayward thoughts under control before I remember that I had set my phone up to record from the side table. Having the newest iPhone means I can activate night vision in video mode. Time to see who my watcher really is. I take a few deep breaths before I replay the video. My nerves are frayed as I push play and watch. I pause the videos a few times and groan, I look like a fucking hussy copping a feel of him. I have second-hand embarrassment of myself! I zoom on the part where I push his hood off, I can tell he's tanned and has dark hair but it's the ink I can just make out on the side of his neck that captures my attention. I squint my eyes trying to get a better look but it's too distorted. All I can make out is the shape and the letter *A*.

I'm appalled to admit that I rewatch the video at least a dozen times—the way he crowded me and used his body to pin me to the bed, and that kiss. Fuck, that kiss breathed life back into me. It woke me up from a slumber I didn't know I was in until now. I can see now that I was just settling with Dylan, it was convenient to be with him, safe if you will. I drop my phone on the bed beside me and flop back groaning. I cringe when I shift and feel how wet I am. My nipples are hard and begging to be touched so I give into the urge and reach up and tweak my nipples through my camisole, then moan. Fuck, they are so sensitive and it's been so long since I've been touched or this turned on. I continue to roll my nipple between my fingers as my other hand slowly skates down my flat stomach and slips beneath my bed shorts.

"Shit," I cry out the moment the pad of my finger brushes my clit. I swirl it around my entrance and moan when I feel my own arousal. I slowly push a finger inside my tight wet pussy relishing in the feeling. I pump in and out of myself slowly coating my finger in my slickness before drawing it out and circling it around my clit, my hips bucking upward on their own accord. A frenzy takes over. I had planned to draw this out and tease myself but I can't, I need this release too fucking much! Within minutes my back is arching off the bed and my mouth parts with a silent scream as my orgasm rips through me and tremors wrack my body as I continue to play with my clit, drawing out the high I'm riding.

I stop teasing myself and bring my hand that is covered in my own juices to my mouth and suck it clean, moaning at the musky taste of my own cum. Utterly spent and bone tired after that orgasm, I settle back into bed ready for sleep to claim me except my phone pings with a text. Groaning I reach over and swipe it open. My jaw unhinges and my eyes bug out of my head as I reread the message three times before it finally sinks in.

UNKNOWN NUMBER

The next time you get off, it will be my cum you're swallowing not your own.

That motherfucker was watching me get off! I flick the bird toward the ceiling and huff. "I hope you enjoyed the show, you creep!" I try to sound annoyed and repulsed by the idea of him watching me come, but the reality is I had hoped he would be watching as I touched my greedy little cunt. That must say a lot about me and the type of person I am.

# Chapter Seven

## CHAOS

Coming home last night, without fail Lani tried to end my life but failed, yet again. Instead of fighting with her last night, I just disarmed her and went to bed, my head was too fucked up over kissing Cassandra. I sat in my car for a minute to gather my thoughts and compose myself. Because I'm a sucker for punishment, I brought up the camera feed on my phone and was stunned to find her getting off, the sight of her hard nipples and the way she fingered her cunt had me pulling my cock out of my jeans and stroking myself, I didn't give a fuck that I was in the car or someone could walk by and see me, I needed to cum with her.

The moment I came all over my hand, guilt slammed into me, I was fucking disgusted with myself for kissing her and then getting off to the video of her. I can't allow myself to ever get distracted by her again. She is the last blood relation to the cunt who had a hand in killing my brother, which is why I am currently sitting at the breakfast counter waiting for Lailani. If this plan is to go smoothly I need to get her on my side with the plan. I made the call to invite Royal and Sin over this morning. Lani walks into the kitchen pulling me from my thoughts. She freezes at the sight of me, her hair is still wet from the shower she just had and her face is slightly pale. I take a good look at her for the first time in weeks. Her eyes are dull and red, like she has been crying, her shoulders bunch as she makes her way toward me and claims the seat on the opposite side of me.

"Say whatever it is you have to say and then disappear until tonight so I can try and kill you again," she says brokenly.

"Even if you did kill me, you wouldn't escape this place."

Her eyes narrow. "You don't think I know that you need a PIN code to get out?"

I raise a single brow and rest my elbows on the counter. "Let me guess, you think you know the code?"

"26.07." I'm powerless to stop the shock from showing on my face.

"How the fuck do you know that?" I murmur.

Her lips pinch as she shrugs her shoulders. "It was a wild guess until you just confirmed it now."

"You've been watching me," I accuse her, and she shakes her head.

"No. I knew it wouldn't be Havoc's birthdate or death date so the only other date would be the day he left me to go back to you." The bitterness in her tone is evident but I ignore it.

"If you had a hunch on what the code is, why not leave?" I eye her carefully watching for any sign of deceit.

"What's the point when I know you would just hunt me down again and it's not like I can return home, my father would kill me on sight. Plus, the only chance I have of you not hurting my son is to remain here and wait for you to formulate a plan to take down my family so you can get your hands on my son for a DNA test."

My lips twitch in surprise. "You're smarter than you look." She rolls her eyes and huffs.

"I mean it, Chaos, I won't do anything to risk you turning your anger on Ryat."

"You don't think trying to kill me daily will push me to harm the kid?" She pins me with a bored stare and shakes her head.

"Me trying to kill you is a sport. You and I both know I can't kill you." I frown.

"Why is that?" I push, she drops her gaze to her lap and twiddles her thumbs.

"You and him may be polar opposites internally but externally, you are mirror images and for that reason alone, I would never be able to kill you." I grit my teeth.

"You won't survive this," I force out.

She nods her head somberly. "I know. I'm okay with dying as long as you promise me to protect your nephew. Ryat is innocent, Chaos. I wish more than anything I was able to tell Havoc about his son... that is something I will live to regret for the rest of my life."

"If he is who you say he is, I will torture you because you robbed my brother of the chance of ever being a father." The venom in my tone is tangible.

"I understand," she mutters. The sound of a knock on the door has her bolting to her feet. I ignore her surprise and leave her in the kitchen as I let Chanel and Royal in, the both of them eye me warily saying nothing as they follow me inside. I know they are trying not to judge but the truth is, the house is bare of furnishings and has no personal touches. I like it that way. I lead them into the kitchen, Lani's eyes widen at the sight of my cousins.

"Well, she is alive," Sin deadpans.

"She looks like shit," Royal adds.

"*She* is standing right here!" Lani snaps, and the three of us ignore her outburst.

"Have you informed your..." Royal purses his lips and cocks his head to the side as he assesses Lani for a moment. "Pet?" I snort out a laugh, Lani balks and mutters under her breath about Royal still being a dick.

"I was just about to," I answer. I motion for them to have a seat around the counter. Lani is the last to claim her seat, she is stiff and any trace of tiredness from a moment ago has vanished. I find it comical that she is more wary of my cousins than she is of me. "I need you to lead the Albanians so I can kill your father and brothers. Do it and I'll get your son back."

"Jesus, Chaos."

"Fucking hell," Sin and Royal both say in unison, clearly they expected me to deliver the news in a different manner. If she were someone I cared for, then I would have but I don't like her so she gets it straight without any sugar coating it.

"You want me to do what now?" Lani sneers back at me. I harden my expression and glare at the bitch.

"Watch your fucking tone," I growl.

"Why? You said it yourself you're gonna kill me so why delay it?" she taunts.

"Want your son to pay the price?" I clap back.

Her eyes crinkle at the corners. "You would harm your brother's child?" I slam my fist down on the marble counter causing her to jump.

"Don't you dare speak about him!" I shout.

"Fuck you, I loved him as well and I have every fucking right to speak about him." I leap to my feet ready to jump over the counter and ring her fucking neck but Royal grips my arm and holds me back. I shoot him a glare but he ignores it.

"We need her for the plan to work, take a minute to calm down." I hold his gaze as I take some deep breaths and try to contain the rage swirling inside me. Since losing my brother I've had a hard time controlling my anger, it's my default setting these days and I'm struggling with it. I give him a curt nod and he releases me so we can reclaim our seats. I meet Lani's stare then tell her my plan for taking over the Albanians and, I even fill her in on how I plan to capture both her brothers the night of the gala. By the end of it she is wide eyed and nodding robotically, Chanel is eyeing her oddly, she is taking this way too well.

"You good?" I ask. She scoffs, rolling her eyes and throwing her hands in the air.

"Don't act like you give a shit, Chaos. Even if I didn't like this plan you would force me to go along with it because if I don't you would threaten to hurt my son." I don't respond because she's right. "What is my guarantee that Ryat won't be harmed in the crossfire because there is no way this plan is going off without a hitch." Chanel answers her question.

"You have our word that we will protect Ryat with our lives." Sin shoots me a loaded look before turning back to Lani. "He may not accept that Havoc is the father of your son but *we* do. He shares our blood, which means we would die to protect your son." I'm more shocked at Sin's declaration than the fact Lani is silently crying.

"Thank you," she mutters as she wipes the tears from her face and turns to me. "I'll do it, but you should know that my father won't be coming to the event without his best men—" She clamps her mouth closed as I begin to laugh.

"You don't have to worry about that, I've taken care of all your father's men even Philly met his maker." The surprised look that crosses her face annoys me, clearly she didn't think I would be able to uphold my word and dismantle her father's empire. We spend the next twenty minutes discussing how we are going to contact the Albanians and set this plan into motion. I don't relish the idea of using the cunts but I don't see another way.

"This is all well and good, but no one aside from the men that died that day know about my marriage to Halil, how are we going to convince them that I speak the truth?" My cousins and I share a look before I turn back to Lani.

"You have a marriage license, right?" I ask.

She shrugs. "I assume so but my father would be the one who has it."

"You really married that fuck because your dad was gonna hurt your kid?" Royal asks Lani. She looks directly at him as she answers.

"Yes. I would do anything to protect Ryat. I received beating after beating from my brothers and my father's men while I was pregnant and after I gave birth because they wanted to know the name of the man that tarnished me." I grip the edge of the marble counter in a death hold.

"They tried to hurt the kid?" I snarl.

"Of course they did. You didn't think that I would get away unscathed, did you?" She doesn't give me a chance to answer. "Imagine what they would have done to Ryat if they knew he was a Murdoch. My father would have murdered his own grandson just to hurt your brother and father. I would go through all the broken bones again and again if it meant my son would be safe. I have no reason to lie to you, Chaos. Shit, if I was just trying to save my own ass I could have said you were his father." I reel back in disgust. "I'll do whatever I have to in order to protect my son. When you meet him, you will see the truth in his eyes because he has his father's eyes." Pain stabs me right in the chest, I can see it in her gaze that she isn't lying, Havoc really is the father of her son.

"He was a father," I whisper brokenly.

"No, he *is* a father. Never allow my son to forget about where he came from. You tell him every fucking day that his father and mother loved him with everything they had. You make sure he never wonders about his worth. You make him feel cherished daily, do you hear me?" Before I can formulate a response, Royal cuts in.

"Why don't you tell him yourself?" She doesn't take her anger filled eyes off me as she answers.

"I won't be around to watch him grow up." Her resigned tone would have any man changing their mind. I hate her and I know she feels the same about me which is why I say what I do next.

"Yes, you will so long as you do as you're fucking told and help us with the Albanians." Her eyes widen to the size of saucers.

"W-what?" she stutters.

"You're the mother to my brother's only living heir. You will not pay for the sins of your family. But you will help us and in return I will reunite you with your son and allow you to live." I stand and walk out; I need to get the fuck out of here and away from this feeling brewing inside me. I can't allow my grief to consume me because there is no way I'll be able to pull myself out of that black hole. I struggle daily just to get my ass out of bed and I'll admit, I am terrified of what is going to happen to me when I finally avenge my brother and have no other purpose in this world.

It's sickening that I constantly find myself sitting outside her apartment. I wanted to get away and escape the feelings that were crushing me so I jumped in my car and drove, but I didn't expect to end up here. Aside from the three Dominico's, she is the last left to take out. I've never killed a woman before which is why I am using that excuse to explain why I am suddenly plagued by thoughts of Cassandra Blake daily. I pull out my phone and open my message thread with her.

ME

How loud would you scream when I fuck you?

I convinced myself last night that fucking her would be a great way to seek revenge. I mean before she dies, she finds out who I really am and then it will hurt her more knowing that she fucked one of the people responsible for her brother's death. My breath hitches when the three little dots appear on my screen.

ROTTEN APPLE

What makes you think you can fuck me good enough to make me scream?

I smirk, I bet she feels really proud of herself for sending that message.

ME

Just the feeling of my cock pressed against your cunt last night had you fucking yourself.

ROTTEN APPLE

That wasn't for you, it was all for me.

ME

Keep pushing me, I dare you.

I frown when she doesn't reply instantly, I wait a few minutes before looking up to her apartment but I can't see her. I'm about to open the camera thread when my phone pings with an incoming picture message from her. "Fuck me." I breathe out as I stare down at my phone. She's standing in front of her bathroom mirror in a purple bra and matching thong and from what I can see stockings to match, but it isn't the outfit that captures my attention, it's the sight of her tiny hand inside her thong cupping her pussy. My cock is rock-fucking-hard at the sight of her perfect tits nearly spilling over the top of her bra and her perfect body on display. I knew she was kinky but this is a whole new level even for me. I'm used to women throwing themselves at me, perks of being the QB but they have never been able to hold my attention. Cassandra doesn't seem to have that trouble. Another text comes through and I practically race to open it.

ROTTEN APPLE

Bet you didn't see that coming on your cameras :)

ME

Nah but I can see me cumming on those tits.

ROTTEN APPLE

Phone sex with my stalker, never thought I
would get to cross that one off my bucket list.

I can't keep the smirk off my face, this little shit is proving to
be entertaining.

ME

Who said I was stalking your ass?

ROTTEN APPLE

The fact you break into my apartment every
night and have cameras fitted throughout it
leads me to think you are in fact stalking me.

ME

Nah, just my way of making sure you don't try
anything stupid before your time is up.

ROTTEN APPLE

Would me fingering myself while texting you
count as something stupid?

I nearly drop my phone in my haste to switch back to the
camera app. I pull it up and growl at the sight of her laying on the
bed, spread eagle with the cups of her bra pulled down exposing
her creamy tits. Her thong is pulled to the side as she works a
finger in and out of her pussy. I jolt when my phone begins to
ring, it's her. I answer the call making sure to keep my tone even,
acting unaffected. I can see the smile on her face and glare down at
the screen.

"It feels so good," she moans. I watch as she places her phone
on speaker, then drops it on the bed and rolls her nipple between
her fingers. I bite my lip when her back arches. "Fuck, just like
that, touch me like that." My eyes widen, she's envisioning that
it's my hands on her.

"Pinch your nipple and keep your mouth shut." She gasps at
the sound of my voice but does as she's told. "I want you to add

another finger and fuck your greedy little cunt hard." My cock is aching and begging for me to storm up there and sink it inside her tight wet heat.

"Hmmm," she moans as she pushes a second finger inside herself. "You feel so good, I want you to suck my clit." I growl and palm my cock through my jeans as I watch her.

"I call the fucking shots, not you. You get what I give you, nothing more."

"Yes, *Sir*." I hum my approval, I've never liked being called sir or having my name screamed out as they come, but hearing that word come from her mouth has my cock twitching in my pants. "Holy shit," she whimpers, I can't take it anymore.

"Stop now!" She stills as her eyes fly open.

"W-what?"

"Turn the fuck over and keep your face buried in the mattress." She hesitantly does as I ask. It's daylight and there is a risk that she will see exactly who I am, but right now I'm not thinking with the right head. I dash out of my car and head for the back entrance, taking the stairs two at a time, eager as fuck to get to her and sink my cock inside her tight little cunt. I stop outside her door and check my phone, she's head down ass up with a pillow covering the top of her head.

I smirk, good girl.

The door is unlocked, forcing a frown to my face. She'll be punished for that. I silently make my way into the bedroom pocketing my phone and the sight that greets me when I cross the threshold has me slamming to a stop. The thin lace that covers her pussy is soaked, her creamy ass is in the air, begging for me to redden it with my hand. I eliminate the space between us stopping at the end of the bed. I war within myself, knowing this is a bad fucking idea and I should either turn the fuck around and leave or kill her now.

"Touch me." The quietly whispered words that tumble from her lips have me throwing caution to the wind. Reaching out, I grip the globes of her ass, drawing a strangled gasp from her.

"You want me to ruin this pussy?" She moans in response. I draw my hand back and lay a swift smack to each cheek, she lurches forward in surprise. "Use your fucking words."

"Yes, I want you to fuck me and destroy my greedy pussy." Her words fill me with glee. I rub her ass, loving the sounds that come from her. I use my index finger to follow the line of her thong from the top of her ass all the way to her pussy. She whimpers and tries to push back against my hand. I withdraw my touch and land another blow to her ass, relishing in the sight of the red handprint. "Ouch."

"You remain fucking still," I snarl.

"Yes, *Sir.*" I growl my approval as I crouch down behind her and press my nose against her soaked panties inhaling her heady scent—Jesus Christ, she smells fucking divine. Unable to stop myself, I flatten my tongue and lick her through the lace. She begins to tremble and whimper. I do this a couple more times before finally giving in and pushing the material to the side. Her glistening pink pussy is on display, she's so fucking wet I can see it slowly leaking out of her cunt.

"You like giving your pussy up to a stranger and getting fucked like a whore?" I don't give her a chance to answer, I dip my tongue inside her greedy little hole. She cries out as I moan at the taste of her. I grip her ass and pull her back against my face, eating her like a starving man. I've never tasted a pussy this good before. I alternate between fucking her with my tongue and sucking on her clit. When I lap at her clit ,she begins to tremble, then I push a finger inside her.

"Oh, fuck yes, you're gonna make me come!" Before she can orgasm I release her and stand. She attempts to shift but I dart forward and grip the back of her neck, holding her in place using my other hand to free my cock from my jeans.

"Stay the fuck still, you move and I leave you on edge. You want that?"

"No," she practically shouts, clearly frustrated that she has been denied two orgasms already.

"You gonna take my cock like a good little slut?" I purr as I begin to palm myself.

"Yes, fuck me like a whore." Her filthy mouth has pre-cum coating the tip of my cock. I release her neck and peel her soaked panties down her legs. I discreetly bring them to my nose and inhale, groaning at the scent of her. I put her thong in my pocket and push my jeans down my legs, then pull her backward so her feet are flat on the floor and she is face first on the bed. I yank my hoodie off and cover her head with it just to be extra sure she won't be able to see me.

"I want to hear you scream," I demand as I line my cock up and slam inside her without warning. She screams so fucking loud I wonder if the floor below us can hear.

"You're too big!" she shouts, and my ego swells inside me as I grip her hips and draw almost all the way out before slamming back inside her. "Fuck!"

"Take it." My pace is unrelenting, my grip on her waist is punishing but I don't care, she feels too fucking good. Her pussy is clenching the fuck out of my cock. I fold forward and reach beneath her to cup one of her tits and bite on the back of her neck.

"I'm coming!" she screams. Her cunt squeezes my cock so tight I wince as aftershocks wrack her body. I press back up and fuck her hard, needing to feel her come all over me again. "Oh, fuck." She spreads her legs wider and shifts so she can fit her hand beneath her. I watch in amazement as she begins to play with her clit. Most women are too shy to demand what they want or tell you how they like it but clearly Cassandra Blake isn't one of those women. "Fuck me like that, don't stop, Sir." I alter my pace, continuing to slam inside her relentlessly. I feel my balls begin to ache with the need to empty inside her. "Fuck, I'm coming!" She is definitely a fucking screamer, there is no denying that. I pull out of her and pump my cock twice in my hand and roar out my release as I spurt jets of cum all over her ass. As soon as I finish, I push my cock back inside her, loving how her pussy instantly clamps down on me.

*This may just be the greatest fuck of my life. Pity I have to kill her.*

I plan to fuck her a lot more before I finally end her, pussy this good is hard to fucking come by and the fact she is willing to give it up so freely, who am I to turn down an offer like that?

# Chapter Eight

## CASSANDRA

*Oh. My. God!*

That was fucking incredible, I have never come that fucking hard before in my life! The instant he pulls out of me, I flop on the bed unable to move, I'm boneless and thoroughly sated. I can hear him moving behind me but I don't have the strength to move, my eyes are heavy and exhaustion is weighing me down but I don't give into the urge to nap, I don't trust him enough to be that defenseless. I snort internally, I can't sleep around him but I can allow him to fuck me like a dirty little whore. I remain still as I hear him shifting behind, zipping his pants, I can feel his gaze on me but he says nothing—neither do I. The awkwardness is palpable and it would be better if he just left, either he came to the same conclusion or read my mind because he leaves without a word, all the tension flees my body when I hear the front door click shut.

I roll over and groan up at the ceiling, my body aches but in the best possible way I can still feel the ghost of him pulsing inside me. I have never been fucked so thoroughly; the way he commanded control and bent me to his will had my pussy gushing, being told when I can and can't come was fucking hot. I know without a shadow of a doubt I want to do that again–soon.

I look beside me and gasp, he left his hoodie behind, like an addict looking for her next hit. I gather the material in my hands and bring it to my nose inhaling his scent, cedar, leather and pine, such a strange mix but it also fits him. I look around the bed for my thong and when I don't find it, I stand and search the room for it but it's nowhere to be found.

"Did he steal my underwear?" I ask aloud. The sick satisfaction I get out of that should have me feeling ashamed of myself but I don't, the other part of me loves the fact that he took a piece of me with him while leaving a part of him behind.

After showering I spent the rest of the day catching up on work emails and staying up to date with all things. I sift through all the notes I have on the Murdochs, with the event coming up I need to make sure I'm prepared and have all the questions I need to ask ready. I researched the founder of the event, *Ricardo Dominico*. I've heard of him a couple times but he's never been a big name in the mafia world until recently. My eyes nearly fall out of my head when I find an article that states Ricardo and his men were involved in the shootout that killed my brother and Havoc Murdoch.

My fingers fly over my keyboard as I try to find as much information about Ricardo as I can. According to a quick Google search, he will be in town a week before the gala at a club opening in the city. I fire off a text to Tabby to tell her we are attending this opening. I'm not going to miss the chance to bring this son of a bitch down, he may not be the one who pulled the trigger but he was still a part of whatever the fuck went down that day. I spend hours scouring the web for every ounce of information I can find about the Dominico family. He has two sons and one daughter, he doesn't live in Miami but on the border and owns a lot of businesses here. He's as crooked as they come and the fact he has gotten away with this shit for so long tells me he has the cops in his pocket.

My phone ringing pulls me from my thoughts, I answer without checking the caller ID keeping my eyes on the screen of my laptop.

"Yello?"

"Cassandra?" I sit up straight at the sound of Dylan's mother's voice.

"Mrs. Cross, hi."

"I just wanted to call and let you know that Dylan will be released to us on Monday, we plan to take him straight home so if you wanted to... say goodbye, Monday would be your last opportunity." I bristle, that was her way of not so subtly telling me I'm not welcome at his funeral.

"Thank you, I would very much like to say goodbye." The slight pause on her end is a clear indication that she didn't expect me to accept her offer. Dylan and I may have ended badly but that one fall-out doesn't erase all the good times we shared together because there were a lot of great moments before shit went downhill. She rattles off the address and gives me a time to meet them there. Thanking her, I end the call and flop back on the couch.

*How did my life become so fucked up and messy?*

I decide to not dwell on that and start typing up my article that I've titled *My Watcher*, I know with every fiber of my being that *Sir* is somehow linked to the Murdochs or their children. I begin to formulate my story and recount all the details of when he first broke in and all the events up until today. I may be a reporter and I know we get a bad rap for not telling the truth but I'm not that type of reporter, I pride myself on always being transparent and open with my readers, even when some of my articles paint me in a not so good light. By the time I finish drafting up my article my eyes are burning and my body is aching. I power down my laptop and tidy up all the papers littering the floor of my living room, then stack them in a neat pile in the corner before heading to bed. I moan as I slip beneath the sheets,

I love my bed so fucking much it feels like I'm sleeping on a cloud.

I toss and turn in my sleep, the feeling of being watched has me consciously sleeping, you know that feeling when you're awake but still sleeping? I'm in that limbo. When the hairs on the back of my neck raise and awareness begins to spread throughout my body, I know that it's not the cameras causing me to have a shit sleep, he's in here with me. I slowly push the covers back and sit up, my gaze immediately goes to the chair in the corner by the window that overlooks the city below. He's illuminated by the light of the moon. My mouth drops open as I drink in the sight of him in a dark shirt and jeans. It pisses me off that he's sitting at the perfect angle so I can't make out his features thanks to the shadows and dim lighting.

"Nice hoodie." His husky voice sends a shiver down my spine. I look down at myself and bite my lip. I know, I'm sick in the head but fuck it, YOLO and all that shit.

"I figured since you stole something of mine you wouldn't mind me borrowing your hoodie." His rich laughter has my mouth parting at the sound, he doesn't seem like he smiles or laughs often and that notion makes me sad for some reason.

"You seem to think we are on an even playing field, we aren't. I will always be ahead of you and above you, fucking you doesn't change that." Ouch, that hurt more than it should have. I decide to be bold and ask him the question that has been burning a hole in my mind all evening.

"Do you know who Ricardo Dominico is?" If I wasn't watching him so raptly, I would have missed the subtle shift to the right and the way his body tensed.

"Don't fucking dip your nose into shit you have no idea about." He sneers.

"Thing is, I just discovered he was a part of a shootout that led to my brother dying, another person died that day—"

"Shut the fuck up!" His cold harsh tone has me reeling back. "You know nothing about what happened that day."

"But you do?"

"You go digging where you shouldn't, you just might wind up in the hole next to your piece of shit brother quicker than I had planned." I gasp.

"You were there that day?" I breathe out. He ignores me and stands, turning his back to me as he gazes out the window. My mind begins to reel with possibilities—if he was there that day then that means my hunch is right, he is either with the Murdochs, Ricardo or the Albanians, because there is no way he was working with the feds. The prison escape was all pinned on Kacey Vaughn, a former agent with the bureau and from what I have found out, he worked alongside my brother, No one has seen Kacey since he escaped. "Are you here because my brother did something to you?" I hate the quiver in my voice, some of the things I have found out about Quintin since he passed isn't flattering. People are saying he was corrupt and orchestrated the events of that fateful day, but I can't accept that as the truth.

His shoulders relax as I steer the question in a different direction which just tells me I need to dig more into that day when he isn't around. "Your brother was a fucking snake. He died too quickly and deserved so much fucking worse than a quick ending." For the first time since he first broke into my apartment I feel real fear, this feeling in my gut is telling me that I am in the presence of a cold-blooded killer.

"You were there when he died?" I ask quietly. He turns to face me and at this angle I get a clear view of his tattoo on his neck!

It's the Ace of Diamonds!

*Oh. My. God!*

He's part of the new mafia taking over Miami—*Memento Mori*. Holy fucking shit, I need to get the fuck away from him or move somewhere he can't find me. Word on the streets is they are ruthless, kill anyone who fucks with them and they leave bodies all over the city with cards attached to the dead corpses. A source told me that if you receive a card, then that means you are marked. They say there is no escaping them once they have marked you as a kill.

"I wish I was the one who killed him." I gulp audibly, darting my gaze toward the door, wondering if I would be able to make it out before he caught me. "You can try to run." I snap my gaze back to him and open my mouth to deny his claim but no words come out. "I know you've been digging into who I am and trying to find any information you can about Ricardo Dominico. Don't waste your time because that cunt will be dead soon enough." His words send a chill down my spine.

"Who are you?" My voice trembles and the stench of my fear coats the room, but I don't care, I am in a room alone with a man who just admitted to killing people and plans to kill again.

"The bringer of death."

"You're a murderer," I snap.

"And you let me between your legs. What's that say about you?" I flinch as if he slapped me.

"I didn't know!" I defend, my argument sounds weak to my own ears.

"You don't even know who I am, what I do or what I have done, and still you opened those legs like it was nothing. How many others have you fucked without knowing a thing about them?"

"Fuck. You!" I snarl, feeling ashamed and angry at myself for allowing him to touch me.

"Gladly," he replies. Before I can blink, he is on top of me and uses his body to pin me to the bed. I thrash beneath him but I can't shake free. When he smirks, I strike out and slap him across the face. I'm still beneath him, waiting with bated breath to see what comes next. He slowly turns back to face me and I drink in the sight of his face. Green eyes, brown hair and the most amazing bone structure in his face, he has the face of a model and that makes this shit worse. He isn't some ugly hobo who can get me off, he's a hot as fuck young guy who is the first man to ever get me to soak through my panties. "You enjoy that?" he taunts.

"Yes," I lie. When he leans down, our faces are a sliver apart and the scent of his minty breath hits my nose and I tense. Not from fear but from the sheer fact my pussy is pulsing, something is seriously wrong with me because my body and mind are not on the same page where this man is concerned.

"Good," he bites out as he grinds his pelvis into me, drawing a loud gasp out of me at the feeling of his erection pressed against my pussy.

"I'm not sleeping with you!" I blurt out.

The bastard smirks. "If I check and find your cunt soaked then I'm burying my cock inside it, but if you're drier than a desert I'll leave and never come back until it's time for you to be rejoined with Quintin and your parents." I grind my teeth so hard they begin to ache. The triumphant look in his eyes pisses me off as the bastard knows I'm wet for him. He trails a hand down my side. I try with all my might to grip his arm and stop him but he just uses his free hand to grab both my arms and pin them above my head. When he pushes the material of his hoodie up and sees I'm only wearing a pair of panties, he groans. I try to clench my thighs together, trying to stop him but he just uses his knees to widen them. His gaze bores into mine as his hand slips beneath the fabric of my panties. I jerk in his hold when his finger glides through my folds toward my entrance. The moment he swirls the tip of his index finger around my hole, he growls his approval. "Well, well, well, someone is dripping for me."

"Nope, I watched a porno before I went to bed that was Timmy D, not you." His brows raise mocking me. I narrow my eyes back at him.

"Is." He pushes a finger inside me, drawing a sharp gasp. "That." He pumps that finger in and out of me as he continues to speak. "So?" I bite my lip, trying hard to keep from making any sound. I don't want to give him the pleasure of knowing that I'm enjoying his touch even if I hate myself for it. He curls his finger and strokes that sweet spot inside me. I lose the battle and moan loudly. "There it is."

"I hate you," I cry out as he increases his pace.

"Yeah, but your pussy doesn't," he claps back. He presses the pad of his thumb against my clit and sweet baby Jesus, I detonate screaming out my release as I come all over his hand. "That's it, ride my fucking fingers and take what you need like a good little whore." Like a slave obeying their master, I do as he commands and ride his fucking hand, drawing out my orgasm. I expected him to leave once he withdrew his fingers, what I didn't expect however was for him to straddle my chest and ram his cock down my throat. "Fuck," he grits out as he hits the back of my throat. I gag around his thick girth, not only is he wide but he's fucking long and there is no way I will be able to fit all of him in my mouth.

When the taste of his pre-cum hits my senses, I moan. the vibration from my moan has him growling. I reach up and slip my hands beneath his shirt, feeling his abs. He grips my headboard and rises slightly so he can thrust in my mouth harder, making tears leak from my eyes and spittle drip from my mouth... But fuck, this is the hottest thing I have ever done!

"Take my cock like a good little slut, suck it hard." I swirl my tongue around him and relish in the moans that slip past his lips. I dig my nails in his chest and drag them down his torso. "Fuck yes, mark me," he grits out, so I do as he asks and rake my nails down his chest, making sure I leave my mark behind. "Suck it like that. I'm going to cum and you're going to swallow every drop or I won't come back and fuck you tomorrow." His words should have me snapping out of my lust-filled stupor but they don't. The anticipation of what tomorrow may bring spurs me on. I suck him as far as I can into my throat, feeling him begin to swell and a second later hot liquid shoots down my throat. I gag a couple times but he keeps his cock in place, stopping his cum from leaking out of my mouth.

# Chapter Nine

## CHAOS

### *Two weeks later...*

Every day I have spent with Lani, making all the necessary arrangements to meet with the Albanians. Caio and Constance are the two that have taken over in Halil's absence. They agreed to meet with us tonight. One of their clubs is opening tonight in the city, I only agreed because I know this club is one of the ones Halil has gone into partnership with Ricardo in. If the chance arises tonight, I plan to take one of his sons.

Stepping out of the shower, I wrap a towel around my waist and stare at my reflection in the mirror. Bite marks mar my chest, scrapes from her nails cover my abs and shoulders. Cassandra Blake is a real fucking freak in the sheets, the girl is dirtier than the floor in a club bathroom. Every night since the first time she put on a show for me, fingering herself on her bed, I end up balls deep inside her tight little cunt. She's a nymph when we fuck. I know she fears me and what little she knows about me but the second we touch, all her fear evaporates and she changes from fearful to downright hellish. She fucking loves it when I get rough with her and fuck her like a crazed bastard.

Heading into my room, I change quickly before heading downstairs. I find Lani in the kitchen sipping a glass of water. She wanted to come tonight but with the possibility of her father being there we decided it was better for her to remain here. At the sound of my approach, she turns to me, her eyes take on a faraway look for a second before she turns away from me.

"What?" I clip out as I head around the other side of the counter to grab my phone and keys.

"Nothing," she mumbles, her blatant brush-off pisses me off.

"Say what the fuck it is that is on your mind."

"Why do you have to be such a dick?" My nostrils flare in anger.

"It's a default setting whenever you're around." She scoffs. Since the talk on the day Royal and Sin came over, she has stopped trying to kill me nightly but it's not like we talk or are friends. I promised not to kill her and that should make her happy but no, she's still a miserable bitch.

"Hate me all you want but you're partly to blame for how we ended up here, Chaos." My anger peaks.

"You are the fucking reason we are here. Your lying scheming ass forced our hand–"

"No, your fear of your brother not needing you is what landed us here. You don't think I know you lied to him about Rico Vargas?" I still. Motherfucker, Havoc told her about that. "You thought you loved me, Chaos, shit, Havoc even thought you loved me which is why he backed away from me so you would be happy!" She's shouting now and I have to admit her words are hitting me right in the feels.

"He what?" I whisper.

"He told me that he loved me but he loved you more, which is why he had to let me go so you could be happy. He was better off without your selfish ass. His whole world revolved around you! He couldn't even allow himself to be happy with me because you ruined it!" I stumble back a step, shaking my head, denying what she is saying. "He loved you more than he loved himself and sacrificed everything for you. Did you know your brother loved to draw?" She doesn't give me a chance to answer. "He never told anyone but me because he knew what was expected of him. You wanted to play football so he gave up on his dream of becoming an artist, as he knew one of you had to step up and be a part of this life. He chose to free you of the burden and claimed his place alongside your cousins."

My mouth opens and closes but no words come out. I keep backing up until I smack into the wall. Lani glares at me, panting with her fists clenched at her sides. What she just said is killing me inside.

"I...I..." She cuts off my rambling.

"Don't fucking squander the gift he gave you. Havoc loved you, Chaos, even after everything you did to him, to *us*. You tricked the woman your brother loved into bed with you and never once said sorry to him. He was the love of my life and you stole him from me. Whenever I look at my son, I get glimpses of his father but that's all I'll ever get now. I may be your prisoner and locked in this house but you are the one who is really trapped. You can't get free of the emotions inside you because you still think your motives and reasons why you did what did are right. Newsflash, asshole, you were fucking wrong!"

I sit in the back booth, twirling my tumbler of gin as I wait for Royal and Sin to arrive, my argument with Lani is playing on a loop inside my head. Everything she said is true. I fucking ruined my brother and here I am trying to act noble and seek revenge in his name. I'm a disgrace. I loathe to admit that Royal sliding into the booth beside me has me jumping. He frowns but says nothing as Sin slips into the booth on the other side, quirking a brow in question.

"You good?" she asks. I grunt in response which just raises more questions.

"I need you straight for this meeting, Chaos," Royal clips out.

"I got this," I say in a tone that leaves no room for argument.

"We scoped the joint out, there are too many cameras here to nab one of them tonight." I shift in my seat to face my cousin, his pale blue eyes stare directly back at me.

"I'm taking them tonight," I sneer.

"You take one of them tonight, then the event next week will be called off and you will miss your shot at getting your nephew and the other brother. You know Ricardo is already on high alert. Tonight will be the first time he has been out in the public eye and not behind his fortress since..." He lets his sentence trail off, not daring to mention that day. The sight of my brother's calling card tattooed on one side of his neck has pain flaring to life inside my chest.

"There's something else we need to discuss with you," Chanel says, drawing my attention to her. She cuts a glance to Royal, who nods at her. I purse my lips, hating that they have this bond like I had that with my brother and never once felt left out when these two would have silent conversations but now... I just feel bitter about it.

"What is it?" I say to distract myself from these wayward thoughts.

"As the heads of the new family in Miami, we are required to meet with the heads of the Russian, Irish, English, Greek and Canadian families. Uncle Bishop has set up the meeting with them and it will take place in Switzerland, on neutral territory." I frown.

"Why the fuck do we need to meet with them?" I ask.

"They are the families we have a treaty with and now that we can add the Columbians and hopefully the Albanians to that list, we need to pledge our loyalty to them as they will to us. It's just a courtesy and one we can't afford to ignore. My dad was adamant that this isn't negotiable. If I am to take his place one day, I need these connections." I look at Royal, trying to gauge what he is saying but not really understanding.

"There's more to this, what aren't you saying?" He smirks before answering.

"One day I will be the head of the Murdoch Mafia and when that time comes, Erika, London and I will be forced to leave Miami and head back to New York, which means, I will need you and Sin to rule over Columbia and Miami. Once we all get the hang of our new roles, then we will be able to share in the work-load and help each other and eventually merge the Murdoch mafia with the *Memento Mori* and rule the way we want. We need these families on our side, we can't win a war against them." I mull over his words, that's a lot to take in.

"Rika is good with giving Columbia up?" I hedge, Royal sighs and scrubs a hand down his face.

"She doesn't want to but she also knows that London needs her and she can't be in two places at once, so as of right now, the *Memento Mori* now have control over Columbia. The Columbians don't like it but when Erika and I get married, they will have no choice but to fall under our rule." My brows raise in surprise.

"You set a date for the wedding?" He beams back at me.

"Yeah, next fall we're getting married in Aspen." I reach out and pull him to me and pat his back. I'm fucking proud and happy for him that he is finally getting what he wants, he deserves it. When we pull a part, I pat his cheek.

"'Bout time that woman made an honest man out of ya." He snorts while Sin and I laugh. Our laughter is cut short when four men approach our table, the three of us sit tall and slip our masks into place. We all eye each other, sizing the other up, the tension is thick. I slip my hand beneath the table and palm my gun in my waistband, ready to draw it if need be.

"You have three seconds to reel yourselves in before I take the four of you out and send your bodies back home to your momma." The four men scowl at Sin who is twirling a fucking blade on the top of the table. Where the fuck does she manage to hide these fucking things?

The one with a crew cut steps forward and extends his hand toward her. Royal snarls at him in warning. If he tries anything on her, Royal will fucking murder him with his bare hands, that's how deep his loyalty goes for us.

"I am Constance." Chanel just flicks her gaze from his hand back to him, saying without words that she has no plans on shaking his hand. He takes the hint and names each of his friends from left to right. "This is Caio and these are our cousins, Albert and Ardik. May we sit to discuss matters or are we no longer welcome?" The three of us share a look before Royal nods and motions for them to join us. Ardik sits next to Royal while Caio and Constance slip in beside Sin, Albert snags a stool from a nearby table and drags it over to the head of ours and sits.

"Move any closer to me and I'll slice your femoral artery," Sin warns Constance who just smiles at her like she is the most amazing woman he has ever met. I snort drawing everyone's attention to me.

"Save yourself the heartache, man, she is fucking crazy and doesn't make idle threats." Constance opens his mouth but I push on, "Her boyfriend is a good guy but if you so much as look at her wrong, the motherfucker will gut you like a fish. They're a match made in hell." I shoot him a wink as I lean back smiling. He swallows and nods, shifting slightly to give Sin more space. Royal chuckles beside me.

"Now that we have that out of the way, let us discuss business," Caio says.

"Why do you have a woman present?" Albert asks. Royal and I glare at him but from the dumbfounded look on his face, I can tell he is genuinely curious. They don't allow women to lead in their culture, so seeing Sin sitting amongst us is new for them.

"Because she is one of the heads of this family and has every fucking right to be here. If you don't like it, then you can fuck off and we'll go to war," Royal grits out.

"You would risk going to war over a female?" Ardik asks from beside him.

"No, I'd go to fucking war for *her*," I snarl.

Before any of them can respond Sin cuts in. "Now that we have established that I have the biggest dick at this table, can we get down to business or would you like to know if I have the biggest balls as well?" Royal and I shake our heads, smirking at Sin's blatant quip at these fuckers.

"Yes, let us discuss the terms of this alliance," Constance says. "You said you have proof of the marriage between our cousin and this woman?" Royal reaches into his back pocket and pulls out the marriage license I snagged from the database, it was easy as fuck to hack into their records and get a copy. Constance looks it over before passing it to the others. The DJ begins to play in the background, making it hard to fucking hear, so we are forced to shout and risk being overheard but we have no choice.

"Your cousin declared war on us, we never instigated it but sure as fuck ended it," Royal tells them.

"Halil was very ambitious, we tried to steer him away from coming to the US but he never listened," Albert says.

"His marriage to my..." I have no idea what the fuck Lailani is to me, so I go with the easy answer. "To the mother of my nephew means she is able to lead until her son is of age to take over, as per your bylaws you are to honor this." The four of them don't like it but I can see it in each of their gazes, that they will uphold their laws and honor it.

"This is correct," Ardik says.

"Then it's settled," Sin adds.

"We have one condition," Caio announces.

"Which is?" I clip out.

"The woman–"

I cut Albert off. "Lailani, her name is Lailani," I sneer, he nods and apologizes.

"We would feel better if one of us was able to be by her side and guide her through this transition. She will need to learn the ways of our people and how things are done."

"No," Royal snaps.

"Our people would have an easier time and the men she will lead would accept her easier if one of us was by her side," Constance quickly adds. I know what he is saying it is true but it's a fucking bitter pill to swallow. I don't want any of these fuckers around her or my brother's kid... fuck, since when did I start thinking of Ryat as Havoc's?

"Fine, but here is a condition of our own." The four of them look at Sin. "If you so much as try to influence her, set her up or harm her child in any way, I will kill each of your families as you watch. No women or children will be safe from my wrath, am I clear?" Constance's eyes dance with longing as he stares at Sin. That look has me scrunching my face in disgust. The four of them agree to her terms and let us know that Constance will be the one to help Lani. What we don't tell them is that we will be the ones pulling the strings and telling her what to do. For the sake of needing them and the numbers they have, we say nothing. They will learn in time that we rule over this city and all its occupants.

We shook their hands and stood to leave the club. The whole time we sat there, I kept an eye out for Ricardo but the bastard never showed. As we make our way past the dance floor, a gold sequined dress captures my attention. No, it's not the dress it's the fucking woman wearing it. I can feel Chanel and Royal staring at me but my gaze is rooted on Cassandra and her best friend Tabby dancing, men openly staring at her with lust in their eyes. I clench my jaw and fight the urge to march over there and punch each of them in the fucking nose for staring at her. The strapless dress fits her like a second skin, the tops of her tits are practically falling over the top of the fucking thing. The nude six-inch heels she wears creates the illusion that her legs are longer than what they are, having every man in here envisioning those legs wrapped around their waist.

"Is that who I think it is?" I nod confirming Royal's suspicion, they both have done research of their own and know exactly who Cassandra is but neither of them have made a move on her. They don't even know I've made contact with the blonde bombshell.

"The girl's got these fuckers eating out of the palm of her hand." Sin's observation spurs me into action as I march toward the dance floor, ignoring them calling my name. Her back is to me but her best friend's eyes widen when she sees me approaching. She may not know who I am but if the rage I'm feeling inside is mirrored in my expression, then she has every right to look fearful. One of the guys gets ballsy and steps in front of Cass, reaching for her, but before he can lay a single finger on her I wrap my arm around her waist and pull her flush against my chest. She gasps and tries to pull free but I tighten my hold, lifting my other hand to grip her jaw and turning her face to the side as I keep my gaze on the cunt in front of me looking like a wounded bitch. I smash my lips against hers, showing this motherfucker that she is taken. He raises his hands as if surrendering and weaves his way back into the crowd. I break the kiss and stare down at Cassandra, her eyes are wide, pupils blown and her chest rising and falling in rapid pants her gaze flicks to the tattoo on my neck, the Ace of Diamonds.

"*You,*" she breathes out. Gripping the back of her neck as a sly smirk tugs at the corners of my lips, I peer down at her.

"Me," I say before I smash my lips against hers, this time she opens for me willingly.

# Chapter Ten

**CASSANDRA**

*He's here!*

That's the only thought that is circulating through my mind as his tongue swirls around my own, drawing a strangled moan from me. His hold on my jaw slips to grip my throat, the fact he is touching me in such an aggressive way that others can see speaks volumes about the fact he gives zero fucks about what others think. I get so consumed by him and the way he is fucking my mouth with his tongue that I forget where I am until I hear a throat clearing loudly over the music. Reality slams into me as I reel back and stare into his sparkling green eyes that hold so much pain in their depths. The color of his eyes reminds me of the trees that grew out back of my childhood home.

"Should I clear my throat again or are you gonna stop sucking face?" The sound of Tabby's voice snaps me out of my watcher-induced haze. I attempt to step back but his hold doesn't loosen. I shoot him a pleading look that he ignores as he flicks his gaze to my best friend. I suddenly realize the danger that I have put Tabby in by bringing her here, granted I had no fucking idea *he* would be here.

"I plan to suck a lot more than her face later." His crass words have me choking on my own spit and my best friend turning a bright shade of red.

"Who the hell is he?" Tabby demands as she cuts her gaze to me. I open and close my mouth a few times but no words come out. How the fuck am I supposed to explain to my best friend, that the man who is currently holding me pressed against his chest, that I have no idea what his name is but I'm also fucking him every night. "What the hell is going on, Cass?" Concern is thick in her tone. I know this must look really bad, considering two weeks ago she accompanied me to the morgue to say my final goodbye to Dylan and here I am now on the dance floor with a God of a man at my back.

"I'd like to know the answer to that as well." The deep rumble comes from beside us. I dart my gaze toward the sound to see a man with pale blue eyes glaring at my watcher, his black hair slicked back. He wears a fitted black shirt that shows off the ink that covers his arms but it's the tattoos on his neck that have my jaw popping open. He has an Ace of Diamonds and a King of Clubs inked on each side of his neck. I turn to the woman who is fucking stunning, her long brown hair is piled in a messy bun atop her head. She wears form-fitting leather pants that hug her legs like a second skin, the white shirt she wears stretches across her ample chest and the matching leather jacket completes her badass look. She doesn't have a speck of makeup on her flawless face. I'm instantly jealous of the bitch.

"Nothing," comes from behind me, his tone is cold and void of all emotion.

"Shitty call, cousin," the woman says. Is it pathetic that some of the tension inside me eases because she called him *cousin*? Sue me, I'm only human and jealousy is a natural reaction, right?

"Mind ya business, Sin," he grunts, then releases his hold on me and steps back. I instantly feel cold without his heat pressed against me. I take the time to drink him in. The shirt he wears enhances the muscles beneath it, the dark wash jeans he wears hug his thick thighs but my gaze zeros in on the slight bulge at the front of his pants. His brown hair is a tousled mess like he has been running his hands through it for hours. When I slowly trail my gaze back to his face, I find his gaze already on me, lust sparking in his heated stare, sending a shiver of anticipation through me. My pussy thinks now is a good time to start fluttering and making her greedy ass presence known. "Go home, Cassandra."

I reel back at the harsh tone of his voice. "Who the fuck do you think you are?" I balk at my best friend—she has no idea who *they* are but now I do. I grip her arm trying to drag her away but she breaks free and steps up close to him. "You don't get to tell her what to do." He opens his mouth to berate her I'm sure but I don't give him the chance, I push between them keeping my back to him and imploring my best friend with a look to let it go and keep her mouth shut.

"We need to go," I hiss. She places her hands on her hips.

"Why? Because mister holier than thou said so?" Fuck, her mouth is going to get us both killed.

"No, because I am telling you that we need to leave, now!" Her eyes search mine for a moment, whatever she sees in them has her lips thinning and nodding stiffly. I snatch her hand and practically drag her out of the club, not caring that I didn't get what I came here for. I'll get another chance to spy on Ricardo Dominico, but right now my main priority is getting Tabby as far away from here and *him* as I can.

The entire cab ride back to my apartment, Tabby hurls questions at me but I can't answer any of them and I can tell my silence is working on her last nerve, but I don't have a choice. The less she knows the better. The hunch I have about who *he* is, which means he is more dangerous than I thought... I need to get Tabby the hell away from me. When the cab stops out front of my building, we both climb out, neither of us speaking a word the whole way up to my apartment. The anger is rolling off her in waves and I don't blame her. I tell Tabby everything but ever since he broke into my apartment that first night, I've been lying to her.

I open the door and motion for her to go ahead of me. She shoulders past me and I grunt from the force but say nothing. I close and lock the door before following her into the living room. I'm conscious of the cameras throughout the apartment so I know I need to watch how this conversation goes. Call me a shitty friend but I really just want to grab my laptop and comb through my notes to prove if my hunch is right or not. Tabby stands near the windows with her back to me, I'm standing still, waiting for her to gather her thoughts.

"I need you to tell me the truth, Cass," she says as she slowly turns to face me with a stern look on her face, tension rolling off me in waves.

"The truth about what?" My sarcasm is clearly not appreciated judging by the way she scowls at me and places her hands on her hips.

"Who the fuck was that guy and why do I get this dreadful feeling that he isn't someone you just met tonight?" I debate avoiding the question all together or giving her a half truth, the latter wins out after a second of deliberation.

"You're right, I didn't just meet him tonight I met him a couple of weeks ago." Her face slackens in surprise.

"Wow, was Dylan still breathing?" I flinch, that was a fucking low blow.

"I'm not going to validate that Tabby, you of all people should know me better than that!"

"I'm starting to think I don't know you at all. The Cassandra I know and love wouldn't be behaving like... Like..."

"Like what?" I push, starting to get really annoyed.

"Like a... you know what I mean."

"No, actually, I really don't. So why don't you spell it out for me?" I grit out.

"You haven't been acting like yourself since Quintin died. You have been acting reckless and closing yourself off from everyone. Before losing your brother, there is no way you would have accepted an invitation to an event from Alex, you know he expects you to spread your legs for him as a thank you."

I keep my face blank. "And you just assume that I would lay down and allow our boss to fuck me because you think I've been acting like a slut?" She jerks back, only just realizing how far she has pushed me.

"I never said that!" she defends.

"You didn't have to, you implied it and that is fucking low, Tabby. I have always stood by your side and never doubted you. You've known me since we were fourteen, how the hell could you think I would cheat on Dylan or sleep with our boss?" Remorse is evident in her features but I'm past the point of caring.

"I just don't understand what is going on with you lately. You're closing me out and I don't know how to stop that. Cass, you are my person and know I would do bodily harm for you." The fight drains from me and my shoulders slouch.

"Tabby, I know you may not understand this but I have been drowning for years." Her eyes widen at my declaration.

"Why didn't you tell me?"

"How could I tell you the truth when you thought I had this perfect life with Dylan?" I don't give her a chance to answer. "I wasn't happy... For fuck's sake, we weren't even sleeping in the same bedroom or fucking. I never told anyone this but I know for a fact that Dylan was cheating on me for the past six months and honestly, I knew it was bad when the girl reached out to me and all I thought was, if she is giving it up then he won't expect me to."

"Cass–"

"I don't want you to pity me. Dylan died and that is fucking horrible and I am sad because we did have some good times together, but I wasn't living. These past couple of weeks I have felt alive and like myself again for the first time in years. I'm finally not ashamed to embrace my sexuality and my preferences. Dylan always shamed me for what I wanted in the bedroom but he doesn't."

"Holy shit." I frown at her whispered words, she covers her mouth with her hand.

"What?"

"You have feelings for that guy from the club, don't you?" I mull over her words. I've never really given thought to how I feel toward him, but now that she has brought it up, I'm forced to face the fact that she might be right. Before I can answer, a knock sounds out around the room. I frown, wondering who the hell could be knocking on my door at this time of night. I unlock the deadbolt and open the door a smidge, the sight that greets me has my jaw practically hitting the floor.

"We need to talk," he growls. Swallowing loudly, I nod like an idiot and open the door for him as I move back into the living room. Tabby frowns at me as I enter but the moment *he* enters her eyes bug out of her head. The awkwardness could be cut with a knife.

Wanting to get this over with I say to my best friend, "Want to hang out for a bit while we... talk in my room?" She snaps her mouth closed and shakes her head.

"I'll leave you to it and we can catch up tomorrow and talk about... *this*, then." I smile my thanks and nod. She crosses the room to wrap me in a hug that I return. "I love you, Cass, and will always be here no matter what."

Her words have tears pricking the backs of my eyes. "Love you too, always," I whisper in her ear before she pulls back. She leaves without another word, the sound of the door clicking shut fills me with dread. I take a step away from him and gather all the courage inside me to turn and face him, his green eyes spearing me with the intensity in them. He stands there with a blank look on his face, I can tell he is shielding his emotions from me and for some reason that annoys me. "Why are you here?" I blurt.

He darts his gaze above my head and looks out the window. "You weren't supposed to be there tonight." I dart my tongue out to wet my lips, his gaze snaps to me and his eyes heat as he follows the movement of my tongue.

"I was working." I don't know why I feel the need to explain my reasoning but I do it anyway.

"In that thing?" he sneers as he eyes my mini dress. I purse my lips.

"Yes, it's a nightclub and this is generally what people wear to places like that," I quip.

"Why were you there?" The hard edge of his tone has me feeling uneasy.

"I was... I went to gather intel for my article." His eyes crinkle at the corners as he studies my face.

"What article?"

"I'm a reporter, it's my job to report on things like a club opening in the city."

His gaze hardens. "You're a shit liar."

I scoff. "It seems we have something other than fucking in common then." My snide dig has his eyebrows raising. Honestly, I'm surprised that shit came out of my mouth as well. He stalks toward me, eating up the space in a matter of two steps. His chest brushes against mine, forcing me to crane my neck back in order to meet his cold stare.

"You have nothing in common with me. You are a hole I get to sink my cock in without strings attached, nothing more." His words are like a whip. I stumble back a step, shaking my head.

"Nothing in common, right," I snark. "Since we have that established, you should go and find a new hole to sink your sorry ass excuse for a dick into." The fact my bravado hasn't wavered has pride swelling inside me. I was telling the truth earlier, since meeting him something inside me has changed, I'm not willing to settle anymore and hide who I truly am. I will no longer be shamed or allow others' expectations to control me. He strikes out so fast I don't have time to prepare, before he has a hand clamped on the back of my neck and his other arm wrapped around my waist.

He bends until our noses are barely an inch apart. "My sorry ass excuse for a dick, huh?" I open my mouth but the words die on my tongue when he grabs my waist and lifts me, my legs instinctively wrapping around his waist and my hands landing on the tops of his shoulders. My mini dress has ridden up and my thong-covered ass is now out. He backs us up until I'm pressed against the window. I hiss from the cold glass and arch forward, pushing my tits right in his face. His hold on my waist shifts until he's gripping the globes of my ass in his hands.

"What are you doing?" I cringe at the breathy tone of my own voice, yet again my mind and body are not on the same page. My pussy is pulsing and begging for me to grind down his hard length but I manage to control myself and remain still.

"Taking what is *mine*," he growls in a husky tone before he bites down on the top of my right tit. I cry out in pain but it quickly changes to a moan when he licks the same spot. He uses his teeth to pull the front of my dress down exposing my girls, then latches onto my nipple, drawing a loud moan from me as I drop my head back against the window. Oh shit, the apartment across the street will be getting a good view of my ass and what he is doing to me. He switches sides and pays my other nipple the same amount of attention—this is new for us. He's normally shrouded in darkness and I'm unable to get a good look at his face, but not tonight. I can see him clearly and watching this beast of a man ravish my tits is an erotic sight.

He releases my nipple with a wet pop, shifting so my shoulders are resting against the glass but my bottom half is angled out toward him. I lock my legs tighter around him when he grips the bottom of my dress and pulls it up higher so it's bunched around my waist. At the sight of the nude colored thong I'm wearing, he hums his approval as he grips the tiny triangle of lace in his hand

and rips the garment from my body. My mouth opens in shock. He drops the ruined material to the floor beside me and presses his thumb between my folds to rub circles around my clit. My eyes roll backward as I groan at the exquisite feeling of his hands on my greedy little cunt. He runs his thumb through my slit and pushes it inside me. I cry out.

"You dirty little lying whore, you're fucking soaked for me and I've barely touched your rotten little cunt." His dirty words have embarrassing sounds coming from me as I push down on his thumb, needing him to move it inside me, but he lands a smack to my ass drawing a yelp of surprise from me. "I should leave you here panting and on edge but you would just finger this tight little cunt until you came like a whore, wouldn't you?"

Fuck, *this*, this right here is what I have longed for in the bedroom. I love being called a whore and slut during sex, it fucking gets me off.

"Yes," I answer as I meet his lustful gaze, his eyes blazing in response. "I would bury my fingers inside my greedy little cunt and ride them, imagining it was your cock, then I would come with the ghost of your name on my lips."

"Fuck," he snarls as he reaches between us to try to free his cock but he can't do it while still holding me, so I make a bold move and reach down to do it for him. The instant I free his cock, he slaps my hands away and lifts my bottom half up so my legs are draped over his shoulders and his face is buried in my pussy. He plunges his tongue inside me without warning. I slap my hands flat against the glass as I cry out.

"Oh, fuck yes, keep fucking my tight little pussy with your tongue." He growls in warning. I bite down on my lip to be silent, he doesn't take orders from me, I am only given what he chooses to give. The control he wields is so sexy. Every time we have fucked I am always left boneless and sated. He knows exactly what I like and how I like it without me having to tell him. My muscles begin to tighten as my orgasm starts to build, my thighs press against his head pulling him in closer. He rips free of my hold drawing a huff from me. He shifts me and wraps my legs around his waist. As he lines his cock up with my entrance, anticipation thrums through me as his eyes lock with mine.

Something about this moment feels different, we have never looked each other in the eyes before as we've fucked. There has always been darkness between us but not tonight. We are raw and open, and it's got me feeling a type of way that I can't explain. Without warning he slams inside me. I scream so fucking loud there is no way my neighbors can't hear.

"Suck your cunt juice off my tongue." I press forward and do as I'm told as he opens his mouth and pokes his tongue out. I suck it into my mouth and moan at the taste of myself. I swirl my tongue around his pretending it's his cock I'm sucking. Muffled moans come from the both of us as he thrusts inside me. When the pleasure becomes too much, I stop my tongue fucking and throw my head back.

"Fuck me like that," I scream out. He wraps an arm around my waist and uses his other hand to grip the back of my neck. His tempo changes and his thrusts become harder, fuck I can feel his cock scraping against the sweet spot inside me. I'm seconds away from coming all over his glorious cock.

"Come for me, my little rotten apple." His words are my undoing. I shatter screaming out my release as my pussy walls strangle the fuck out of his cock. I don't get a chance to ride out the aftershocks tearing through me, before he pulls out of me and places me on my feet and spins me so my naked front is plastered against the window. Stepping up behind me he kicks my legs apart, then he's slamming inside me again, this time we both cry out at the feeling. Reaching down I grab one of his hands from my waist and place it against my throat. He growls his approval as he wraps his hand around my neck tight enough to slightly restrict my airway but not too much.

He leans down and sucks the soft flesh of my neck into his mouth before he bites down. I cry out with a mix of pain and pleasure, the mixture is a heady combination. He switches sides and does the same thing to the other side, I know without a doubt I will have bruises on my neck but I don't give a fuck. All I care about is him not stopping and fucking me harder until I come again.

"You want to come?" he rasps out as he nibbles on the shell of my ear.

"Fuck yes."

"You gonna be a good little whore and suck the cum off my cock after I blow my load deep inside this greedy little cunt?" His dirty talk has me moaning and muttering promises to do whatever he wants me to do as long as I get to come again. True to his words he has me coming again in a matter of seconds, following after me roaring out my name. Hearing that sends a shiver down my spine. He's barely finished emptying himself inside me before he's pulling out, spinning me around and forcing me to my knees, then ramming his cock down my throat. I instantly gag and try to pull back but he grips my hair and holds me in place as he continues to fuck my mouth like a savage. When the taste of both our releases hits my senses I reach up and grip the backs of his thighs holding him in place as I take control and suck him clean, needing to taste more of the both of us.

He pulls his cock out of my mouth panting and breathless. I drag in lungfuls of air and try in vain to wipe the spit dripping down my chin, but he bats my hand away and smears the mixture of spit and our cum all over my face. When he is satisfied that my entire face is covered, he releases me, tucks himself back into his pants and straightens his shirt, then steps back running a hand through his hair.

"Next time you try to tell me no, I'm fucking your tight little ass. This ends when I say it fucking ends. Stop digging into Ricardo Dominico and the *Memento Mori*, that is your only warning," he says before he turns and walks out, leaving me on the floor looking like the used up whore he's turned me into.

# Chapter Eleven

## CHAOS

Pulling into my driveway, I groan at the sight of Royal and Chanel leaning against the hood of his car. I park beside them, take a calming breath before stepping out. I had planned to come home and fall into bed now that my balls were empty and I left my mark on Cassandra, but apparently these two didn't go straight home after I left them at the club and chose to come here instead and wait for me. I bet they didn't expect to be waiting this long. I move around the other side of my car and lean back against it, crossing my arms over my chest, waiting for them to say whatever it is they need to say so they can leave.

"You reek of sex," Sin sneers in disgust. I say nothing, I don't see the point when we all know I was definitely having sex less than an hour ago,

"You are playing a dangerous fucking game here, brother," Royal says with an edge to his tone.

"Exactly, this is a fucking game and right now I am winning, so what the fuck is the problem?"

Royal throws his hands in the air. "She is the sister of the fucker that—"

I push off my car and step right into him. "Don't fucking say it," I yell right in his face, my breaths coming out in loud angry huffs. His chest is rising and falling just as fast as mine, a lick of adrenaline courses through me at the thought of going a round or two with my cousin. I could use the outlet.

"Both of you need to back the fuck up now before I get trigger happy and have to explain to my aunts why I shot both their sons in their legs for being dumb fucks." We glare at each other but do as Sin said and take a step back, reclaiming our spots against our cars. "Now, why don't you explain to us what the fuck you are doing, because if this blows up in your face, it will blow back on all of us." I turn my attention to Chanel and scowl.

"My plan is the same as it always has been. I have four–now three Dominico's left to kill since Lani now has immunity."

"What about *her*?" I keep my gaze on Chanel as I answer Royal.

"She is the last, her end will be slower than the others. She is going out of her fucking mind trying to figure out who I am and what I want with her. I want her crazy and out of her mind before I strike, then and only then will I kill and dump her body on top of her cunt of a brother's grave with my card nailed to her chest, so every motherfucker will know who wiped out the Blake bloodline," I say with finality.

"What happens to the Dominico empire? Have you thought of that, because we have. They own the territory to our border and own clubs and hotels in Miami."

I pull my gaze from Sin to look at Royal as I answer his question. "The *Memento Mori* will take over the Dominico turf and after we control theirs, we will wipe out the Marga's, then we will have secured control of Alabama and Georgia, therefore Florida will be untouchable and no one will be able to come for us." The surprised look on both their faces is fucking comical. They thought I wasn't thinking things through and going off half-cocked but they should know better. I was always the twin that planned and thought things through, Havoc was the one to pull the trigger first and deal with the repercussions later.

"That means, we would have the three states. Columbia and Albania on our side as well as the alliances with the other families in the world and our own. Uncle Bishop has control of New York, Texas, California, Montana and Washington." Chanel breathes out, her wide eyes darting between the both of us. "Our family would be untouchable. If we seized control of South and North Carolina as well as Mississippi, we would practically own this half of the country. If our fathers keep taking over states throughout the US, we would be the most powerful families in the *world*."

"We would never be able to own the entire US, our family has treaties with some of the other smaller families in Idaho, New Jersey, Tennessee and a few other places but yes, we would run a majority of the country," I say. They both remain silent, lost in their own thoughts. Unlike them, I haven't been playing a quick game of checkers, I have been playing the long game of chess while I sought revenge for my brother. I will not allow his death to be in vain. I will help this family fucking prosper in his name and make sure every cunt knows that we will never allow anyone who harms our family to live, their entire bloodline will be erased from existence.

"How do we make this work?" Royal asks, the awe in his tone gives me pause. He isn't used to being the one not in control or being a step ahead of the rest of us, so this is a humbling moment for him.

"We take out Johnny and Ricardo Jr at the gala, then we go after their bastard of a father and make an example out of him. I want everyone at this meeting with the other families to know what happens to those that come after us. The Dominico line will be no more."

"One Dominico will remain though," Sin adds. I scrub a hand down my face and decide to tell them what I have planned for Lailani.

"No. The day Ricardo Sr dies, is the day I will make her a Murdoch." Both their eyes widen to the size of dinner plates.

"Come again?"

"Say what now?" They both shout in unison.

"It's what has to be done," I snap back.

"You're going to marry the mother of your nephew?" Royal hisses in disbelief. I scrunch my face in disgust and shake my head.

"Fuck no!" They both sag in relief at my answer.

"Then what do you mean?" Sin asks.

"I plan to have her name changed, she is the mother to the future of our family so it seems only fitting she shares the same last name as her son since Hav..." I take a deep breath and push the words past the lump in my throat. "Since my brother never got the chance to marry the love of his life," I whisper brokenly as I scrunch my eyes closed to try to stave off the pain rising inside me. A moment later a hand lands on my shoulder. I snap my eyes open to see Royal standing before me.

"He would have loved that. What you're doing is a great honor to his memory, Chaos. Just don't lose yourself in this war of redemption for him because that isn't what he would want and you know that." I nod stiffly, unable to speak. "Do not sacrifice your happiness because you believe you need to suffer. Never be a prisoner of your past, it was just a lesson for you to learn from, not a life sentence."

After sending Chanel and Royal on their way, I make my way inside. I'm still on high alert as I enter the house, not trusting Lani not to take a stab at me even though she has stopped for a couple weeks. I should have chained her crazy ass up in the basement but I couldn't bring myself to do her like that because of what she meant to my brother. That is the only reason I have gone easy on her, the same courtesy will not extend to her father and brothers. I close the door softly behind myself and round the corner waiting for her to jump out, but the stairwell light is on and she is sitting on the bottom stair with tears trailing down her cheeks and her phone–the phone I had hidden in my bedroom–clutched in her hand.

At the sound of my approach, she looks up and startles at the sight of me. Quickly wiping away her tears, she turns her phone face down in her lap. I move past her, ready to call it a night but when I reach the third stair I pause and war within myself. I should go to bed and leave her the fuck alone, but another part of me knows that deep down inside I need to treat her better for the simple fact that she is my nephews mother—the latter wins out. I grit my teeth and turn around, dropping down on the stair beside her, my leg brushing against hers and she tenses.

"Why are you crying?" I ask. When she huffs at the gruff tone of my voice, I try again, gentler this time. "Why are you so upset?" She turns her face to me and scowls, the hatred in her gaze is on full display. The look pisses me off but I also know I deserve it for the way I have treated her.

"Like you fucking care. All I am is a way to garner more men for your stupid little gang, you're no better than my father." Instinct has me reaching out to grab her throat but she reels back. I freeze with my hand in the air, then drop it back to my lap after I get my temper under control.

"I am nothing like him," I spit at her.

"No? So, you don't plan to use the safety and wellbeing of my son against me when we get him back?" Now, I recoil.

"I would never hurt the fucking kid," I sneer.

"Bullshit, you threatened to kill me and take away my son. I lied to you, I will not allow you to kill me willingly, I will fight you because Ryat deserves to have one of his parents raise him." Her words are like a red-hot branding iron, the reminder that my twin isn't here to meet his son or raise him kills me.

"I told you, I won't hurt you and I meant it."

"And I'm just supposed to take your word for it?" she throws back at me.

"Yes."

"I can't believe a thing that comes out of your mouth. You are fucking crazy, Chaos. Everything you have said to me since the first time we met has been a lie!"

I turn away from her and stare down at my lap, hating that she is right, again. We sit here for a long time in silence lost in our thoughts. Mine always drift back to the day I lost my best friend. Nightmares plague me every time I close my eyes, I wake with a fright every night and without fail I always call his name expecting him to come smashing through my bedroom door but... he'll never come through any door again. Lani lifts her phone and unlocks it, then hands it to me. My eyes mist at the sight of the picture on the screen. It's a photo of Havoc smiling happily, he has his arms wrapped around Lani from behind as she takes a selfie of them.

"I loved him so fucking much, Chaos," she chokes out, sobs clawing their way out of her throat. She buries her face in her hands as she breaks down beside me. I scroll to the next photo and the lump in my throat reappears, it's another photo of Havoc but this time he's sleeping in her bed back at UNLV. Even while he sleeps, he has a smile on his face. It's too much, I lock the phone and drop it into my lap as I fight back my own tears. "I miss him so fucking much it's hard to breathe," she cries. I do the unthinkable and wrap my arm around her shoulders, drawing her into my side. She fights me at first but I hold firm, the struggle leaves her after a minute and she melts into me as she cries for my brother.

Holding her through her grief is so fucking hard considering I haven't even allowed myself to deal with my own, I can't. If I allow myself to break then I won't get back up, it will eat me alive until there is nothing left. I haven't even spoken to my parents since the day we left for Miami over a month ago, I can't handle seeing them or hearing their voices. I don't want to hear the resentment in their voices or see the hatred and blame in their gazes as they look at me. I know it should have been me that died and so do they. Havoc spent his life protecting me and I couldn't do the same for him when he needed it the most.

I don't know how much time passes before I realize Lani has stopped crying and fallen asleep in my hold. The asshole in me wants to wake her up, but the other half that wins out knows she has been through hell. So I scoop her up in my arms and carry her up to her room, then place her gently on top of her covers where she stirs. I grab the blanket at the end of her bed and pull it over her. Her eyes lazily open but I can tell she is still half asleep when a smile graces her face.

"Havoc," she whispers, causing me to tense. "He looks so much like his daddy," she mumbles as she rolls over. "I love you both so much." She yawns then closes her eyes as sleep claims her again. I stand here for the longest time staring down at her. I don't think I really realized until now that she really was–is in love with my brother. She loved him so much that she fought her family and was beaten to try to harm her unborn baby in the hopes she would miscarry, all because she protected the identity of her child's father.

*My brother.*

The next morning I leave the house before Lani wakes, after last night I need some space to deal with all this bullshit swirling inside me and fucking my head up. I drive aimlessly until I reach the beach. It's barely dawn when I park my car and head down to the shore where I drop to my ass and thumb the ring on my finger that contains the ashes of my brother. I close my eyes and allow the pain to bleed through. It robs me of breath, call me a coward but I quickly put a lid on that shit and push my feelings down. I'm thankful for the sound of my phone ringing to distract me from my thoughts. I pull it out of my pocket and the sight of

Amelia's name lighting up my screen has curiosity eating me so I answer the call saying.

"Meelz?"

"Do not hang up!" I still at the sound of my dad's voice and debate ignoring his demand but I'm frozen in place unable to move.

"Why do you have Meelz's phone?" I mutter, unable to say anything else.

He scoffs. "Who the fuck taught you and your brother to hack?" He doesn't give me a chance to answer. "It was simple to switch her number to mine, I knew your nosy ass wouldn't be able to ignore her call." I flinch, I haven't just been ignoring my parents, I've blocked out my aunts and uncles as well.

"What do you want, Dad?" I rasp out feeling utterly caught off guard with this call and the fact I'm sitting at the beach watching the sunrise alone like a pussy.

He sighs dejectedly. "I've already lost one son, Chaos, I am not going to lose you as well. Your mother and I wouldn't survive that." I slam my eyes closed and fight back the tears that prick the backs of my eyes as guilt gnaws at my insides. "We need you, Son." I shake my head even though he can't see me.

"No. You need *him*. It was my fault and I'll make this right, Dad. I'll fix everything and show you and Mom that I am worthy of your forgiveness and then you won't hate me for not protecting him."

"Chaos–"

"You'll see. I'll prove to you both that I am capable and you will see that I won't fail him in death, just watch me." I end the call with a renewed sense of determination flowing through me. I needed that call with my dad to remind me what is at stake. I silence my phone when he continues to keep calling, then stalk back to my car, ready to move this plan along and lay waste to any fucker that tries to stop me—not even Cassandra will sway me from my end goal.

# Chapter Twelve

## CASSANDRA

*One week later...*

I haven't seen him since he fucked me against the window of my apartment. I waited for him Sunday night, then again on Monday night but I gave up waiting when he didn't show by Thursday. Tabby has been distant since I returned to work on Monday and I can't blame her. She pushed me for an explanation on Sunday but I couldn't give her one, so she told me until I could be honest with her she and I were done. It fucking stings that she won't even look at me. The gala is tomorrow night and I know that is the reason she is extra pissy today. She has been snapping at everyone all day. I tried to talk to her but she just ignored me.

Just before we left for the day, Alex stopped by and dropped me off a garment bag that contained the dress I forgot to choose for myself. He said he took it upon himself to choose one for me since he saw I didn't use company funds to buy it myself. Tabby glared at the bag like it was the bane of her existence. I didn't want to anger her further so I haven't opened the bag to see the dress. Carrying the garment bag up to my apartment I expected to feel excited at the fact that I'm going to a gala and have a swanky dress to wear that no doubt costs more than I make in a year, but I can't find it within myself to care.

I drape the bag over the back of my sofa and dump my purse on the counter before heading into my room, where I freeze at the sight of the woman from the club sitting on the end of my bed. At the sight of me in the doorway, she slowly stands and runs her gaze over me. After spending this past week digging through every ounce of information I have gathered on the *Memento Mori*, I know for a fact that she is one of them. I may not be able to prove that she is Chanel Murelo except for the fact she was with the Ace of Diamonds–I've been calling him *Ace* all week—and the other guy who had the King of Clubs tattooed on his neck. She looks like a right badass dressed head to toe in black with her hair in a high ponytail, and yet again she is free of makeup—this woman is beauty personified.

"Cassandra Blake, we meet at last." I stand tall and meet her accusing stare with one of my own.

"Do you have a habit of breaking into people's homes?" She shrugs like it's not a big deal.

"Only the ones I need a moment alone with." I swallow audibly. If the rumors about the *Memento Mori* are true, then this woman could kill me in the blink of an eye.

"What do you want?" The quiver in my voice has me wanting to slap myself for allowing her to hear fear in my tone.

"I need someone who won't cower under the pressure or succumb to the demands of others. From what I have gathered about you, you don't seem to bend to anyone's will when it comes to exposing the truth."

A frown has my brows drawing in. "The truth about what exactly?"

She reaches into her back pocket and pulls out some folded

pieces of paper, then hands them to me. I eye them and don't make a move to grab them. "There is a list of names on these papers. Each of them are corrupt federal agents and some of them are politicians, their crimes are listed in here as well."

My face slackens. "Why would you give this to me?"

She pins me with a deadpan look. "Don't play coy, I know you have a hunch about who I am and who *he* is." I reel back, shaking my head trying to deny her but she just pushes on. "I can't stop what he has in motion for you, but what I can do is hand you this proof that not everything you hear and see is black and white. You spend your free time taking down crime families and exposing them for the pieces of shit that they are but have you ever stopped to ask yourself how they got away with committing the crimes they have for so long?" It's a rhetorical question so I don't bother to answer. "All crime families have many powerful people in their pockets. Here is a list of names of those people."

I tentatively reach out and take the papers from her. "I'm guessing a list of the names that help *your* family aren't listed in here?" She smirks.

"I never said I was a part of any family."

"You also never told me your real reason why you want me to print this article," I shoot back.

"Print it or don't print it, I don't give a shit but this was my way of offering you something before I tell you what I take from you if you print the secret article you are writing now."

I gulp. "I-I—"

"Whenever you open a document on the Google drive, it is connected to the web, I... know some people that can hack and the article you have there titled *The Watcher*, needs to be buried." The venomous tone of her voice tells me she isn't asking.

"If I print this article, what do I get in return?"

"What do you want?"

"Freedom from the Ace of Diamonds." Her brows draw in for a split second before understanding shines in her brown eyes.

"*The Jack of Spades represents the coming Chaos and Ace of Diamonds is for the Havoc.*" Her reply is cryptic and unhelpful.

"That explains nothing," I shoot back.

"I just told you more than you deserve, there is no escaping him. He will claim his pound of flesh and there is no outrunning that. Print the article first thing tomorrow morning and you may be surprised at the changes that follow."

She brushes past me without another word but before she can leave I ask, "How do I convince him to not kill me?" She peers at me over her shoulder.

"You can't, he needs to convince himself that he is worthy enough to live." Again, her reply is so fucking unhelpful. The moment the door clicks shut behind her, I crumple to the ground and suck in lungfuls of air. I need to get a better lock for my door or move the fuck out because random people showing up at my house anytime they like isn't good.

My eyes are burning from staring at the screen of my laptop for hours and my fingers are aching from moving across my keyboard at warp speed. The information contained in these papers is groundbreaking. The crimes committed by the chief of police are disgusting, he was being paid to look the other way as women were sold and shipped from these ports to other countries to become enslaved sex workers. I am appalled to think that some of these names on these pages are people sworn to protect us but in fact, they just use us to line their pockets. This article is going to cause mayhem and uproar but it needs to be printed—the backlash can get fucked. I flip to the last page and freeze at the sight of the name at the top.

*Quintin Blake, Director of F.B.I*

I read through the crimes he is accused of. My hand covers my mouth as tears cloud my vision, my brother helped the mafia and the Albanians sell drugs, import guns, sell women and children. He fucking sold *children!* Bile rushes up my throat. I push off my stool and dart around the counter to empty the contents of my stomach in the sink. I can't stop heaving even after I have brought up everything I have eaten and drank today.

Turning the tap on, I cup my hand and bring water to my mouth, rinsing it, then swallowing some before splashing more on my face to snap me out of my stunned state. When the splashing water on my face doesn't do the trick, I shove my face under the running water. I reel back gasping, finally feeling like I can breathe again, I use the back of my hand to brush away the water from my face.

"Get your ass back over there and read that fucking paper!" I scold myself aloud. It takes me a solid minute or two to convince my legs to move and carry me to the other side of the counter and drop onto the stool. I blow out an exaggerated breath as I shakily reach out, grab the paper and read over the remainder of the crimes my brother was accused of. I make it to the last paragraph feeling queasy again at the horrible things that he did. "Oh my God," tumbles from my mouth as I read over the last part, not retaining any of the information, I read it aloud in the hopes it will help it sink in.

*"Quintin Blake ambushed agent Kacey Vaughn and set him up to be taken hostage and killed by the Albanians that had murdered his brother weeks prior in a prison incident. The three vans carrying Agent Vaughn and other agents were gunned down. An outside special ops team managed to rescue some of the agents from being killed and helped Agent Vaughn escape the scene. Director Blake was shot in the back of the head after he pulled the trigger on his service weapon killing a twenty-year-old male who was later identified as Havoc Murdoch."*

Before my mind can spiral any further, I march my little ass over to the cabinet above the stove and snag the bottle of Hennessy, pop the top and guzzle the liquid until it burns my throat. I nearly cough up a lung, only then do I make my way back over to my laptop and spill the truth about the dirty FBI agent that sold children, hurt women, received bribes, sold drugs and killed the son of the most powerful family in the United States. By the time I have finished writing the article, it's nearly two in the morning, half the bottle of Hennessy is gone and my vision is fuzzy from being half drunk. A smart reporter would look over her work and make sure everything is correct but tonight, I'm feeling reckless and I also know if I read back through it, I will lose my nerve. I attach the document and email it through to my editor marked *urgent* and telling her it needs to be printed by tomorrow evening at the latest.

The moment I push send I feel sick again, rush into my bathroom and drop to my knees in front of the porcelain throne, throwing up every ounce of alcohol I just drank. Crossing my arms over the bowl I rest my cheek atop them and close my eyes to try to stop my head from spinning.

"Fuck off, fly," I snap when the sound of the insistent buzzing continues. I roll over and freeze when I feel a body beside me. I slowly crack an eye open and prepare myself to come face to face with... I don't know what I expected but the sight of my best friend lying beside me isn't it. My head thumps to the beat of an imaginary drum, the buzzing happens again, this time I realize it's not a fly but my phone. I snatch it off the side table and don't bother to check the caller ID as I answer.

"Yello?" I croak out, my mouth is dry and my throat is scratchy.

"What the fuck were you thinking?" is screamed down the phone.

"Alex?"

"Of course, it's me, Cassandra! You just fucking ruined not only your career but mine as well!" I sit up regretting the move instantly when the whole room begins to spin. I close my eyes and try to breathe through the nausea, this is why no one should drink hard liquor, the hangovers are a bitch.

"What are you talking about?" I ask as Tabby begins to stir beside me.

"That fucking article you published has not only gone viral but it's streaming on all major news channels." Hangover forgotten, I jump off my bed and race into the living room with Tabby hot on my heels and switch on the TV. Alex's voice becomes white noise as Tabby snatches the remote from my hand and turns the volume up.

*"Breaking news, a local reporter, Cassandra Blake has released an article pin pointing politicians, police officers, FBI agents and many more supplying proof of their crimes."* I jerk back, I didn't supply any type of proof, I only sent the article. The camera changes to display officers leading the majority of the people I named in my article out of their homes, offices, restaurants and so on in handcuffs. *"This article has caused a frenzy across the nation, cases some of these high profiled lawyers tried will be thrown out and many criminals will walk free."* I stumble back and drop down onto the sofa staring at the screen.

"Cassandra!" I startle at the sound of Alex's voice, scrambling and bring the phone back to my ear. "Are you even listening to me?"

"Y-yes, I am."

"I will have Beth clear out your desk, you're fired effective immediately."

"What?" I screech, Tabby spins around with wide eyes at my shout.

"You have tarnished the name of this company."

"I told the truth!" I defend.

"You broke company policy by publishing an article through another source."

"No, I didn't. I sent it through to Margaret to be edited last night. I never published this, Alex, you have to believe me," I plead.

"I don't. You're fired, Cassandra," he shouts before ending the call. I lift my gaze to Tabby's, the look on my face has her rushing to my side and wrapping her arms around me as I cry at the injustice of the situation.

"He fired me," I cry out.

"The article was published by an unknown source, babe," she replies hesitantly. I pull back and search her gaze. When she refuses to look me in the eye I know there is something she is hiding.

"What do you know?" I push.

She deflates and pulls her phone out of her pocket and hands it to me. I stare down at the text message.

UNKNOWN NUMBER

Suck up your pride; she didn't tell you the truth because she can't, so deal with it because she is going to need her best friend when this article hits the news in the morning. She is going to have a lot of heat and will need a friend, go to her.

I reread the message twice and before handing her phone back to her, I can already tell that the message wasn't sent from Ace so that leads me to believe that it was Chanel.

"I'm sorry, babe, I had no idea that you were hiding stuff because you didn't want it to blow back on me." I open my mouth to correct her but I decide against it, knowing she will ask questions. She doesn't need to know the truth right now.

"I couldn't live with myself if something happened to you because of me." Tabby spends the morning screening calls from other outlets trying to get me to comment on the article I wrote *and* how I managed to gather images and voice recordings. I have no idea where the proof came from. I double checked my emails and the one I sent with the article was definitely sent to my editor, so what happened?

That's when the thought hits me like a ton of bricks. I ignore Tabby's worried look as I dash into the corner of the living room and rifle through the boxes of intel searching for the list I composed years ago.

"Babe, what ya doing?" she asks from behind me. When I find the sheet of paper I cheer and spin around to face her holding in front of her. "Uh, what's that?"

"Their skillsets!" I say like it's obvious.

"Who's?" I wave her off as I read over my notes—there it is.

*Knight Murdoch - Fighter, stays out of the public eye, older twin, hacker, father to twins, husband to Koby Murdoch.*

He did this!

Well, given the text message Tabby received it was either him or Chanel that hijacked my email and sent it to every outlet with the proof they gathered attached to it but why would they use me? Why not send the email themselves?

"Cass?" I look over at Tabby and frown at the sight of her holding the garment bag from Alex and two lanyards.

"What are you doing?"

A devilish smile lights up her face. "Alex the dumbass left yours and his passes inside the dress bag."

Shrugging my shoulders. "And?"

She rolls her eyes. "*We* have passes to go to the gala!" My brows raise to my hairline.

"Tabby, my name is hot right now and I don't think—" I clamp my mouth closed when she slips a lanyard over her head and walks toward me pressing the other against my chest. I look at the tag she's wearing and frown when she holds her hand out for me to shake. "I'm Cassandra Blake, nice to meet you." I gape at my best friend.

"You can't, Tabby, you will be eaten alive by the press—"

"Shhh, this may be our only chance for you to get close enough to the Dominico's, let me help you."

I soften. "I got my answers from that article. Quintin wasn't who I thought he was," I say bitterly.

"I know, babe, but us going tonight means you may be able to find out why your brother did what he did, plus, what the hell do you have to lose? Alex can't fire you twice." I can't help but laugh because she's right, I'm already jobless why the fuck not?

"Let's do this!" She squeals and jumps up and down laughing, her happiness is infectious and I find myself smiling and laughing along with her, time to stop chasing ghosts after tonight and get the answers I need to move on.

# Chapter Thirteen

## CHAOS

Against my better judgment I agreed to go to the gala with the others instead of arriving alone. I park my car out the front of Royal's house and turn to Lani. She hasn't uttered a single word since we left the house, she sits there looking like a proper mafia princess in her Victoria Beckham evening gown and her red bottom Jimmy Choos. Her hair is done and her makeup is on point, but none of the glamour can hide the haunting look in her brown eyes.

"Tonight is important–" I start but she cuts me off.

"I know!" she snaps, earning a glare from me.

"Then snap the fuck out of it and look the fucking part. I didn't buy you this shit so your sour ass face could spoil it." She looks at me and sneers.

"I don't care about this shit." She motions down her body with her hands. "All I care about is my son." Her eyes begin to grow hazy with unshed tears. "You and I will never be friends, Chaos. We may not be enemies one day but we'll never be more than prisoners of our past, but I am asking you as the brother of my son's father to protect him. Tonight shit will pop off because it always does."

"What are you asking me?" I grit out.

"I'm asking you to put the safety of your nephew first and above your need for revenge against my family. Get him out safely and then go after them but I am begging you—"

"Don't fucking beg." She recoils at my clipped tone. "You control the Albanians, they are there to protect the future ruler of their people and will die for him. As soon as you have eyes on Ryat, you tell Caio and he will have them move and extract him." I don't stick around, climbing out of the car I head toward the house, not bothering to check if she is following or not. Rather than go through the front door, I head around the back and drop down onto the porch steps not caring if the suit I wear gets wrinkled. I snap my head up at the sound of her approaching. I narrow my eyes at Lani when she claims the space beside me, the sound of laughter and loud voices can be heard from inside the house, forcing me to deal with the fact I can't hide from my parents any longer.

"Your family is inside, why are you out here?" I pull the blunt from my pocket and light the bitch up, dragging that sweet herb into my lungs and savoring the taste before blowing the smoke into the sky.

"Why the fuck do you care?" I ask her after a couple more drags.

"I don't. I just think someone who preaches about not being scared or whatever, you sure are acting like a pussy hiding out here." I don't take the bait, instead I just laugh lightly.

"Go play Dr. Phil with someone who gives a fuck. I don't have time for this shit—"

"Too late, they're coming out." I tense at the sound of the back door opening. Lailani climbs to her feet and stares down at me, the challenge in her eyes sparks me to life. I would never allow her to be able to hold this over me, so I stand and slowly turn around and come face to face with my parents who are flanked on either by Sin and Royal. Dad stands there stoically with his hands in his pockets while my mom keeps darting her eyes between me and Lani. When her eyes widen slightly, it dawns on me that she thinks Lani is my girl or some shit so I correct her pronto.

"Don't look at me like that." Mom's questioning gaze remains fixed on me as I speak. "She isn't mine, she's... Havoc's." I whisper his name, it still hurts to speak aloud or hear someone mention his name. Koby Murdoch is a badass, but missing is that inquisitive look in her eyes she had a second ago, replaced by one of warning as she eyes the woman who stole her son's heart. When Mom steps forward, Dad tenses but doesn't stop her as she comes closer. Lani shifts closer to me but I do nothing, if my mom chooses to beat the shit out of her I won't stop her.

"Who the fuck are you?" The deathly calm tone of Mom's voice has Lani steeling her spine and standing taller.

"My name is Lailani... Dominico." At the mention of her last name my mom shifts into action, she moves her leg, exposing the slit on the thigh of her royal-blue ball gown and pulls a knife from her garter, ready to hurl it at the woman.

"She's the mother of your grandson!" Royal shouts. Mom's arm freezes mid-air as Dad shifts to face my cousin and Mom darts her gaze to me. The look in her eyes steals my breath. I expected to see pain and anguish but what I didn't expect was to see happiness at the sight of me. How the fuck she could be happy to see me after what I did?

Mom holds my gaze as she speaks. "Is that true?"

"Yes," Royal answers but I can tell from the way my mom is looking at me that she will only listen to me.

"Yes, she is the mother of your grandson," I answer. Dad comes to stand by Mom's side, gently pushing her arm down and taking the knife from her hand.

"Which one of my sons is the father to your child, Ms. Dominico?" My dad asks just as the rest of the fucking family comes to join us. Great, let's just have a fucking family reunion right here! My aunts and uncles all share looks with each other trying to figure out what's going on. It's the sight of Uncle Rook stepping forward to stand on my dad's other side that has my chest cracking. I'm about ready to bail but before I can move Lani speaks.

"Ryat is Havoc's son," she answers in a tone that holds strength, I didn't think she had it in her.

"Ryat?" my mom questions.

"Yes, my–your grandson's name is Ryat," Lani answers, I can hear the pride in her voice.

"Where is he?" Dad demands.

"He's with my father." Mom's eyes turn cold. She descends the stairs but when she is about to reach Lani, out of nowhere I shift and block my mom from getting to her. I don't conceal the shock from showing on my face. My mom searches my gaze for a second before reaching out and cupping my cheek. The feeling of her warmth has me closing my eyes and deflating slightly.

"I love you and I know we have a lot to discuss but right now you need to move out of my way before I make you." A snort escapes me and I flinch. I shoot my mom the best *I'm sorry* smile I can muster before I step aside. Mom and Lani standing in front of each other sizing the other up, Dad comes to my side as Royal and Sin move to join us. "What mother leaves her son with the man who killed his father?" Mom spits. I wait for Lani to drop her gaze and cower but... she doesn't.

"The type of mother who had no fucking choice. Think of me what you will but I love my son, and will do whatever the hell I have to protect him. You don't know me so don't you dare judge me."

A smirk tugs at the corner of Mom's lip. "Who are you to my son?" Lani cuts her gaze to me as if debating how much she tells my parents. I remain stoic leaving her to make the choice on if she should rat me out and tell them what a piece of shit I am for tricking her or not.

"The mother to his nephew," she answers.

"And, to my other son?" The slight tilt in Mom's voice spears me.

"I can't tell you what I was to him but I can tell you that he was my savior. Havoc gave me the strength and courage I needed to fight for a better life for myself and our son."

"Did he know he fathered a child?" Lani drops her gaze at that question and shakes her head. "Why not?" Mom clips out.

"Because I never told anyone who the father was or I risked my father hurting my baby and I couldn't allow that."

"I'll kill the bastard," Dad growls.

"No." My parents snap their gazes to me. "You will not do a thing, we have a plan to get the kid–"

"I'm not standing back doing nothing," Mom shouts.

"Ricardo will kill him if he finds out Havoc is the father. You need to let me handle this," I shout back. Before Mom can come back at me Dad cuts in.

"I want my grandson home by the end of the night or I'll blow your little revenge plan out of the water and nuke their entire compound killing them all, and just to fuck with you, I'll leave a chess piece on the pile of ashes." Royal and Sin snicker beside me at Dad's jibe about our calling cards but that isn't what has me raging inside, it's the fact he is doubting me.

"Would you have given Havoc the same ultimatum or am I just special?" Mom gasps while Dad just stares at me with wide eyes. Everyone knows Havoc was the one to execute every plan he made while I was the one who fucked around and allowed my brother to do all the work. The fact my dad is calling me out like this just shows me that everything I have been thinking is right, they do wish it was me that died and not my brother. I don't stick around, I shoulder past my dad and grab Lani's arm, dragging her after me. I release her when we reach my car and get behind the wheel, she gets in after me but before I can get out of here the back doors open and Royal and Sin climb in.

"Don't bother arguing, just fucking get us to the gala. Erika and Kacey are going to follow us." I peer at Royal over my shoulder. "You have three minutes to get the hell out of here before that gate stays locked for the night. Want to be stuck here with our parents?" Not needing to be told twice, I floor it. Kacey and Erika are right on our asses as we exit the property. The gates close behind us, sealing our parents in there for the night.

"They are going to be pissed," Sin says laughing.

"Serves them right for doubting us. This is our city and it's about fucking time they learned that," Royal growls. I nod my agreement. I hate that my father questions my abilities, though I didn't realize until tonight how much I was trying to prove to my parents that I am capable and good enough for them to love me.

"A parents' love is indefinite, no matter the trauma or pain, a parents' love never diminishes, it only grows." I spy Lani out of the corner of my eye, she twists her hands in her lap staring out the window. "They don't hate you," she whispers. I say nothing because I refuse to acknowledge that she was able to read me and understand my hurt, like she said, we aren't and will never be friends.

I toss my keys to one of the boys wearing red to park my car just as Kacey and Rika pull in behind us. Royal goes to his girl as Kacey does the same, placing a kiss to Sin's cheek. That will never be me, I'll never have what they share because I'm too broken to offer a woman more than shattered pieces of my heart. My soul left my body the day my brother left me, I have nothing left to give. Caio appears near Lani, shooting me a nod before he leads her inside the gala. When she looks back at me, I keep my face blank, a lot of our plan tonight is riding on her and if she fucks it up then we're all fucked. Kacey claps me on the back on his way past, I glare at the fucker as he smirks. I follow after them, Royal and Rika. As we enter the opulent building, we are led to the ballroom that is decked out in whites and gold.

"Seriously?" Erika whisper shouts, we follow her line of sight to the middle of the room where a large ice sculpture stands, my fists clench at my sides.

"He's taunting us," Sin snarls.

"No," I say, drawing their attention to me as I keep my gaze fixed on the large ice sculpture that is carved into a card, the motherfucker had the Ace of Diamonds carved into it. "He's trying to get in our heads and throw us off our game. He has no idea who the card belongs to, he's just guessing."

"How do you know?" Royal asks.

"Because I have been nailing the Jack of Spades to all the victims I send him," I answer.

"He's using the Ace because it was the card that was left at the scene of the shootout," Kacey adds, I nod my agreement. Ricardo knows my brother died that day but he has no idea what we look like. Our identity is kept a secret for this very reason. Our parents being here tonight would have raised too many questions and it would have taken a matter of hours before people started connecting the dots on who we are, which is why I never wanted them to come.

"He's here," Chanel says, motioning to the back of the room. I inhale deeply at the sight of Ricardo and his two sons—Johnny is the oldest out of the two at eighteen and Ricardo Jr is the youngest at seventeen. Their age means nothing in this world. At those ages. They are able to take over and run their father's empire. I won't allow that to happen. My breathing accelerates when I see a little boy in a tux dash out from behind Ricardo Sr and run across the room. Johnny tries to grab him but the boy is too quick. I follow his movements. Lailani is on her knees with her arms open and tears trekking down her cheeks across the room as her son runs to her.

"He looks like..." Sin lets her sentence trail off.

"He's a replica," Royal breathes out. The sight of the little boy who looks exactly like his father has my chest splintering open, there is no denying it now. Lani was telling the truth, Ryat is

Havoc's son. The little boy clings to his mother as she wraps her arms around him and holds him tightly against her chest.

"Incoming," Kacey says. The five of us cross the room and reach Lani and Ryat at the same time her father and brothers do. Ricardo Sr eyes us warily for a second until his gaze drops to the tattoo peeking out of the collar of my suit, his eyes widen as he realizes exactly who the fuck I am. He darts his gaze around the room looking for his men no doubt, he won't find them.

"Looking a little lonely there tonight, Mr. Dominico," Kacey taunts. There are too many people here to kill them where they stand. Lani climbs to her feet with her son still clutched in her hold. Johnny reaches for them, I strike out and smack his hand away as I push her behind me glaring down at the punk bitch.

"You're no match for me, boy." His eyes blaze at my words.

"She isn't leaving here with that bastard," Ricardo Jr growls. I snap my gaze to his ready to tear the fucker a part but Rika beats me to it.

"And you won't see the sunrise tomorrow, you disgusting little boy." Pride shines in Royal's eyes as he stares down at his woman. At the sight of the press being allowed through the doors I look to Kacey.

"It's time for you to go, keep them safe," I say. Kacey places a kiss to Sin's forehead before ushering Lani and Ryat out. The poor fucker is still on the most wanted list so he can't be seen by the press. The fuckers in front of us try to step up but we don't move, they are outnumbered.

"You thought you were smart," Ricardo Sr says as he smiles and winks before taking a step backward. I keep the uneasiness from showing on my face, something isn't right. I cut a glance to Royal who is staring at the smirking pussies in front of us.

"Not all Albanians hate us," Johnny taunts before rushing after his father with his brother in tow.

"Call Caio now!" I clip out. Royal pulls his phone out and dials Caio, a sinking feeling begins to churn inside me as Sin pulls her own phone out and tries to call Kacey.

"Fuck!" Sin grits out, the hairs on the back of my neck rise as realization sinks in.

We got played!

"No answer," Royal says with a slight panic in his voice.

"Kacey isn't answering either!" Chanel snarls, cutting her gaze around the room trying to find the fuckers. When she spots them, she steps forward but Royal grips her arm and pulls her back.

"There are too many people," he says.

She yanks her arm free and glares up at him. "He has Kacey." The worry is evident in her tone.

"I know, but we need to be smart and play this out like we had planned. We need to get those two away from their father, we use them as leverage." I listen to Royal but I'm not hearing a word of it thanks to the sight of Cassandra. Her long blonde hair is out in loose curls, wearing a purple silk gown that clings to her body, enhancing her curvaceous body. Her best friend stands beside her but my focus is on the blonde that has my cock twitching in my pants. I can see from here that she isn't wearing a bra and it grates on my nerves knowing every cunt in the room can see her nipples poking through the fabric.

"I have a plan." I tear my gaze from the woman that has taken up too much time in my head to stare down at Sin. "Do you trust me?"

"Yes," I answer without thought.

"Remember that," she says before she crosses the room toward where Cass and Tabby stand sipping champagne. Her best friend has cameras flashing and reporters in her face, she cuts Cass a look that has her shifting away leaving her friend to deal with all the attention.

"What's that about?" Royal asks me.

"No fucking idea," I grit out as I watch Sin approach my girl.

*Where the fuck did that shit come from?*

# Chapter Fourteen

**CASSANDRA**

I feel awful leaving Tabby to deal with all the press but she insisted that she would be fine and let's be real, my bestie loves the spotlight so she is right in her element. I take a sip of my champagne as I walk away ready to go in search of Ricardo Dominico and get my answers. I don't make it more than a few feet before I'm being ambushed by none other than Chanel Murelo.

I thin my lips at the sight of her. "You set me up!" I accuse.

"You are going to help me right now or I will slit her throat." She flicks her gaze to where Tabby stands, fielding off questions from the relentless group of paps. My jaw unhinges as tears prick the backs of my eyes.

"Don't hurt her," I plead.

"Help me and she gets to live to see another day, refuse or fuck it up and she will die slowly." She may never have admitted to being Chanel but it isn't needed now after that threat. I know exactly who this monster is.

"What the hell do you want from me?" I force out. She leans in close and whispers what she wants me to do, my eyes snap wide and I jerk backward. "Are you out of your fucking mind?" I whisper shout, earning a dirty look from the couple standing nearby.

"Do it or I end her now." When I take too long to answer she takes a single step toward Tabby.

"Fine!" The bitch smirks.

"You have five minutes, get moving." I grind my teeth so fucking hard my jaw aches, then stomp across the room not giving a fuck what I look like as I go in search of these little fucks. I spot them across the ballroom talking to some older gentleman near the bar. I slow my steps and smooth down the front of my dress, fluff my hair and taking a deep breath to work up the nerve to approach them. I take a single step forward only to have an arm snap around my waist and draw me into the shadows of the room. I don't scream, I know who it is without having to see him. He keeps his front plastered to my back as he speaks.

"Don't fuck this up."

I scoff. "Like I have a fucking choice!"

"Get it done," he snarls as he releases me with a shove. I shake off his threat and move toward the bar, ignoring the eyes of the men lingering, I can feel their eyes glued to my ass.

"What can I get ya, darling?" the bartender asks. I twirl my hair around my finger playing the part of a clueless blonde and nibble my bottom lip.

"I like sweet," I say, then giggle. I spy one of the dick bags moving toward me out of the corner of my eye, it takes everything inside me not to flinch away when he places his hand on my lower back—on the top of my ass is more like it. I tear my gaze from the bartender to look at the... my God, up close he looks so young, he can't be older than eighteen.

"Try a Shirley Temple, that's sweet and... tasty," he says the last word as he runs his gaze up and down my body suggestively. A shiver runs down my spine, drawing a smirk from him but it's a shiver of revulsion not arousal. I spot my watcher over his shoulder in a black tux that should be illegal for him to wear out in public. The sight of him has my thighs clenching. His cousins and a woman stand around him, at the sight of Chanel I snap out of my staring and smile at the *boy*.

"What if I don't like it?" I say in a hushed tone, his eyes shine with approval.

"Oh, trust me, sweetheart, you'll *love* it." I hood my eyes allowing him to think that I am getting horny—honestly I want to barf, the thought of this kid's hands on me makes me feel ill.

"Why stop at one when you can have two?" the other brother says as he comes to stand on my other side. The three older men they were chatting to laugh and tip their glasses toward me.

"Oh, my... I... I've—" The one with his hand on me reaches out and shushes me with a finger to my lips.

"Say yes." I want to laugh, this kids trying to sound all dominant and in control is fucking comical. I want to tell him that the guy glaring holes into the back of his head from across the room is the master at demanding me to do shit but I don't.

"*Yes,*" I breathe out. The two idiots high five each other, making me want to face palm myself. I know the one with his hands on me is the older brother, Ricardo Jr., the fact he is willing to share me with his brother is disturbing. I thread my arm through the older one's arm when he offers it.

"Don't wreck her too much, boys, we might want a piece after you finish." Disgust rolls through me at the fat man's words. These men are fucking pigs. The brothers laugh at the three fuckers at the bar.

"Let's go," Johnny says as he leads us in the opposite direction of Ace and Chanel. When they lead me down a dimly lit corridor toward the emergency exit, I start to panic and sweat. Ricardo Jr. is at my side while Johnny leads the way. I peer over my shoulder to check if we are being followed but the corridor is empty. Johnny pushes the door open— I pray that an alarm will sound but it doesn't, it fills me with a foreboding feeling. The crisp air hits my clammy skin as they lead us toward the car park and that's when I snap out of it.

"I changed my mind," I blurt out. Ricardo's hold on me tightens. I dig my heels in and pull back, the bastard counters and yanks me forward into his brother who wraps his arms around my waist and lifts me off my feet. "Let me go!" I shout and begin to struggle in the fucker's hold. I was wrong, they weren't taking me to a car park they were taking me to the trees behind the building.

Oh my God.

*They're going to rape me!*

I struggle and scream but the fight leaves me when Ricardo punches me in the stomach. I flop forward in his brother's hold, coughing and wheezing, tears falling on their own accord. I'm dropped to my knees and cry out when sticks dig into my tender flesh through my gown. Ricardo comes behind me, grips my hair and yanks it, drawing a cry of pain from me. Johnny silences my scream with a backhand that has me swaying to the side, but their grip on my hair keeps me from falling. Johnny grips the front of my dress and tears it down the middle, exposing my breasts. I cross my arms over my chest to shield myself from their gazes.

"Fuck, I'm so hard let me fuck her first," Ricardo says from behind me, bile rushes up my throat.

"Be quick, Dad will notice we're missing soon enough," Johnny answers. Ricardo moves to stand in front of me, the bastard reaching for his zipper and without thought I punch him right in the dick. He screams out. I jump to my feet and make a run for it but I don't make it two feet before I'm tackled to the ground. I scream and fight as the fucker flips me to my back, ready to hurl threats at him. As I meet his gaze they die on my tongue when he punches me, my vision turns fuzzy, my head begins to swim as bile rushes up my throat but doesn't come out.

"Fuck!" I hear roared above me before Johnny's weight disappears. I roll to my side to finish heaving but I can't. I'm lifted and cradled against a chest, screaming and fighting even though I still can't see clearly.

"It's me, stop fighting." At the sound of his voice and the knowledge that I'm not about to be raped, the adrenaline flees me and I begin to sob in his hold. I wrap my arms around his neck and bury my face in his chest. I feel him tense but I don't care, and don't pull my face from its hiding place when I feel him sliding into a car. "Give me your jacket," he barks, then a second later drapes it over me, shielding my exposed body which I am grateful for.

"I hate you," I mutter against his skin. I feel the tension flee his body as he sighs and sinks back into the seat.

"I fucking hate you more." The painful part about hearing those words from him is the truth is unmistakable, he means what he says. He really does hate me but unlike him I lied, I want to hate him but I can't.

My head is pounding, I try to move but I can't. I blink my eyes open and startle at the sight in front of me, Ricardo Jr. and Johnny Dominico are chained to metal chairs. I dart my gaze from side to side to see I'm chained to a fucking wall like an animal! Hysteria begins to rise inside me as I tug against my restraints trying in vain to get free. Both assholes are gagged but try to speak to me, I ignore the fuckers as I stare down at myself and frown. I'm in a shirt that is definitely not mine—someone changed me out of my dress!

My train of thought is cut off when Ace stumbles out of the shadows with a bottle of Jack Daniels dangling from between his fingers. He stumbles toward the boys. The closer he gets to them the harder they fight against their restraints, there is no way they are getting free but it doesn't stop them from trying.

"Ace, they are just boys," I blurt out, not knowing why the hell I am trying to help these bastards when they had planned to violate me. He spins around and launches the bottle of Jack at me. I scream and shift slightly. The bottle smashes beside my head as shards of glass cut my skin. I stare up at him with hatred in my eyes, he is a fucking bastard.

"You don't fucking speak. You remain silent. Be seen and not heard, you washed up bitch." His words hurt but I don't let it show. I don't know what the fuck happened to turn him into this version of himself but it must have been something bad. I knew he was angry when he found me earlier but I don't understand why he is this mad. I did everything they fucking told me to and I still somehow managed to wind up chained to a fucking wall!

I watch as he walks around the boys, letting the tips of his fingers brush their shoulders. Johnny whimpers in fear, he's not so tough now, is he.

A moment later the smell of urine saturates the air and I drop my gaze to the floor to see a small puddle forming around Johnny's feet.

"What a little bitch," Ace snarls.

Ricardo Jr tries to speak but it comes out muffled thanks to something being shoved in his mouth. Ace yanks the cloth out of their mouths and steps to the side, crossing his arms over his large chest.

"Do you have any idea who the fuck we are?" Johnny screams at Ace, the fear is heard in his voice no matter how hard he tries to mask it.

"I know exactly who the fuck you are. I am going to give you both a choice, a choice that was never given to me–"

"Who the fuck are you?" Johnny screams, but the way his eyes keep darting to his younger brother gives him away, he's scared out of his mind, if the urine on the floor isn't indication enough, then the way his lip keeps wobbling should be.

"I'm the motherfucking Reaper, bitch and you're here to meet your maker. Now, it's time to choose." Ace sneers.

"Choose what?" Ricardo shouts.

"Which one of you dies first?" They both shout and scream while thrashing against their metal chairs to get free. It's no use and they know it but their fight or flight instincts have kicked in.

Ace moves so fast I don't even see him pull a knife until he plunges it into the top of Ricardo Jr.'s thigh. The boy throws his head back and screams out in pain. Johnny turns to his brother and pales at the sight of the blade sticking out of his brother's leg.

"Him!" I gasp, he just turned on his brother!

"For the display of weakness you have shown, the Jack of Spades chooses to enact its pound of flesh from you."

*The Jack of Spades!*

My mouth hangs open at his admission—he isn't the Ace of Diamonds like I had thought. Johnny opens his mouth to plead but he doesn't waste a second as he yanks the dagger from Ricardo's leg and plunges it directly into Johnny's open mouth. My own mouth hangs open and my eyes burn from not being able to blink. I'm frozen by the fear that is gripping me at the sight of him murdering a boy in front of me.

"You motherfucker!" Ricardo screams as he struggles against his restraints, trying to get free.

I barf on the floor as I watch Ace scalp the young boy in front of me. He passes out from the pain until his kneecaps are shattered by the sledge hammer Ace uses. He wakes screaming in agony. I fight against my restraints wanting to cover my ears to block out the sounds of his screams. I close my eyes and try to block out the sounds of bones breaking and the screams of pain but I can't escape them. Tears trail down my cheeks as whimpers force their way out of me.

He lifts his gaze from the hunched over body of his victim and glares down at me. "They were just boys," I choke out. He moves toward the corner where there is a camera set up and flicks it off before turning back to me.

"And you were just an innocent reporter who happened to be related to the wrong FBI agent and yet here you are. You will be last on my list to kill and believe me, Cassandra, I will make you fucking suffer for the life your brother took from me!" He's threatened me numerous times but I never really believed him. But now, I can see the devil in his eyes and know without a doubt that he means what he says, he is going to kill me and there isn't a fucking thing I can do to stop it.

"I never hurt you," I scream at him feeling hysterical.

"You can't hurt what's already dead, your days are numbered."

"Chaos?" someone calls, his eyes narrow as mine widen. His nostrils flare as anger courses through him at me learning his identity.

"This changes nothing," he grits out through clenched teeth.

I meet his heated stare with one of my own. "I already knew who you were." Surprise flickers in his gaze before he snubs it out and leaves the basement, leaving me alone with the bodies. When the light flicks off and I'm bathed in darkness fear grips me. I know they are dead but I've watched too many zombie movies! I try to remain calm and remind myself that they aren't going to wake up and eat me—I lose the battle. I begin to scream for help and beg whoever the fuck may hear me for help. I don't know how much time passes before my throat begins to protest and I finally give up yelling for help and sag against the wall crying.

Quintin's crimes are what landed me here, but Chaos's fascination with needing to see me burn is what is keeping me here.

# Chapter Fifteen

### CHAOS

I'm only partially listening to Royal drone on and on as I pop the top on another bottle of Jack. I bring the bottle to my lips only to have it yanked from my grasp. I snap my gaze to Chanel and glare at her.

"The fuck is your problem?"

"You're my fucking problem, Chaos!" I reach for the bottle she has gripped in her hand but she bats my hand away. "Pull yourself together for fuck's sake!"

"Get the fuck out of my house and leave me alone," I sneer. Royal ends the call he was on with our men and focuses on me.

"You want to get wasted, go for it. Sin and I will pick up the pieces of your fuck up like always." My upper lip twitches.

"Fuck you."

"No, Chaos, fuck you!" he claps back, rounding the counter and pushing into me. I press my forehead against his.

"You sure you want to do this?" I taunt.

"You reek of booze and blood. You're spiraling and I refuse to let you take us down with you. You need to snap the fuck out of this haze and wake up!" he yells in my face. I shove against his chest, pushing him back into the counter. He rights himself and tries to come at me again but Sin and Erika appear out of nowhere and stand between us.

"Enough!" Rika shouts, then she stands off to the side keeping her gaze on us both.

"Baby—"

She shoots Royal a look that has him clamping his mouth closed. "This isn't about either of you, this is about us needing to work together to bring Kacey, Lani and Ryat back home. Put your shit aside until they are home." At the reminder of yet another failure, I drop my gaze and turn away from them. "Your parents are on their way over." I spin around so fast I nearly lose my footing.

"What?" I roar. Rika doesn't cower under the pressure of my glare.

"We need all the help we can get. With Marco and some of the men being in Columbia, we only have Benny, Terry and half the men available." What she says has merit but that didn't give her the right to invite them to *my* house!

"You had no right—" Before I can finish the sentence, Chanel is in front of me with a fiery look in her eyes.

"Fuck you! She had every right to do it because I am not losing Kacey. You want to drown yourself in a bottle, then go right the fuck ahead, keep spiraling but I won't help you. He would never have wanted this for you, you dishonor him by acting like this." It dawns on me then, both of them have said the near exact same thing in the space of a few minutes.

"You both been talking shit about me?" I ask.

"What?" comes from Royal.

"They're only concerned about you, Chaos." Erika's words may have been meant to calm and soothe me, but all they did was confirm that in fact my cousins have been talking shit about me. The two people who were meant to have my back and be there for me without question are the ones who stood by and judged me.

Stuffing my hands in my pockets I nod my head. Sin and Royal both look tense.

"How am I supposed to be acting?" The calm tone of my voice has them looking uneasy. "Should I be over the death of my brother? Should I be smiling and happy that I am the one still breathing and not him?"

"Chaos—"

"Answer my fucking questions!" I roar. Erika shrinks back into Royal who pushes her behind him. I scowl at the bastard. "That move right there just showed me what your words couldn't, you don't trust me."

"It's not about trust, it's about us needing to be able to rely on you," he defends.

"When haven't I been reliable?" I throw back.

"You don't think we can't see it? We see you dying inside a little more every fucking day. I know you've been drinking daily and getting high to numb the fucking pain. That shit won't work forever, Chaos!" Laughter breaks free from me, the two of them stand there gaping at me like I have lost my fucking mind—maybe I have.

"Chaos–" I shake my head, cutting Chanel off.

"You two were supposed to be the foundation that I rebuilt myself on. You were both pillars that I was always able to rely on to keep me standing, but now I see I was wrong." The hurt that crosses their faces is evident but I don't care. I thought they would always be there for me while I tried to navigate my way through this shit. "I'm on my own for the first time in my fucking life and I am struggling not having him by my side. I am doing the best that I fucking can here, can't you see that?" Pain is rippling through me, I haven't spoken this shit aloud before, but it seems that liquor really does loosen your lips.

"You stupid son of a bitch," Royal growls as he steps up beside Sin. "You think we were the fucking foundation?" He doesn't allow me to answer. "The fucking foundation for all of us was your brother!" he says with so much conviction I feel it in my bones. "Havoc was a pillar for all of us, he was the fucking glue that kept the *Memento Mori* from becoming what we are now. He was the fucking one that *we* all relied on. You lost your brother but we lost him as well, he was a brother to us too. We want to break down and give into the pain that his loss has caused but we don't have that luxury because we have to keep it together so you can crumble." I shake my head denying him, he sighs and drops his gaze to the floor in exasperation.

"Know this, Cousin," Sin says, bringing my attention to her. "You can crumble, break apart and be the mess that you are and continue to try and push us away, but we will never leave you."

I scoff. "Yeah, because of the *Memento Mori*," I spit.

She shakes her head. "No, because we love you and you are our blood. We will go to fucking war for you, Chaos. The *Memento Mori* was built on the foundation of love, trust and loyalty and you will always have those things from us, but it's time you remember that we deserve those things too because we are here. We may not be the person you want most and I am fucking sorry I didn't take that shot sooner... I should have shot the cunt but—" When a tear slides down her cheek, realization robs me of breath. She has been harboring this guilt of my brother dying because she was a second too late to put Quintin down and I've been acting like a fucking prick not helping her at all. I dart forward and shock the fuck out of everyone including myself when I wrap my arms around her and pull her against me.

She wraps her arms around my waist and breathes me in as I hold her tight. "I'm so sorry, Sin," I whisper as I drop my chin to the top of her head. I've hidden from them since Havoc died nearly two months ago and shut them out. I thought I was the only person grieving for his loss because everyone seemed to just carry on with their lives and acted like he was a just memory but for me, I feel like I am fading and only barely existing.

"It's my fault, Chaos, I should have got to him sooner—"

I cut her off. "No. It wasn't your fault, Sin, he chose to save... London. We all know that Havoc loved her like his own." I close my eyes, there is only one person I blame for my brother's death and the little shit celebrated her tenth birthday two weeks ago. If she hadn't snuck into the back of the fucking car, Havoc wouldn't have died protecting her. She sniffs and pulls out of my hold, turning away from us to wipe her face and act like we didn't all just see her cry. Chanel doesn't do emotions, she's practically allergic to them.

"What happens now?" Royal asks. Before I can answer him a knock sounds out at the front door, a whoosh of air escapes me knowing my hasty exit is out of the question and I'm gonna have to deal with my parents.

"Now, we deal with the olds, then get our people back so I can deal with the banshee in the basement." The three of them look surprised at my offer to help, I ignore it as I go and let in the people I have been trying to avoid unsuccessfully. My aunts and uncles greet me on their way in. I hug my aunts awkwardly and shake hands with my uncles but when they all disappear and leave me alone with my parents, apprehension takes control of me.

"Why are you hiding from me?" Mom blurts.

I run a hand through my hair and sigh. "I'm not hiding."

"Bullshit!" I snap my gaze back to my mother and frown. "You want to lie to everyone then go the fuck ahead, Chaos, but you won't lie to me. You haven't spoken to us since the day you came back here, why? What did I do for you to shut me out?" I reel back, shaking my head as tears cloud her vision and her bottom lip begins to tremble. My mom is the strongest fucking woman I know and she's a badass that can put men twice her size in their place, seeing her so vulnerable and broken spears me.

"Mom—" I start but she cuts me off.

"I lost my son!" she cries out. Dad wraps his arm around her in support, shooting me a look of warning telling me without words if I hurt her, he will beat my ass. "He was my fucking baby, Chaos. I loved you both from the moment I found out you were growing inside me. You weren't the only one who lost him, we did too. No parent should ever have to bury their child, except I felt like I buried both my boys because you blocked us out from that day. I need you, Chaos." Sobs tear out of my mom. It takes me a second to get over myself and how I feel, then for the second time tonight I'm hugging someone. Mom clings to me like a lifeline as she buries her face in my chest and cries, I cup the back of her head and hold her close.

"I stayed away because I knew it hurt you both to see me." Dad flinches, neither of them deny what I say because they know it's true. "Each time you looked at me, you saw him. I couldn't bear the pressure of living up to the image of you both seeing him in me, so I left. I'm sorry I wasn't strong enough to be able to give you both the chance to see him through me but... I'm not Havoc and I can never be him." Mom pulls out of my hold and stares up at me as she cups my cheeks, Dad comes to stand at her back.

"I know you're not him, I swear I do." I drop my gaze to the ground unable to bear the sight of the pain in her eyes. "We always thought that it was Havoc that couldn't survive without you," she whispers.

"Turns out you were wrong, huh?" I say.

"No, I was wrong to assume one could live without the other because you two have always been a pair. I am so sorry you lost your other half, Son, but if anyone can share in your pain, it's us because we lost half our heart the day our son closed his eyes for the final time." Dad's words hold so much weight that I struggle to take a full breath as the weight of what he is saying sinks in. "I'm a twin, Chaos. Rook is more than my brother, more than my best friend... he's just more, when I thought I lost him I broke. Believe me, Son, I have been where you are and done some things that still to this day make me feel sick." Mom turns away from me and grips Dad's hand in hers.

"You didn't mean it," she whispers. I frown and look between the both of them confused as fuck.

"Point is, what you are going through and dealing with is normal, Son. Just remember that we are here, I don't know if we are the right people for the job but someone around here will be."

"Right job for what?" I ask my dad.

"To pull you out of the black hole you will wind up in when you finally allow yourself to feel the pain and loss of your brother." I lead my parents inside where we find everyone congregated in the sparse living room. For the first time I see I really do need furniture and to make this into a home instead of a cage.

"Who gave the intel to the reporter?" Uncle Bishop asks the three of us in a clipped tone. I frown and shake my head not knowing what the fuck he is on about.

"I did." I drop my gaze to the side, staring down at Sin. Uncle Vincent curses from across the room.

"Chanel–" She cuts Uncle Gage off and stares directly at Uncle Bish as she speaks.

"I did what I had to, we are taking Miami by force and in turn, after we rid ourselves of the Dominico's, we are taking over the surrounding states," she says in a matter-of-fact tone.

"We aren't stupid, we know we have to meet with the other families and turning up only having one major city under our belt is pitiful," Royal adds on, I eye both of them.

"You used Cassandra to print the article because everyone would believe it coming from her since her brother is one of the accused." It's not a question, it's a statement because I know without a fucking doubt that they did it. They both look at me and nod. I nod my head deciding not to call them out on this in front of our parents, they don't need to know that we have issues within our own family unit.

"How did you get close to the sister?" Uncle King asks. Sin and Royal both look around the room avoiding looking my way, motherfuckers!

I grit my teeth and face my uncle as I answer, "They didn't, *I* did." The looks on all their faces are shock, surprise and doubt.

"How?" Dad asks.

I snort. "I don't think my mother wants to hear about me fucking some chick into submission." Mom cringes and scrunches her face in disgust, my aunts mirror her expression while my dad and uncles try to hide their smirks.

"Atta boy," Uncle Rook says, earning a glare from my mom. He coughs and darts his gaze around the room, trying to act innocent.

"That article is going to bring heat to a lot of families. You outed high ranking members of congress, Chanel. Not only did our family rely on them and their pull, but so did the other five families." The clipped tone of Uncle Bishop's voice tells me that he is pissed.

"They were corrupt," Royal says in defense of Sin.

"That was the fucking point! We needed them so our shit could run smoothly, you fucked us all by outing them!" He's in Don mode now as he rips his son a new asshole. "That girl is going to have a target on her fucking back, they will kill her—"

"The fuck they will," I growl before I can stop myself, gaining the attention of everyone in the room.

"If she isn't already dead, she will be soon," Uncle Gage says.

"Pretty hard for someone to kill her when she's chained up in Chaos's basement," Erika snidely says from the other side of Royal. I shoot the little shit a look that promises retribution.

"That's perfect, we'll use her as leverage against Ricardo." Everything inside me turns to stone at Uncle Bishop's words. "We'll trade his sons and the girl for the safe return of Kacey, the child and his mother." Royal snorts earning a glare from his father. "Problem?" he grits out.

"Chaos is not going to give that girl up, he may hate her but she's his pet and we can't trade the sons," Royal answers.

"Why not?" Aunt Kiara asks her son.

"Chaos already killed them," Sin answers. All the olds begin to curse and start talking amongst themselves, trying to come up with a plan to save my brother's kid and Sin's man, oh and Lani if we have to. All the arguing stops when the sound of someone screaming for help below us sounds out around the room.

"Let me the fuck out of here, you bastard!" I purse my lips, shove my hands in my pockets and rock back and forth on my heels ignoring all the eyes on me.

"Is that her?" Aunt Anya asks but I ignore her, acting like I can't hear her.

"I am going to fucking kill you, I'll never let you touch me again, you prick!" I scrunch my eyes closed and take a deep breath. I was beginning to feel okay a minute ago but the sound of her voice has the monster inside me raising his head.

"You can't keep her chained up—" I snap my gaze to my mom and narrow my eyes.

"Yes the fuck I can and I will." Dad steps forward ready to defend his wife but I push on. "We'll handle Ricardo, the mother-fucker will give me what I want because soon enough I will know where they are."

"How?" Royal asks, I smirk at the bastard.

"The necklace around Lailani's neck has a tracker in it. It won't be able to be picked up by scanners until she activates it. I knew there was a chance she would be taken so I had a plan in place. Kacey has a tracker on him as well." Sin's brows practically touch her hairline.

"He knew about this?" she snarls.

"I told him at the gala and he agreed it was a good idea, at least I'm a functioning drunk though, huh?" Her and Royal both cringe but say nothing. At the sound of Cass spewing more threats, I stalk out of the room and head toward the basement ready to deal with her and maybe get her to help me out with the semi I'm sporting—talking about death gets me off.

# Chapter Sixteen

## CASSANDRA

"Help–" I clamp my mouth closed when I hear the door opening, press myself flat against the wall and try to squint my eyes trying to see in the darkness but it's fucking futile, I can't see in front of me. I heard the door close but I haven't heard any footfalls. I close my eyes and try to hone in on my other senses but I hear nothing. My heart begins to beat erratically in my chest. I breathe through my nose trying to calm myself but the fear grips me, why haven't they turned the lights on?

The hairs on my arms and the back of my neck stand on end as I feel someone drawing near, my chains clanking against the wall and I try to shrink further back into the wall. My breathing comes out in pants, I try to quieten it but it's no use. My pulse pounds in my ears muting all sounds around me. My legs begin to shake, I clench my hands into fists at my sides and pray to whoever the fuck is listening that I don't die down here. I gasp when I feel someone in front of me. I'm about to scream until a hand locks around my neck and my scream is silenced by his mouth on mine.

I try to clamp my mouth closed to deny him entry, I don't need to see him to know who it is. I've done this dance enough with him in the dark to know his touch, the way he feels and the way he can make my body hum. His grip on my neck tightens in warning, forcing a gasp from me. Instead of inhaling air, I inhale him. I want to fight him off and claw his face but I'm stuck, literally. He presses his body against mine, holding me firmly against the wall as his tongue devours my mouth and teases me.

He breaks the kiss, resting his forehead against mine, we're both gasping and trying to fill our lungs with much needed air. "You're a toy, nothing more. Only I get to use you, do you understand?"

I press my head against his getting right up-close, ghosting my lips over his. "I hate you! I'm not yours to do anything with," I sneer. I feel him smile against my mouth.

"They want me to trade you for another, doing that means Ricardo gets to play with this pussy," I gasp when he cups me right between my legs, "that I have claimed as mine." I rise up on tiptoes trying to get away from his touch but he's relentless, he uses his hold on my neck to push me down. He pushes my panties to the side and runs a finger through my folds. I bite down on my lip to remain silent when he pushes a single finger inside me. "You hate me but you're wet as fuck, how does that work?" he taunts.

"I fucking hate you," I grit out as he continues to work that finger in and out of me. I try to fight it—to fight him and the pleasure he is inflicting on me—but the second he hooks that finger and glides it against that sweet-fucking-spot inside me, I can't stop the moan from tumbling from my lips.

"You disgust me, you're nothing but a dirty little whore that likes to be fucked next to the bodies of my enemies." My eyes snap wide at the reminder of the two dead kids. I open my mouth to tell him to stop but then he presses the pad of his thumb flat against my clit, then covers my mouth with his, swallowing my scream. I ride his finger shamelessly needing to come so fucking badly. I almost cry when he pulls free and steps back. I'm about to hurl insults at him until I feel him kneel before me. Lifting my leg, he hooks it over his shoulder and buries his face in my pussy.

"Fuck yes!" I cry out when he pushes his tongue inside my greedy pussy. He alternates between fucking me with his tongue and sucking my clit into his mouth. My orgasm is right there, but no matter how hard I try to reach it I can't. As if he can sense this, he pushes two fingers inside me while he sucks my clit into his mouth. I scream so fucking loud as the orgasm rips through me, then I'm fucking boneless and trembling but he isn't done with me. He stands in front of me, the only sound in the room is my ragged breathing and his zipper. He hooks the same leg around his waist and lines his cock up with my entrance.

"I hate you," he snarls as he slams inside me. I smack my head against the wall as I cry out at the feeling of him filling me, stretching me perfectly. His hands grip the globes of my ass as I balance terribly on one leg as he continues to slam inside me at a punishing rate. I know I'll be able to feel him inside me tomorrow. "You like that, you little whore?"

"Yes, I fucking love it," I moan as I try to wrap my arms around his neck but the chains don't allow it, so I lift my other leg locking it around his waist. His hold on me shifts automatically, securing me to him. Before he can protest, I slam my mouth against his and grind on his cock, smirking against his lips when a groan rumbles inside his chest. I've never been able to take the lead before and granted this is awkward as hell since my arms hang limply at my sides, but I do my best. I arch backward when he meets my thrust and hits that fucking sweet spot, sending me into a moaning mess.

"I can feel your cunt trying to milk me, you want me to cum in you like a good little slut?" His crass words call to this vixen inside me that I've buried for so long I forgot she even existed until he came along and brought her back from the brink. We may despise each other and loath the existence of the other but the monsters that live inside us rejoice each time we are connected. It's fucked up and toxic as hell but I would be lying if I said I didn't enjoy it.

"Yes, I want to feel you deep inside me, I want all of it." The words slip free without permission. I wish I could blame it on an alter ego or some shit but I can't, when he's fucking me like this and using my body for his own gain, I love it. He makes me feel like a livewire, almost like I could conquer anything with him beside me or in this case—inside me.

"That's my *Rotten Apple*," he growls as his fingers dig deep into the soft flesh of my ass and he pounds into me. Cries of euphoria erupt from me as another orgasm tears me in half, I'm nothing but dead weight in his arms as aftershocks rock me to my core. He throws his head back and grunts loudly as I feel his cock swell inside me and his cum fills me. He leans into me, resting his head on the top of my shoulder as the concrete wall behind me digs into my back, I say nothing. Too stunned that he hasn't pulled out and escaped like he always does. Our breaths are the only sounds that can be heard. It takes us a couple minutes to get our breathing under control and a minute longer for him to pull back, I may not be able to see him but I can feel his eyes on me and it's unnerving. "I hate you for making me feel," he murmurs before he pulls out of me and steps away. I feel cold without his presence but I'm more confused by his words than anything.

"I hate you for waking me up," I whisper back. I was fine living my life the way it was but now that he has awoken the vixen within me, I know I will never be able to shove her back in the box and enjoy a vanilla relationship. I crave the dirty crass words that tumble from his sinful lips each time he takes me. I love that he doesn't ask permission or worry about how I feel, he just takes what he wants from me—granted, I always wind up sated and wrung out from the orgasms he gives me.

"Your feelings mean nothing to me." His tone is harsh but his words lack heat.

"I mean enough to you for you to keep fucking me," I clap back.

His dark laughter fills the space. "An hour ago, you hated me and wished me dead and yet, one finger in your cunt and you're spreading those legs for me like a whore. If that's hate, I dread to know what it would be like if you actually liked me." I grind my teeth hating that he is calling me out.

Rather than dwell on that, I change the subject. "Are you going to trade me to Ricardo?"

"And let you escape the plans I have for you?" I know it's a rhetorical question so I don't bother answering him. "I'm having too much fun watching you hate yourself a little more each time I slide my cock inside that greedy little cunt of yours to allow someone else to play with you."

"Fuck you and fuck your crooked family for tricking me. I never did anything to any of you and all of you have ruined my fucking life!" I scream.

"Your brother ruined mine when he killed my brother!" he roars so loud I smack my head against the wall, my heart is beating so fast I fear it may burst out of my chest. "You think you are better than us because you expose the evil in this world. You are nothing but a bottom feeding whore who is trying to play saint to the world. I see you, Cassandra, you are no fucking saint, you are the evil that lives in plain sight."

His words feel like they are crushing me from the inside. "If I'm evil, then what does that make you, *Chaos*?" It's the first time I have said his name aloud, the hitch in his breathing tells me I've shocked him as well. I think I've known who he was for a long time now but I was lying to myself and trying to deny the truth of who he really is.

He avoids my question by asking one of his own. "You know my face, you know my name, you know the secrets I have allowed to let slip, why not expose me in that article you published?"

His questions throws me, I assumed he was the one who sent Chanel to my place with the information. I may look like a ditsy blonde but I'm not stupid, I would never expose the mafia like that. If I was going to do it I would use my blog but I haven't...

Why the hell haven't I exposed him? I try to think of a reason why I wouldn't have exposed him, but when my mind starts to veer down a path I don't approve of I shut it down.

"Answer the question," he snaps.

"No." I cringe as I feel his cum start to leak down my thighs.

"*What?*" The disbelief in his tone is evident.

"I don't want to answer," I mutter.

"I don't give a fuck, answer my question now before you lose a kneecap." I want to tell him to go fuck himself but after witnessing what he is capable of first hand, I relent and answer the question.

"I don't know!" I shout.

"Bullshit."

"It's the fucking truth. I don't know why I didn't rat you out. I should have done it but... the thought never crossed my fucking mind." Silence stretches between us. I don't know how long we stand here before he grunts and leaves me alone again in the dark with two dead bodies and his cum dripping out of me.

# Chapter Seventeen

## CHAOS

I lock the basement door behind me and round the corner, only to be met by the disapproving stare of my dad. He looks me over before shaking his head. I bristle at his judgment but say nothing, I don't need to explain myself to him. I don't have to abide by his rules anymore, I live by my own set now.

"When Rook went missing, I blamed your mother." My intrigue is peaked, Dad has never spoken about this before, even when Havoc and I begged him to tell us the story. We asked our mom but she would just tell us that we didn't need to know. I move into the dining room and lean against the wall opposite him, Dad keeps his gaze focused out the window that overlooks the backyard.

"Why?" I ask.

He flicks his gaze back to me. "I thought she was a spy." He gazes back out the window and sighs dejectedly before continuing. "When we arrived at the ports, Rook was nowhere to be found. Maverick had Koby in his arms and at that stage I was denying the way I felt about her, I didn't want my brothers to know that I was falling in love with the enemy. Your uncles used to call me the *Dark Knight*, they would joke and say I lived in my twin's shadow. I denied it but the truth was that they were right, I hid behind Rook because it was easier than dealing with people, so when I thought I lost him I was forced out of hiding and became unhinged. I'm disgusted at myself for what I did." He hangs his head in shame.

"What'd you do?" I push.

"Your mother was shot from the Russian's that ambushed her at the port, I didn't care. I couldn't think straight or see reason, so I took her home and chained her to a chair in the bunker and tortured my wife." My eyes bug the fuck out of my head. "I allowed one of the men to hit her because I couldn't bring myself to do it, I starved her and hurt her."

"Why?" I grit out, anger thrums inside at the injustice my mother suffered through because of my father.

"I blamed her for losing my brother," he answers without hesitation.

"Why'd you stop?"

"Her bullet wound got infected, I had no choice but to get her seen by a doctor. I was lucky she didn't die, Chaos. I nearly fucking lost her!" He scrubs a hand down his face before his eyes slowly meet mine again. "On top of nearly losing the love of my life, I found out she was pregnant." My mouth parts in surprise. "My selfishness nearly cost me the lives of the three people I love most in this fucking world, I will never forgive myself for what I did to your mother and what I nearly did to you and your brother."

I study him for a moment unsure why he is telling me this now. "What does that have to do with me?"

A sad smile plays across his lips. "I thought Havoc was more like me. I was wrong, Chaos. You are every bit just like me."

"Huh?"

"Do you not have a woman chained up in your basement who you have been sleeping with and have feelings for?" I open my mouth to argue, but he holds his hand up, silencing me. "Been there, done that, save it." I glare at the fucker. "Deny it all you want and tell me I'm crazy because you, yourself believe you feel nothing for her except hatred. You don't continue to sleep with the same woman you hate, Son." I narrow my eyes at the bastard. When a sly smirk appears on his face, I'm ready to battle the fuck out of him and prove he's wrong but then my phone begins to beep. I pull it from my back pocket.

"We gotta move," I say to my dad as I rush from the dining room in search of the others. I find them all sitting on the hardwood floor in the living room, I cringe at the sight. I need to get furniture ASAP! "I got the location, lets bag the heirs and get the fuck on the road."

"Where are they?" Sin asks as she jumps to her feet. I hand her my phone and motioned for Royal to follow me, he does without complaint. This time when I enter the basement I flick the lights on, and ignore the sight of Cassandra as I get to work spreading out some tarps.

"Jesus," Royal snaps. I ignore him as I spread a tarp out beside Ricardo Jr.'s body.

"You have got to be kidding me." I flick my gaze to the side to see my dad, Uncle King and Uncle Vin standing there with their gazes focused on the far wall behind me.

"Meet Chaos's pet," Royal snarks, I get to work undoing the chains that hold the fuckers corpses not wanting to be distracted.

"Where's the key, Son?" I drop the chains to the floor and spin around to see my dad standing in front of Cassandra. I glare at Uncle Vin as he brings a water bottle to her lips, the little whore guzzles the liquid greedily.

"Key for what?" I snarl.

"For her chains," Dad snaps back. I stand tall and hold his icy stare, I won't let him try to assert himself over me. This is my motherfucking house.

"She remains where the fuck she is, you may live with regrets about what you did but I don't. She is not and will never be my wife or the mother to my fucking children should I decide to curse the world with more of me. She is on borrowed time, that bitch's brother is the one who murdered your son." Cassandra drops her gaze to the floor beneath her bare feet. Dad doesn't shy away from her like I expected him to at my declaration.

"She is innocent, Chaos, you are punishing her for a crime she never committed—"

I cut him off tired of this argument. "I don't give a fuck what you think, you either help get theses bastards out of here so we can go and save your fucking grandson or just leave. I don't need a lecture from you if you're going to sympathize with the bitch who shares DNA with the cunt that killed my brother!" An unreadable expression flickers across his face as we stand here staring at each other, I refuse to be the first to look away. I'm tired of being told what everyone thinks I should fucking do.

"I'm sorry for what Quintin did." The sound of her pathetic voice has me breaking the stare off. I drop the mask so she can see the full effect of my emotions, I want her to see the disgust and hatred I feel for her, had she been related to anyone else things may have been different.

"No you're not, but you will be," I answer calmly.

Royal, Sin and I are in one of the *disposable* cars I had stashed at my place, we keep cars like these around in case we need to transport certain things that we don't want being traced back to us if we were ever raided and they tested our cars for blood or other substances. My dad and uncles follow behind us in two separate cars. I would have preferred them not to come with us at all but unfortunately, we needed the man power that they have. Luka brought a plane full of soldiers with him and will be meeting us at the location, the joys of being rich and owning your own plane means you can fly wherever the fuck you want when you want.

"How far out is Luka and the others?" I ask Royal.

"They should be landing now so they won't be far behind us. I got our guys meeting us there," he answers.

"I never want to be caught shorthanded like this ever again, it's embarrassing we have to ask our dads for man power," Sin grumbles from the back seat. I can't argue with her because I feel the same.

"We have some of the Columbians returning. Once we take the Dominico territory we'll have more men take the other states and then we'll never have to worry about needing our dad's help again." The brisk tone from Royal tells us all he isn't happy about needing help from his father either. We drive toward the Georgia border, the closer we get the more alert we become. Royal pulls his phone out and dials Benny, telling him we're two minutes from their location and to take the lead with two other cars and leave three to trail behind our dads.

"We cross that border we're in their territory, the only way out will be killing every motherfucker, you get that, right?" I ask.

"They signed their death warrants the moment they took something that belonged to me, I am going to enjoy slicing every single one of their fucking throats!" Fuck, Chanel is worse than me! Royal agrees that this needs to end tonight. I know he just wants this over with so he can get his ass home to his bride to be. Erika didn't stay behind with my mom and aunts, she chose to return home to London because the fucking nanny called and said the demon was having nightmares. It's not nightmares, it's the way her father, Lucifer contacts her. I snicker at my own thought but don't comment when the others ask me what's so funny.

"What's the bet that Aunt Anya and your mom figure out how to crack your pin code on the basement door?" I glare at Royal and white knuckle the steering wheel when the fucker begins to laugh at my expense. As we cross the border, his laughter dies off. I accelerate and go around the three cars in front of us taking the lead, I don't need a GPS, I know how to get to the Dominico compound with my eyes closed.

The moment the red dot appeared on the map on my phone showing me Lani and Kacey's location, I knew exactly where they were. I want to ram his gates and drive my car through his house but I also don't want to give the bastard the chance to harm the kid and the others. It was fucking hard for my dad to convince my mom to stay behind.

"Are you fucking kidding me!" Royal shouts, I look over at him to see him clutching his phone in his hand.

"What happened?" I ask.

"Your mother, Aunt Anya and my mom stole your car and apparently are right on our tail." Chanel chuckles while I just shake my head. I should have known there was no way my mom bought my dad's story about needing to keep her safe and wouldn't be able to concentrate if she was there.

"I guess they won't be breaking into my basement after all," I clip out earning a laugh from Sin. Royal just glares and begins to stab his screen as he replies to a message. I veer right and take the next turn that will lead us to the back of the property where we have the trees to shield us from the cameras and this side gives us an advantage to scope out the place since the bastard has the Albanians on his side now. All the vehicles form a line behind ours and kill their lights as they park. The three of us climb out and wait for the others to join us. I glare at my mom and aunts as they approach us. Uncle Gage, Uncle Bishop and Dad look furious at the sight of their wives.

"You are fucking going to regret this," Uncle B snaps at his wife who rolls her eyes.

"Promises, promises, baby," Aunt Kiara sass's back.

"Why the fuck are you here? I told you to stay put," Uncle Gage whisper shouts, Aunt Anya just raises a brow at him.

"I used to fight men in a cage for my life daily, you don't fucking scare me." Me, Sin and Royal cough to mask our laughter at our Uncle getting his ass handed to him.

"Before you try joining in on this macho man shit, don't. That cunt had a hand in helping hurt my baby, he also has my grandson in there. That boy is the last link I have to my son, so you shut the fuck up and deal with the fact I am coming with you, got it?" Dad doesn't argue back he just smiles proudly at my mom and nods.

"I knew your crazy ass wouldn't stay behind, I was just surprised it took you so long to catch up." Mom smirks and wiggles her brows.

"We were on your ass the moment you hit the interstate, we just kept a car between us the whole time." My aunts laugh while my uncles frown. I ignore them as I pull out my phone to check the location of Kacey and Lani. Frustration rises inside me when I see that they are on either side of the mansion, that makes a snatch and grab impossible. We discuss possible strategies and try to make a plan to infiltrate the compound but none of them are good.

"We don't know the layout of the place to go in blind," Uncle Vin says.

"We don't have a man on the inside so we have no choice," Uncle Rook claps back.

"We need to scout the property and count how many men they have," Uncle B says. Before the fucking Albanians fucked us over, I knew Ricardo only had twenty men here which meant our numbers could overpower him.

"If someone didn't get murder happy we would have had some leverage," Royal snarks, pinning me with a pointed look. I flip the fucker off.

"Those motherfuckers were marked weeks ago, they knew their time was coming," I answer.

"Enough, bickering amongst ourselves doesn't help us," Aunt Kiara says. "We need to find a way to get eyes on the inside. Anyone have an idea on how we can do that?"

"Unless one of us is willing to be captured, then, no," Uncle King says as he hands us all ear pieces to remain in contact when we manage to get inside. I run a hand through my hair, knowing what I need to do but also knowing no one here is going to let me do it. I look to the side to see Sin's gaze already on me. She searches my eyes for a moment before hers widen slightly, then gives me a subtle nod. She's on board with what I have planned, the problem we face is getting away from our parents and Royal.

"Chaos, get the map from the backseat," Sin says as the others continue talking and trying to formulate a plan. I nod and head in the direction of our car, opening the back door and pretending to look.

"Can't find it," I call back, she rolls her eyes dramatically before stomping over to me. Royal must sense something is up because the moment she opens the driver's door, he is sprinting toward the car calling out for us to stop. I jump in just as Sin plants her foot on the gas. The door slams closed, I sit up and stare out the back window only to be greeted by the sight of fucking Royal hanging onto the back.

"You fucking bastards!" he roars, now is not the time to laugh but I can't help it, of course the fucker couldn't be left behind and had to catch us somehow. I know our parents are going to be pissed, but at least this way with the two—now three of us being captured means they are able to get a layout of the house and come save our asses. It grates on my nerves I need my mommy and daddy to save me, but right now I don't care. I just want to save my brother's kid. Sin stops the car in front of the gate, Royal leaps off the back and rushes to the side of the car and slips in beside me. "I am going to beat the shit out of you both!" he snarls as we all place the ear pieces in our ears just as a couple guards come into view behind the gate with their guns raised.

"Check, check," I mutter as the gates slowly begin to open and more guards appear.

"You little shits are in so much fucking—"

Royal cuts his father off. "Six guards approaching the front." The six guards surround the car with their guns raised.

"Get the fuck out!" one of them shouts. We all step out with our hands raised, I'm shoved to my knees then cuffed. I smirk up at the fucker as his buddy checks to make sure my cuffs are secure, the cunt uses the butt of his gun to slam into my forehead, I grunt in pain. My vision blurs but I'll never give him the satisfaction of letting him see me in pain.

"Call the boss," one of the other fuckers says. The bastard behind me grips the back of my shirt and drags me to my feet, I allow them to manhandle me and don't fight back but their faces are marked in my memory, they won't see sunset tomorrow. The other guards drag Royal and Sin near the front by me. When Sin tries to shrug the fucker off that has his hand clamped on the back of her neck, he spins her around and backhands her. Royal and I thrash against the bastards that hold us. I manage to headbutt the son of a bitch that pistol whipped me, Royal knocks one of his guards down, I'm about to launch myself at the second one but freeze at the sound of a gun being cocked. I dart my gaze to Sin, who is on her knees with a gun pressed against the back of her head, flashbacks play through my mind, freezing me to the spot.

"Make another move and she dies." The cunt with the gun pressed to her head sneers, Royal and I immediately stop fighting. The guards we knocked down come at us, throwing a couple punches, I grunt when the fucker gets me right in the nose.

"I'm gonna enjoy killing you," the fucker sneers in my face.

I smile. "How about you pop the trunk and take a look at the surprise I brought for your boss." His face slackens and he darts his gaze to his buddies waiting for one of them to direct him. I laugh at the bitch earning another hit to the gut.

"Chaos, how many times have you been told not to taunt weaker men?" Royal chastises me, I turn to him with a look of regret and nod my head.

"Yes, I know, it's not nice to pick on boys with little dicks." We both laugh as the fucker in front of me begins spewing threats in Albanian, then suddenly another four guards come toward us.

"You needed four more guys to help you out, I'm appalled," Royal says mockingly before he cops a coward punch from the side. He only said that so our parents and our men would be able to hear and keep count of how many men are here.

"Hold on, Son, I'm coming for you." Hearing those three words from my dad bolsters my confidence, I know without a shadow of a doubt that my dad is going to burn this fucking house down to get to us with my uncles, aunts and mom by his side.

# Chapter Eighteen

**CHAOS**

After finding the surprise in the trunk of my car, we were marched up the driveway with guns trained on the three of us the entire way. None of these pussies had the balls to call Ricardo and tell him what they found in my trunk. Excitement begins to build inside me as we get closer to the house. I see the son of a bitch standing at the top of the stairs just outside his front door flanked on either side.

"Wow, he needs six guards just for himself," Sin says.

"Shut up, bitch!" She shoots the asshole at her side a glare, I know he is going to die painfully for calling her that. We're stopped at the base of the stairs, I peer over my shoulder to see my car being driven up the drive by one of them. I can't keep the smile from my face as I turn back to face Ricardo and wag my brows.

"Surprise, Ricardo," I say in a chirpy tone, it earns me a swift kick to back of my legs that has me landing on my knees. I am going to enjoy killing every single one of these bastards. Ricardo slowly comes down the stairs toward us but my gaze darts over his shoulder to Ardik and Caio, glaring at the two-timing mother-fuckers. They follow Ricardo and stand on either side of him as he stares down at me.

"The two of you are going to pay for double crossing us," Royal growls, Caio just shrugs and purses his lips, Ardik shrugs.

"He pays us, you don't and he understands that a woman can never lead," Ardik snaps back.

"What about Constance and Albert, they in on this as well?" Sin asks.

"No, those two are soft," Caio sneers.

"Enough," comes from Ricardo, drawing my gaze up to him, hatred simmering inside me as I stare up into those shit-colored brown eyes. "You are foolish to think you had the power to over-throw me."

"I managed to wipe out your second, your capo's and your sons." At the mention of his precious boys he stiffens and his eyes harden.

"The fuck did you just say, you little cunt?"

I smile up at him. "I left you a couple surprises in the trunk, I hope you love them because I made sure to take my time and drag it out, making sure the final product was perfection." The taunt is clear in my tone. Ricardo is a picture of rage as he stands before me. I begin to vibrate with the need to kill the fucker, he cuts his gaze to one of the fuckers behind me.

"Pop the trunk."

"Sir—"

"Pop the fucking trunk, Miguel," Ricardo roars as he steps around me. I watch over my shoulder as he hastily makes his way toward the back of my car. I wait with bated breath for his reac-tion, the second the trunk pops open he stumbles backward and falls to his ass. Laughter bubbles out of me when he screams out in pain at the sight of his sons' mangled bodies, unlike the other ones I dropped at his gate with a card nailed to their foreheads, I chose to carve A and a diamond beside it in their foreheads, marking them Havoc's prey in the afterlife. The guards rush over to their Don and help him to his feet. He's muttering incoherently until his gaze lands on my smiling face. Without warning, he shakes off his men and rushes me, I'm on my back with the son of a bitch straddling me landing punch after punch to my face and sides. I hear Royal and Sin shouting but I block them out, relishing in the pain he is inflicting.

Ricardo is pulled off me by his guards, my face aching but it's nothing compared to the damage Royal has done when we've sparred, the oily fucker doesn't pack a hit. The painful look in his eyes is a balm to my battered soul.

"Now you feel half the fucking pain I do," I spit out as I awkwardly push myself to my feet.

"My boys were innocent," he screams.

"You weren't, you will all die for your part in taking away my brother. None of you will make it to sunset tomorrow evening." His nostrils flare in indignation.

"Take them to the chamber and string the two of them up, take her to the parlor wing, she can entertain the men with my daughter." Royal and I fight as hard as we can when the bastard drags Sin away, but we're pulled in the opposite direction.

"I'll kill them all, Chanel, I'll fucking kill them all," Royal screams as Sin is dragged out of view. We're dragged up some stairs when we're inside the house and pulled down a couple different hallways—I make sure to keep note so I can tell our parents when I get a chance.

"You have five fucking minutes to give me a lay out, I'm getting into position and I'm going to start taking them out," Uncle Vin's voice comes through the coms. We're thrown through a partially open door and both tumble to our sides awkwardly, I dart my gaze above us and balk at the sight of Kacey hanging in the middle of the room from chains—two from the roof keep his arms above his head, two from the ground that keep his legs anchored to the ground. His chins rests on his bloody chest, his hair is caked in blood. I shoot Royal a worried look.

"Kacey?" Royal shouts before he's kicked in the gut, the

fuckers drag us to separate sides of the rooms and wrap chains around our waist that are attached to the wall and secure them with a padlock before they leave the room locking the door behind themselves.

"Up the stairs, left, left, right fourth door on the right, Kacey's in here and he's injured," I alert the others.

"Where did they take my daughter?" comes from Uncle Vin.

"Lower level, first door on the left as you enter through the front door," Royal answers. "I saw five more men on the second level. I heard voices on the main level but I couldn't get eyes on them to count how many."

"There's at least ten that are out back that I managed to count through the window," I add on. Before we can explain more the door is thrown open to reveal an angry Ricardo, the sight of him all angry and hurt makes me feel fucking giddy, it's the same feeling I used to get when I would wake Christmas morning as a kid and think Santa had been there. His gaze snaps to mine and narrows.

"You are going to pay for what you took from me, I am going to kill your bitch downstairs while you watch." Royal scoffs.

"Good luck killing her, chances are she's already killed your men and making her way up to free us as we speak." Ricardo tries to act unaffected but I see him flick his head discreetly to the guard behind him who scurries off to check. The three remaining men move into the room and unhook Kacey. He drops to the floor with a hard thud, the sound has me cringing. When a groan of pain comes from him, I sigh in relief, thank fuck he isn't dead because Chanel would have killed us. Two of them grab his arms and drag him across the room beside Royal, not bothering to chain him, the other three come to me. I can see it in their eyes that they are wary and unsure how to proceed.

"Get his fucking ass hooked up," Ricardo snaps. The one with the crazy eyes in front of me draws his gun while the other two come to my sides, undoing the chain around my waist and lifting me to my feet. Once I'm in the spot Kacey just left, they uncuff me and secure the chains to my arms. Ricardo shifts and pushes a button on the wall that has the chains attached to my arms lifting them. I look up to see a pulley system attached to the roof, grunting when I'm lifted off my feet. I grip the chains to take some of the pressure off my wrists from holding my weight, my ankles are secured with the chains on the ground. Ricardo smirks when he pushes another button that retracts the chains into the floor stretching me. I grind my teeth and breath through the pain not giving him the satisfaction of making a sound.

"Give me all you got," I grit out.

"Chaos, what's going on?" comes through the coms, I shoot Royal a look telling him without words not to reply to Uncle King. They are watching us too intently right now and will know we have back up. The two guards move behind me. I hear clanking and metal hitting metal but I can't see shit until they wheel a metal table in front of me.

"Not so tough now are you?" Ricardo taunts as he steps forward and grabs a corkscrew opener from the table. I keep my eye on him, waiting for him to continue talking but the motherfucker doesn't do as I expected, he darts forward and plunges the weapon into my side, this time I can't keep the roar of pain from tearing out of me.

"You cock-sucking motherfucker, I'll fucking kill you!" Royal shouts as he yanks the fucking thing free and jams it into my other side, as I cry out in pain.

"Chaos!" I hear my mom scream in my ear, hearing her voice sends a surge of strength through me. I feel the cold sweat dotting my brow as I lift my head to smirk at the fucker in front of me.

"Your sons screamed like bitches." He roars before dropping the corkscrew and swapping it for a hammer, I tense in anticipation trying to prepare for the blow but no preparation can prepare you for the feeling of a hammer being smashed against your shin. I throw my head back and roar out in pain.

"I'm gonna fucking gut you like a pig!" Royal threatens but Ricardo ignores him as he continues to swing that fucking hammer. When he finally stops, I'm limp in the chains barely clinging to consciousness.

"Bring her in," Ricardo barks to his men.

"Chaos?" I hear Royal call but I can't lift my head. "Fight brother, don't you dare fucking give in, do you hear me! You are Chaos motherfucking Murdoch and you can handle this shit. We are the *Memento Mori*, brother, and you have him marked, earn your kill." His words are empowering and mean to spark a fire inside me, but I'm fucking spent and bleeding out here.

"How touching," I hear Ricardo taunt. "He is going to die tonight and join his bastard brother." Hearing that has me snapping my head up and growling.

"You don't speak about him!" I roar, ignoring the pain radiating throughout my body. "You are going to feel the full force of the Murdoch name tonight, you will learn that you cannot escape us–" My words are cut off when the door bangs open to reveal two guards dragging Lailani inside the room. She has a black eye and her lip is split, the gown she wears is torn and her arms bruised. They throw her to her knees before me where she stares up at me and weeps. I tear my gaze from her to stare back at her father. "She's your fucking daughter!" I shout at the heartless cunt.

"She is a traitor and will die like one." Another guard walks in carrying a little boy in his arms, a burlap sack over his head and his little hands are cable tied in front of him. His quiet sobs shred me open. Horror fills me when he is placed on his knees beside his mother. Lani tries to reach for him but stops when her father points a gun at the boy.

"Please!" she screams. "Not him, you do whatever you want to me, sell me, use me, kill me, do whatever the fuck you want but don't hurt my son!" I watch Lani break before me, all the strength and the fight flees her as she pleads for the life of her child prepared to exchange her life for his.

"You touch that boy and I swear on my brother I will fucking slaughter you like the pig you are," I warn him in a calm tone.

"Hold on, Son, we're breaching the fence line, I'm coming for you, Chaos!" Dad's voice is like a balm to my battered soul.

"You will remain fucking silent," Ricardo snaps. He keeps the gun pointed on the boy, I thrash against the chains restraining me but it's fucking useless, Royal attempts to try and get free to save the boy but we're useless and bound.

"Please, I am begging you—" He lifts his gun and fires a shot that sends Lani tumbling backward with a scream. I spew threats and fight harder as I see the blood oozing out of her shoulder, he just shot his own fucking kid.

"Shots fired, shots fired," Uncle Bishop's voice comes through the ear piece.

"Royal? Chaos?" Uncle Rook says.

"Lani?" I call out, she groans and rolls to her side only to chuck up bile. Ricardo cocks his gun and yanks the bag off and presses the gun to the side of Ryat's head. His eyes collide with mine and I'm robbed of oxygen, he looks exactly like his father. Flash backs play out in my mind of Havoc staring into my eyes as he took his last breath. The boy's tear-filled eyes widen at the sight of me chained and bleeding. I force a smile to my face for his benefit.

"Say goodbye," Ricardo sneers, Lani screams, Royal fights to free himself to save the boy, while my eyes remain locked on his.

"He's my son!" I scream. Ricardo snaps his head to me, the surprise is evident in his eyes. "You want to destroy my family, you want to end us all then you hold the key to doing that in front of you. That child is the only living blood descendent to the Murdochs, he is the next generation. Kill me, raise him in your image and when he is of age, he will be the oldest and able to claim not only the Murdoch mafia but the *Memento Mori*. You have the fucking key at your feet to end us all." I hear the plea in my own my voice but I don't care, I just need to buy enough time for my dad and the others to get here, as if on cue, shots ring out and then Chanel is bursting into the room throwing daggers at each of the guards as my dad, Uncle B, Uncle King, Aunt Kiara and my mom come barreling into the room. Lani screams and pushes forward to cover her son with her body as a shield. A shout comes from me when Chanel takes a shot to the side protecting Royal, Mom spins around and shoots the guard between his eyes.

"Enough!" Ricardo roars and that's when I feel the blade at my back, pressed right against my kidney, and the gun pressed to the other side. He has the kill shot and he knows it. My family all freeze, Dad's eyes blaze while my mom's fill with fear. "Drop your weapons–" He doesn't get to finish his sentence, the window shatters from the bullet sailing through it, then Ricardo is on the ground crying out in pain. Dad rushes forward with his gun raised ready to finish him off but I stop him.

"I want him alive, he's mine!" He eyes me for a beat before nodding stiffly.

"Get him down, we need to get the fuck out of here and get him seen, the cops are on the way," Uncle Bishop clips out as he helps free Royal. Uncle King and Sin help Kacey to his feet and wrap each of his arms over their shoulders to lead him out. Aunt Kiara and Dad help me down while Mom goes to Lani. It's the sight of my mom kneeling down in front of her grandson that has a smile tugging at my lips before I pass the fuck out.

# Chapter Nineteen

## CASSANDRA

I wake to the feeling of being watched. I groan as I slowly blink my eyes open only to slam them closed immediately as the light blinds me, I didn't expect it to be on. I blink my eyes open slowly this time and balk at the sight of the women in front of me—I want to piss myself. I've written about these women, stalked them on the web and tried to dig up any information on them and their families for the longest time and here they stand in front of me in the flesh. Carlina Murelo, Allison and Clare Murdoch all stand before me smiling kindly.

"Well, you don't look comfortable," Allison says.

"How did you get down here?" I blurt without thought. The three of them chuckle and shake their heads as Carlina steps forward with some metal tweezer looking thing in her hand and starts to do something to the padlock.

"Honey, my husband is the best tracker in the world, my brothers also possess a set of skills each that no other in this world could rival aside from our own children. Us ladies have learned a few things from them over the years," Carlina says just as the padlock that secures my right wrist clicks open. I gasp. She shoots me a wink before moving to the other side and picking the lock. The moment she frees me, I rub my raw wrists, they are red and inflamed and will be bruised for days. She slowly pushes to her feet and offers me her hand with a kind smile. I stare at it unsure.

"We are the only ones here, at least let us get you upstairs and cleaned up and maybe even convince you to eat something before they get back," Allison says, the kindness I see in her eyes is so unexpected. I had built up an opinion about these people based on what I had read and heard, none of them aside from Chaos has shown me anything but kindness which is why I shakily place my hand in Carlina's and allow her to help me to my feet. I'm stiff and aching as we walk toward the stairs, I can still feel the ghost of Chaos's cock inside me with each step I take.

We walk through a kitchen and past a bare living room, I spot the stairs expecting them to lead me that way but when we reach the foyer, I frown at the sight of Erika and a young girl by her side. I dart my gaze between them and suddenly feel like this is a trap until Erika steps forward and places her hand on my shoulder.

"We won't hurt you. I'm just here to offer you all a ride back to my place where you can shower, eat and get checked over by a doctor." I nod numbly and allow them to lead me outside, barefoot and clad only in a soiled thong and Chaos's shirt, I slip into the backseat and remain silent as Erika drives us away from the house of horrors. A shiver rolls through me as the memory of watching Chaos torture those boys runs through my mind. I could see the devil in his eyes as he slaughtered them. He smiled the whole time.

"Cassandra?" I jolt awake and recoil back into the seat. Clare raises her hands and tries to hide her frown at my reaction but fails. "We're here, you fell asleep." I shake my head and nod, then slip out of the car when she steps back. I keep my head down and follow her into the house. I still don't look around—I don't want them to think I'm trying to gather intel or some shit, I just want to get some clothes, wait for them to leave me alone for a minute and then make a run for it before Chaos gets back. I need to get the fuck away from him!

We come to a stop on the outskirts of the kitchen. "Can I get you something to eat?" Erika asks softly.

"No, thanks, I just want a shower and to rest... please." I can feel their eyes on me but I keep my head down.

"Follow me," Erika says as she leads me upstairs. I don't count the doors or look at the walls, I just focus on her back. She opens a door for me and motions for me to enter, I do but then stop in the middle of the room when I notice that this is someone's bedroom. It's not bare, there are clothes strewn all over the floor and cologne, pictures and other knickknacks on the dressers. I turn to face Erika to ask what I'm doing in here but the look on her face has mine slackening.

"This is *his* room." It's not a question but she nods.

"It is, well, it was when he was living here."

"He'll be angry if he finds out I was in his private space." She shakes her head.

"He would be furious if I put you in any room other than his own." I frown.

"Let me go," I blurt, her eyes dim and they slowly lower unable to hold my stare all that does is piss me off. "I don't belong here, I haven't done anything! Please, I swear I will never say a word about this. I'll leave the country and never come back. I have a best friend who will be worried sick—"

"Tabby was slipped a note by one of our men telling her that you would be in contact when it was safe." My mouth drops open in shock.

"You what?" I shriek.

"Believe it or not, Cassandra, I have been where you are."

"Yeah, right," I snap.

"I was tortured by Chanel and Havoc when Chaos was kidnapped by Royal's deranged cousin. I was also shot by Chanel and beaten by Chaos's mom, so yes, I do understand what you're going through."

"Why the fuck are you still here?" I ask exasperated. This woman is out of her mind, I would have ran the first chance I had and never looked back.

"Why didn't you move to escape him?" I bite down on my lip to keep from telling her to fuck off. "Look, I know this situation isn't ideal but given that you saw some things you..."

"You mean how I saw him murder two boys?" I add for her, she sighs and nods her head.

"Not everything is as black and white as you think it is–"

"What did they do?" I ask.

"You read the file Sin gave you. What that file didn't mention was that Ricardo was working with your brother and had planned to kill Royal and the others."

"What?" I breathe out.

"Chaos did what he did tonight because Ricardo and his sons were in the loop of what was planned that day."

"What day?" I snap.

"The day his brother died protecting my daughter," she whispers somberly, my brows jump to my hairline in surprise. "Havoc was shot in the neck protecting my little girl. Havoc loved her like she was his own. Chaos can't stand the sight of her or being near her because he blames her for the death of his twin. London barely sleeps and is plagued by guilt and nightmares over what happened."

"I had no idea," I whisper.

"I know, you learned the truth about your brother and I am sorry you had to find out the way you did but he wasn't a good man, Cassandra. Chaos is hurting so badly right now and lashing out."

I snort. "You stand there and defend him but the man has promised to kill me more times than I care to count, remind me again why I should care about how the fuck he feels?"

She pins me with a pointed look. "If you didn't care you wouldn't be here right now, you would have fought to get free. You know as well as I do that if you run he will hunt you down.

Chaos is just as good at tracking as Chanel, there is nowhere you can run without him finding you."

"What a fucking life," I growl in annoyance.

"The bathroom is through that door, get cleaned up and I'll bring you something to eat and drink. The doctor will be here in an hour."

"I don't need a doctor."

"The bruises around your neck and arms say otherwise," she retorts before turning and leaving. I hear the lock click into place and narrow my eyes, bitch. I rush into the bathroom and flick the light on, stand in front of the mirror and yank his shirt over my head. My eyes bulge out of my head at the sight of the hand print bruises that mark my sides, arms, neck and teeth marks are dotted along the column of my shoulders. I turn and peer over my shoulder and cringe—my ass is bruised from his grip. I tear my gaze from the mirror and push my ruined thong down my legs, kicking it to the side before stepping into the opulent shower. The rainfall shower head is fucking euphoric, I stand beneath the scolding spray allowing it wash over me and hoping it will wash away the confusion inside my mind.

"What are you doing, Cass?" I mutter to myself before the urge to vomit hits me. I place a hand over my mouth and swallow until the feeling passes. I use his products to wash myself and my hair, the petty bitch side of me emptied the remainder of his stuff down the drain before stepping out and snagging a towel off the rail. I dry myself, then use the towel to dry my hair before I run my fingers through it to try to rid myself of the tangles. Wrapping the towel around my body I step back into the bedroom to find a sandwich and a glass of milk on the side table. I scoff at the sight of it.

I tug open his drawers. searching for a shirt. The first two are just boxers and socks but when I get to the third I stop, there are photo frames stuffed in here. I pull one out and gasp. It's a photo of him and his twin brother smiling, they have their arms around the other's shoulders, they look so happy. I return the frame to grab the next one, it's a picture of the twins, Royal and Chanel when they were younger, laughing. The sight brings a smile to my face. I scold myself for feeling anything but hatred for him. I drop the frame back into the drawer, pull a shirt out, then slam it closed.

I pull the shirt over my head and drop my towel on the floor, not giving a fuck about the mess I have made in the bathroom or the fact I'm leaving my towel on the floor. I want to destroy his fucking room and break his things like he did to my life but something keeps me from doing that, call it my conscious or some shit. I spy the window and quickly rush toward it, then yank it open, hoping to find a way down but I see nothing. I'm fucking trapped!

"Fuck my life!" I growl as I stomp over to the bed and flop face first onto it. I want to scream at the injustice that is my life but I can't because it's my own fucking fault! I should have run after the first night he broke into my apartment. I should have fought him, I should have fucking done something other than allow him to weasel his way into my body and into... nope, I shut that train of thought down before it can continue.

I yawn and stretch out smiling when I recall the dream I had about me and... I snap my eyes open and gasp, I fucking dreamt about him! I bolt upright in the bed and cringe, I fell asleep in his fucking bed! How did I end up under the covers? I wrack my brain for a second. I remember laying face first and berating myself but that's it. I know I didn't see the doctor either so what the fuck happened?

"You escaped." My gaze snaps to the far corner of the room, eyes widening at the sight of him sitting in the wingback chair. My greedy eyes drink in the sight of his naked chest but I frown at the sight of the bandage that is wrapped around his stomach. I lift my eyes back to his and frown at the sight of the bruises that are present on his handsome face–no, not handsome!

*You hate him, Cass!*

I school my features and keep my face blank. "Rough night, dear?" I taunt, his jaw locks and his eyes narrow as he clenches the arms of the chair.

"A victorious night more like it," he clips out.

"Murder more people, did you?" I sass, he pushes to his feet and the tightening of his features indicates that he is in a shitload of pain but would never allow me to see it—too late buddy. I should be appalled that I am able to read him that clearly, to know he is hurt, instead I count it as a victory of my own. If I can read him that means I can use it to my advantage to escape.

"Not as many as I would have liked," he snarls as he stalks toward me. It takes everything inside me to remain rooted to the spot and not scramble away from him. I have to keep reminding myself that he's injured and can't hurt me, I could fight him off now, right? He stops at the side of the bed. I lift my gaze slowly back to his and am met with the eyes of the devil. The green of his eyes seems to slowly disappear and fade the longer he stares down at me.

"Why are you doing this?" I whisper when the silence begins to get too much.

"Revenge is all I have." I hear the truth in his words and it gives me pause. I see it in his eyes that he means what he says, he truly thinks that revenge is all he has in this world.

"Is revenge worth the cost of your soul?" I ask hesitantly, he and I have never exactly had a conversation that meant shit aside from arguing, so this is new for the both of us.

A shuddering breath leaves him. "My soul was ripped out of me two months ago."

"You're wrong." My answer clearly stuns him.

"You don't know shit."

"Maybe not, but have you ever thought that his soul lives on inside you?" His eyes crinkle at the corners. I dart my tongue out to moisten my lips and his eyes track the movement. Silence stretches between us for a moment before he sighs and shifts forward to join me on the bed. I scramble to the other side, earning a glare from him. He flinches in pain as he situates himself so he's resting back against the headboard, this feels... weird. I've never been in *his* bed or in his space before, this is foreign territory for us. I attempt to slide off the bed but he snaps his arm out and grips my wrist. I turn back to him in fright, I can see the movement has caused him pain but he ignores it.

"You allow me to fuck you like a whore, bruise you and leave my mark behind but when I'm not fucking you, you can't get away from me fast enough." His tone is one I don't recognize.

"You're kidding, right?" I bark at him as I yank my arm free of his hold and slip off the edge of the bed.

"Where the fuck do you think you are going?" he growls in a tone I know well, anger. I ignore him and stalk into the bathroom, slamming the door behind myself and locking it. The bravado rushes from me in an instant and I sag against the counter gasping for air. I meet my reflection in the mirror and cringe, I look like shit! I turn the tap on and splash some water on my face to try and rid myself of this queasy feeling, then decide to take a shower and put off facing him for as long as I can. Seeing him hurt had me feeling the need to nurse him back to health and ease his pain anyway I could, that shit needs to stop. I'm not some girl who falls for the guy who treats her like shit. I can't be that girl, I'm better than that.

# Chapter Twenty

## CHAOS

I haven't slept a wink since I regained consciousness in the car ride back here in the early hours this morning. I was rushed inside and stitched up by the doctor Royal now has on retainer, I've got some bruised ribs, fractured shin and some other shit but the place I hurt most is inside, every other physical injury pales in comparison to that. I left my mom to tend to Lani and Ryat, knowing she needed this time with her grandson. My dad tried to talk to me but I waved him off and told him I needed to sleep. What I didn't expect was to walk into my fucking room here at Royal's and find Cassandra face down on my bed. I planned to drag her ass off my bed and make her sleep on the floor but the moment I saw she was in my shirt and wearing no panties I froze.

Her pussy was on full display and despite the immense pain I was in, my cock leapt to attention inside my pants, it took more self-control than I wanted to admit to turn away from her and take a cold fucking shower to rub one out. I came with her name on my lips. The doc had to rewrap my dressing. The fucker tried to scold me but shut his mouth when I glared at him. I returned to my room only to find myself tucking her into *my* bed while I sat in the corner and watched her like a fucking creep. I've never slept with the same chick more than twice, the fact I have been fucking her for nearly a month is out of character. I keep telling myself it's to break her before I kill her, why does the thought of killing her not hold the same feeling of joy it once did?

The bathroom door opens and she stands there in a towel with steam billowing out around her. She has her blonde hair piled on top of her head in a messy bun and her eyes are red and puffy like she has been crying. She ignores me as she moves toward *my* dresser and helps herself to my shit. She drops the towel, I grit my teeth and will my cock to remain placid but the sight of her bare ass with my mark on each cheek has the fucker twitching in my pants.

She lifts the shirt to slip it on but stops at the sound of my voice. "Come here."

Peering over her shoulder at me with her arms still raised as she is about to slip the shirt on she asks, "What?"

I narrow my eyes. "Drop the fucking shirt and get over here."

"You're not fucking me!" she snaps, shocking herself clearly by the way her eyes widen.

I smirk. "Nah, you're going to fuck me though."

Her brows raise. "What?" she squeaks, the pink tinge that coats her cheeks is proof that she likes the idea.

"Fuck. Me." I announce the words so there is no way she can misunderstand my meaning; I need her to do this so I can remind myself that she is nothing more than a hole for me to sink my cock into. Nothing more than that. She nibbles her bottom lip debating if she should defy me.

"You're hurt..."

"That a question or a statement?"

"An observation," she sasses as she turns to face me, my shirt dangling from her fingers, her tits and pussy on display. My mouth waters at the sight of her blush colored nipples, I watch as they slowly begin to harden the longer I stare at them. "I... I don't want to hurt you," she mutters under her breath. I hide the surprise from showing on my face.

"You give a fuck about hurting me?" She glares before scoffing and shaking her head.

"Some people do have a heart you know," she fires back.

"Not me, now shut the fuck up and get over here so I can taste your pussy." A gasp comes from her, but it takes her two seconds flat before she's standing at the edge of the bed beside me with a stern look on her face.

"I get to be in control?" she asks, my nostrils flare and I grind my teeth. I'm fucking horny and need to get my dick wet but I also know I'm in no state to take the fucking lead so I have no choice but to nod stiffy. She beams at me.

"Don't fucking smile," I growl, she ignores me as she climbs on the bed careful to not jostle me. She straddles my thighs and stops. We both take a second to take in this new position. It's taking everything inside me not to throw her on the bed and fuck her, but if I rip my stitches it will take longer for me to heal and get my revenge on Ricardo who is chained up in Royal's basement.

I jolt when her tiny hand cups my cheek, I can feel her trembling and see the nervousness in her eyes as she slowly leans forward, giving me every chance to end this and turn away before she can kiss me but... I can't. Her soft lips press against mine hesitantly, her tongue prodding at my mouth begging for entrance. I relent and give her what she wants. She moans as her tongue swirls around mine and grinds her naked pussy against my cock, drawing a hiss from me. She jerks back and stares down at me with a panicked look on her face.

"I'm sorry, I knew this was a bad idea, you're fucking injured," she scolds. "What the hell were you thinking?" she snaps, but doesn't allow me to answer. "You need to fucking rest." She tries to shift off me, so I clamp my hands on her waist and hold her in place.

"You try to escape, I'll rip these fucking stitches open fucking you against the wall." Her mouth parts, forming a perfect O. "Get my cock out and sink that pussy on it." She shakes her head earning a glare from me.

"I hurt you—"

"You didn't!"

"You hissed," she shouts and tries to pin me with an angry look that just makes me want to laugh at her.

"You rubbed your pussy on my cock, I hissed because it felt good."

"Oh." Her cheeks turn a bright shade of red. I can tell she needs me to take the lead in the only way I can right now.

"Stand the fuck up and sit on my face, I want to taste that rotten little cunt." Her eyes spark to life at my words. She scrambles to her feet and does as she is told, gripping the headboard as I carefully slide down the bed until I'm flat on my back so she can kneel down either side of my head.

"What if–"

"Shut the fuck up and sit on my face." She huffs but from this angle I can see how wet she is already, this dirty bitch needs to fuck as much as I do right now. I grip the globes of her ass and press her flat against my face so all I smell, taste and breathe is her. The taste of her cunt is like none I have ever tasted before, I push my tongue inside her.

"Holy fuck," she cries out as she begins to grind against my face, the chemistry between us is purely from hatred that is mutual. She despises me and I loathe her but the sex, it's fucking catastrophic. Her hand tangles in my hair as moans continue to tumble from her lips, I feel her begin to tense in preparation of her orgasm. I suck her clit into my mouth and relish in the strangled scream that rips from her. "Chaos!" Hearing my name come from her sinful mouth has something in my chest tightening. I push her off my face, careful not to injure myself and position her above my cock. She's still trembling from the orgasm I gave her. I smirk cockily when I see the blissed-out look in her eyes.

"Ride me." She nods shakily as she grips my cock and lines it up with her pussy, we both moan as she slowly sinks down on me. I groan when I'm balls deep inside her tight wet heat, feeling her cunt spasming still. She leans forward and places her hands on either side of my head, bringing us face to face. I open my mouth to protest, not liking the intimacy that this position brings but then she begins to bounce up and down on my dick while looking me in my eyes. The power I feel from holding her gaze as she fucks me is like none other, I've never felt this before during sex, I am *always* in control.

"Chaos," she whimpers as I begin to meet her thrust for thrust, the pain in my abdomen is crippling but the need to cum overrides my self-preservation.

"Fuck me like a good little whore." She moans and a thrill shoots through me. I fucking love this shit in the bedroom, I've tried it with girls before but you can tell when they are faking and they all fucking did but not Cassandra Blake, she fucking needs this. "You like being my whore, don't you?"

"Fuck yes." She slams down on my cock, I grunt in pain. She tries to pull away so I grip the back of her head and smash my lips against hers, silencing whatever she was about to say.

"Make me cum you dirty little slut." She obeys me like a perfect student, she rides my cock like a master and has me spilling everything I have inside her. I bite down on my lip to keep her name from slipping past my lips. She places a shy kiss to my lips that shocks me still, then leans back, refusing to meet my gaze as she lifts off me and disappears into the bathroom. I lay here with my cock out, not giving a single fuck. I'm exhausted and need at least a week worth of sleep. "The fuck!" I snap as I push up to a sitting position, Cassandra stands there with a frightened look on her face as she stares down at me.

"I'm sorry, I was trying to help to..." She clamps her mouth closed.

"What were you doing?" I ask.

"I was just trying to clean you up so I could... return little Chaos to his cave." I glare at her.

"There is nothing fucking little about my cock!" She giggles but quickly smacks a hand over her mouth to hide the sound as she brings the wash cloth to my semi hard cock and wipes it clean before tucking *big* Chaos back into my sweats. She disappears inside the bathroom for a few minutes then returns wearing one of my shirts. I open my mouth to tell her to get her ass back in the bed but then the bedroom door flings open.

"Chaos, we need to—" My dad clamps his mouth closed at the sight of Cassandra standing there in nothing but my shirt.

"Have you ever heard of knocking?" I sneer, the old man just smirks and shakes his head.

"Never thought I would see the day that I would need to knock, it's not like you have ever brought a girl home before." I groan and flop back against the bed ignoring him introducing himself to Cassandra. "Ignore him, his bark is bigger than his bite." She giggles, that fucking sound is going to drive me crazy.

"Time to get up, shithead." I lull my head to the side to see Royal standing in the doorway with a stunned look on his face. "I fucking knew they would bust you out, can't trust the women in this family I tell ya."

"Both of you get the fuck out!" I shout then flinch when pain explodes in my abdomen. Within a second I feel her tiny hands on my chest, her eyes are filled with concern and it pisses me off. "I don't need your fucking help."

"You did five minutes ago when you couldn't get yourself off." The moment the words flee her mouth, I watch as her face turns a bright shade of red as she remembers we are not alone in the room. I want to laugh at her stupidity and the only reason I don't is because I know it would fucking hurt.

"So, I'll send your mother up with the doctor." I turn to my dad to tell him no but I'm too late, he and Royal are already gone and the door is shut.

"Fuck," I grit out.

"Your mom is coming!" Cass hisses.

"So?" I snap.

"I just fucked her son and have residue of his cum still inside me, she is going to fucking murder me."

I smirk darkly at her. "Her doing it would save me a job."

Cassandra narrows her eyes down at me. "I fucking hate you."

"I hate you more."

*Why does it feel like those words don't hold the meaning they used to?*

# Chapter Twenty-One

**CASSANDRA**

I've been hiding in the bathroom for the past five minutes. I want to say that I stood by Chaos side and waited for his mother to arrive so I could tell her that her son was a deranged asshole who was holding me against my will, but the moment I heard a knock on the door, I squealed like a school girl and dashed into the bathroom, locking myself inside and away from his mother. I have no fucking idea why I am so scared to meet his mom—no, that's bullshit, I do know why but I also misjudged his aunts who turned out to be nothing like I read or perceived about them. I look at myself in the mirror and scowl.

"Woman up, Cass. You're not dating him and have nothing to be ashamed about. He hunted you not the other way around," I quietly chastise myself. I face the closed door, steel my spine and pull it open. I freeze in the doorway the moment Koby Murdoch's gaze lands on me. I'm robbed of air. I open my mouth to say something, anything but nothing comes out. She is fucking flawless, I hate to admit it but I can see why her sons are so fucking gorgeous when they have her as a mother and Knight as a father, these boys had no chance of being hideous.

"I'm guessing you're the woman my husband was smiling about." I pale and shake my head.

"I didn't mean to make your husband smile!" I rush to say, earning a frown from her and a glare from Chaos.

"Shut the hell up and sit your ass down," Chaos snarls, this time I don't argue with him. I march my ass across the room and claim the chair he was occupying earlier, tuck my legs under myself and pull the hem of his shirt over my knees—the thing is long enough to be a dress on me.

"Look at me, Chaos." He ignores his mom and keeps his gaze on the ceiling. Koby's eyes pinch at his defiance. "Well, I guess I'll just talk to your friend over—" He cuts his mother off before she can finish taunting him.

"Don't." One word, that one fucking word holds so much weight that even his mother can feel it.

"Then look at me or I'll take her with me when I leave this room and return her to where she came from." I scrunch my face, she makes me sound like an item he purchased and no longer wants that she is going to return to the store.

"Take her, I don't give a fuck." His dismissal of me stings more than I would like to admit. "I'll just hunt her ass down and drag her back."

"I'm not a toy!" I grit out glaring at him, he refuses to meet his mother's gaze but has no trouble meeting mine and showing me just how much he dislikes the idea of me being here.

"You're my fucking toy until I say otherwise."

"No, I'm not!" I shout not caring that his mother is standing right there. "I'm not your anything, you've made that clear. You have also made it clear how much you hate me so why not just fucking kill me or let me go, because I can't keep doing this with you, it's fucking with my head." Now that I've finally started, I can't stop the words from spewing out of me. "You never minded using me to get off but the moment you blow your load you're back to being cold and distant. You hate me because of my brother, I understand that, but I wasn't the one to take yours from you, but you were the one to take mine from me!" I don't remember getting to my feet or even realizing I had started crying until I felt the tears coating my cheeks. "Just let me go... please," I beg brokenly.

He pushes himself up in the bed and rests back against the headboard as he looks at me, but this time it's like he is actually seeing *me*, not the person he thinks I am but the real me standing here in front of him. The pressure of his gaze has me wanting to fidget and cower but I force myself to remain standing and keep my gaze on his, showing him without words that I am a fucking person and I have feelings!

"You done?" I reel back like he whipped me.

"What?"

"Are. You. Done?" he snarls in a cold tone. I feel the tiny ember of hope inside me evaporate to nothing but a distant memory. Tears continue to flow unchecked down my cheeks, how can someone be so cold and cruel and yet be attentive and intuitive in the next minute? This man can make me feel things no one has ever been able to, only for him to destroy me in the next second.

"Chaos, let her go." He slowly turns his head to face his mother with the same harsh look he just gave me.

"No." I muffle my sob behind my hand and drop back into the seat.

"Why?" Koby asks.

"You know who she is, you know why I have to do this."

"You don't have to do anything. We have been gifted a fucking miracle, a part of your brother, but you refuse to acknowledge his child. You saved that boy–"

"I did it for you!" he shouts so fucking loud his mother stumbles back a step. "I saved his kid for you so you would have something left when I—" He clamps his mouth closed and turns away from her, my jaw unhinges when I pick up what he was putting down. Koby misses it completely and continues to beg him to change his mind and come meet his nephew. When he refuses to talk and keeps ignoring her, she finally gives up and tells him she'll check on him later. She doesn't look at me as she leaves the room, the soft click of the door announces that I am yet again alone with him.

Neither of us say a word, too lost in our own thoughts. I don't realize how much time has passed until the door opens quietly to reveal Erika. She pokes her head in and smiles kindly, handing me a plate of food and some bottles of water. I thank her before she leaves again. I look over at Chaos who is fast asleep and sigh. With nothing better to do, I decide to eat the offered food and drink the water. When night falls I decide to give up on trying to sleep in the chair and quietly make my way over to the bed, watching him closely as I slip in beside him, making sure to keep as much space between us.

I want to snort at my idiocy, I've slept with him more times than I care to count and yet lying next to him seems like a larger risk than letting him inside my body. I carefully pull the covers over me, trying not to disturb him as I get comfortable. I place a hand under the pillow and freeze, I run my fingers along the hard edge of a... Holy shit, it's a knife. I slowly pull it out and squint to see it better, the only lighting in here is from the moon. I peer over my shoulder to make sure he's still asleep, then before I can talk myself out of my suicidal plan, I roll as quick as I can and straddle his lap pressing the blade against his throat, my chest is rising and falling rapidly as adrenaline courses through me.

When his eyes open I thought I would see shock, fear or something but all I see is determination. "I heard you the moment you stood from that chair." He has got to be kidding, I didn't make a freaking sound! "You don't think I knew there was a dagger stashed under there?" My plan to have him surrender and let me go seems to be failing by the second. "I put the fucking thing there, I was just waiting to see how long it would take before you found it and ended up here." He tilts his head back slightly offering me better access to his throat. "Do it."

"W-what?" I stutter.

"It's the only way I won't hunt you down, Cassandra. I'll never stop coming for you, I can't. If you want to be free of me, truly free then take that blade and slice my fucking throat or get the fuck off me, now." I press the blade harder against his skin willing myself to do it, it would be so easy to end all my suffering.

"Just let me go," I plead as I feel tears prick the backs of my eyes.

"No."

"Why?"

"I can't."

"You can!" I argue.

"No, I fucking can't."

"Why not?"

"Because I can't fucking kill you!" he shouts, then knocks my arm away, the dagger flying from my hand and clattering against the hardwood floor somewhere.

"What does that mean, Chaos?" I ask in a defeated tone.

"I don't know, I don't fucking know, okay?" This is the first time he has ever been open with me.

"Killing yourself won't change the scars of the past, it would only create more." His sharp intake of breath has me worried I pushed too far on calling him out.

"Ending my suffering is the only way they get to be happy without my darkness ruining everything for them." Pain explodes in my chest, not for myself but for him and the way he is feeling.

"You see darkness but they see light, you think you are their destruction but they need you to be their redemption, don't rob them of that."

"What the fuck would you know?"

"I know that the death of my brother was my demise but I refuse to allow his crimes to destroy me. I will be my own savior and right the wrongs he did, I'll not bow to the demands of others or allow greed to sway me from what is right. Quintin wronged you, he hurt you and did unspeakable things but I am not him, I am not the monster you want to view me as being."

"I don't see him when I look at you." I stifle my gasp from breaking free at his whispered words.

"What do you see?" I push.

He lulls his head to the side and gazes out the window. I wait with bated breath for him to answer me. Time seems to stretch and move at a snail's pace as I wait for him to answer.

"You." He turns back to look up at me, there is no mask in place and he isn't shielding his emotions from me, he's allowing me to see everything and it's scaring the fuck out of me. "I should have killed you that first night I broke in. I was supposed to but then something stopped me. Every time after that I promised myself I would end you but... You called to the fucking beast inside me, stoked the anger and sparked the flame that hungered for revenge. My hatred for you is what keeps me coming back."

"I don't understand," I whisper.

"Hating you means I hate myself a little less."

"I hate you, too." My words lack the heat they need.

"You wished you hated me, if you did you wouldn't bend to my will and let me fuck you any time I wanted. Love and hate are hard to differentiate, you can't have one without the other."

I shake my head. "I don't love you."

"You don't hate me either."

"I could say the same about you," I snap back.

"Difference is, when I tell you I hate you, you know I mean it. You telling me you hate me is the same as you telling me you love me."

"I don't," I grit out through clenched teeth.

"Why do you worry for me then? Why do you care that I'm hurt? Why do you care what happens to me?"

"Because I'm fucking human," I say angrily.

"No. It's because you wished you hated me but somewhere along the way that hate turned to want and then your want turned to lust, then of course lust bled away to love which is why you find yourself here. That bedroom door is unlocked, you could have run anytime you liked but you didn't. As much as you claim to want your freedom, you don't mean it because *I* make you feel alive, you'll be my greatest conquest."

"Why?" I whisper, fear grips me in its tendrils knowing his answer is going to shred me.

"Because I get to break your mind and heart and that is a sweeter victory than death."

# Chapter Twenty-Two

## CHAOS

### *Two weeks later...*

My stitches are finally out and I can move without hindrance, freedom never felt so fucking good! I step out of the shower and stroll back into my room, Cassandra sits on the chair in the corner scrolling through her phone—I gave it back to her last week after I planted a bug so I can monitor everything. She lifts her eyes to me, trying hard to not allow them to roam my naked chest but fails. She tears her gaze from my body, trying to act uninterested as she goes back to scrolling, she says she's job hunting but I know she's full of shit. She's been looking into movers and apartments in Texas, I saw the messages between her and that fucking best friend of hers, the bitches both plan to run and live in Texas until they can get passports.

I yank the drawer open and grab what I need, I feel her gaze on me when I turn my back to her and drop the towel to pull my shorts on. She gasps. I know it's because she is seeing the tattoo on my back for the first time but she masks that by snorting, earning a scowl from me. "What?" I clip out as I pull my shirt over my head, then use my hand to push my hair back.

"No boxers?" she asks with a raised brow.

"Less clothing to remove when I fuck you." Her jaw locks and her eyes spit fire. Ever since our little heart to heart a couple weeks ago, she has shut down and refuses to speak more than two words to me unless I'm fucking her. Yeah, she may be furious with me and what I said but she'll spread her legs willingly for me every night or whenever the fuck I say because she is a feign for my cock. She hates herself for wanting me and the knowledge fills me with pure satisfaction. "Pack your shit, we leave soon."

That grabs her attention, dropping her phone to the seat as she stands and faces me. "Where are we going?"

"Wherever the fuck I say. We leave in an hour," I snap before brushing past her and making my way downstairs. All my aunts and uncles have gone but my parents refuse to leave their grandson. I told Royal to send them, Lani and the kid to my house while I healed. I chose to stay here rather than return home so there were more eyes on Cassandra in case she tried to be stupid and run. Entering the kitchen, I find Sin, Erika, Kacey and Royal all sitting around the counter, sipping on their coffees and eating. Sin got rid of her sling the moment her parents walked out the door, stubborn ass that she is. Kacey is still sporting bruises and a couple of cracked ribs but he's up and moving around easier now —they worked him over real fucking good. The bastard earned my respect, he never ratted us out or gave up any intel on our family—he's loyal.

"Look who decided to grace us with their presence," Royal teases. I shove his chair as I pass by, the fucker laughs.

"What's got you up early?" Erika asks.

"I'm heading back to my place to put an end to this shit," I say as I pour myself a cup and lean against the counter facing them. They all stare at me with a mix of expressions on their faces. "What?"

"You're not taking Ricardo," Royal says with finality.

"Try and stop me," I warn.

"We've called a *royal flush*." I nearly drop my fucking mug at Sin's declaration, then cut a glance between her and Royal.

"He is mine!"

"We are a fucking team, Chaos. He took from all of us, therefore a royal flush has been called," Royal argues.

"A royal flush needs to be unanimous," I fire back.

"Are you going to deny us this?" Chanel says as she sits back in her chair and crosses her arms. I mull over their words for a minute. We have only called a royal flush once before. Them doing this means they are serious and really do want to be a part of the final kill where Ricardo is concerned.

"Fine." I relent. "We do this shit today. I need to grab some shit from my house, when I get back we get down to it," I say as I dump my mug in the sink and stalk toward the front door.

"What about Cass?" Erika calls out, I don't stop moving as I call back.

"She stays here."

I park my car in my driveway and stare at my house, so many emotions churning inside me. I know they are all in there, the people I have tried to avoid and keep at a distance until this was all over.

*Killing yourself won't change the scars of the past, it would only create more.*

Cassandra's words play out in my mind. I hate to admit it, but those words have plagued me daily. Would me no longer existing really bring them comfort and peace or would it be the final straw that destroyed my parents? I thought giving them their grandson would help them but all it has done has my mom doubling her attempts to call me daily, plus she sends me pictures of her and Ryat. Dad is even in some of them, smiling as he holds the boy on his lap. The front door opens and I frown at the sight of Lailani Dominico standing on my porch. Sighing, I grab the papers from the passenger seat before I lose my nerve and step out of the car to meet her. She takes a seat on the edge of the steps, I drop down beside her keeping my gaze forward.

There is tension between us and I don't think that will ever go away, but knowing that she really did love Havoc and went through hell to bring his son into this world helps me hate her a little less, which is why I decide to tell her what we have been doing the past two weeks while I was laid up resting at Royal's.

"The Dominico name is no more." I feel her gaze boring into the side of my head but keep facing ahead. "We have removed your father from his seat of power, all his operations within the mafia world will remain with the *Memento Mori*."

"I understand," she whispers. I slowly turn to face her. Her eye still has faint bruising around it but her lip looks healed. Her eyes seem almost brighter, she even looks... healthy.

"All of your father's nightclubs, shares in the hotels and his houses are yours." Her eyes widen at the same time her mouth drops open. "All the income from those businesses will be solely yours and Ryat's."

"Why?" she breathes out.

I take a deep breath as I force myself to speak the next words. "It's what he would have wanted." Tears shine in her eyes.

"I don't expect you to pay for me, I'll get a job. Your mom and dad have offered to help but—"

"He isn't their son!" She snaps her mouth closed, I growl and scrub a hand down my face trying to get my shit in check so I don't take my anger out on her. "Look, just take the fucking money, that way if anything were to happen to any of us I'll know my brother's... kid will always be taken care of." A sad smile graces her face as she shakily reaches out and places her hand atop of mine giving it a squeeze.

"Thank you, Chaos."

I scoff. "Don't thank me yet, there's more."

"Oh." She leaves her hand where it is so I use my free hand to grab the papers from beside me and hold them out to her, she doesn't take them she just keeps darting her gaze from them to me. "What are those?" The hesitancy in her tone is warranted.

"I cannot allow the Dominico name to remain, after today we'll be ending the line." Her bottom lip trembles as she snatches her hand back.

"You promised you would let me raise him!" she practically shouts at me.

"I'm not going to kill you," I snap.

"Huh?" I shove the papers at her, leaving her no choice but to grab them.

"Your father is going to die today." I search her face for any type of emotion but all I see is relief that her tormentor will no longer be around to harm her or her son.

"Good," she sneers.

"Which is why you are going to sign those papers to end your family name." Her eyes blaze and shakes her head looking like she is ready to argue so I push on. "They aren't marriage papers," I snark.

A whoosh of air escapes her. "Thank fuck."

I shoot her a glare, she just shrugs. "They are papers to have your name legally changed to... Murdoch."

"Chaos–" she breathes out but I keep going.

"I know he would have put a ring on your finger if I didn't fuck things up for you both." A lone tear tracks down her cheek at my admission. "He loved you, Lailani. He knew who you were and didn't give a fuck because he trusted you with the one thing he never trusted anyone else with, not even me."

"I don't understand," she says as tears flow freely down her face.

"Havoc gave you his heart a long time ago, Lani... I guess he never got it back." A sob claws out of her. I don't think as I awkwardly reach out and wrap my arm around her shoulders and pull her into my side. She weeps in my hold for her lost love and I admit I even start to get choked up a bit.

"I loved him so fucking much, Chaos. He was my person." Her quiet declaration has me closing my eyes and fighting back the guilt for what I did to them both.

"He would want you to have his last name. I'm not him so I can't marry you, Lani, but I can give you this so you will share the same name as your son." She pulls back and stares up at me with forgiveness—I don't deserve that shit from her.

"You have no idea what this means to me."

"I'm just trying to fix what I stole from him. You were always meant to be a Murdoch, I'm just fucking angry at myself for not seeing that sooner. I'm the wrong twin to be offering you this gift, I know that, but he isn't... here, so I am trying to do what he would want and you having his name is something I *know* he would have wanted." Talking about him in past tense fucking kills me.

"You have given me something I never thought I would ever receive, I know this is hard for you."

"I wish I was like him," I admit quietly.

"You may be twins but the both of you are opposites, he had his qualities and you have yours. Twins share a bond that no one can never explain, you will heal and live on."

"I'm scared I'll forget him," I admit for the first time, shocking myself that I actually said that shit aloud.

"You'll never forget him because *In Chaos lives Havoc.* He lives on inside you and in his son." The laughter of a child can be heard, shattering the moment. I tense as she smiles and slowly climbs to her feet clutching the papers in one hand and offering me the other. I stare at it for a long time debating if I am ready or not to take this step. "*He* would want you to meet his son, Chaos." Frowning I nod and accept her hand, feeling choked up and strange as we head toward the front door. I'm tense, almost like I'm about to go to battle as I walk through the front door after Lani. She leads us into the living room and I'm shocked to see it has furniture and other shit in it.

At the sound of our approach, Mom and Dad both snap their heads toward us and smile, but my gaze is rooted to the spot on the carpet where a little boy plays with toys. His mop of hair is tousled and in disarray and when he looks up at me, I'm brought to my knees. He frowns and slowly makes his way toward me with a curious look on his face as he stops in front of me. His tiny hands reach out to touch my face, so I lean down and allow him to touch it. He smiles wide.

"Dadda?" Gasps sound out around the room as the tears I have been battling to stay hidden for weeks finally surface, I shake my head.

"Nah, little man, your daddy was way cooler than me," I choke out. The little boy sees the tears on my face and pulls me into him, trying his best to hug me. I snap my arms out and lift him, clutching him against me as I break down holding the last piece of my brother I have left. My parents and Lani stand around us, leaving me to have my moment with my nephew. After a few minutes, I manage to get myself under control and place him back on his feet. Sniffling, I wipe my eyes with the backs of my hands and reach up to unclasp the necklace around my neck that contains Havoc's ashes. I place it around his neck and smile at the sight.

I have the casing for his ashes custom made, it's a 3D style necklace of his calling card the Ace of Diamonds. "Wow," Ryat says as he holds the charm in his tiny hand.

"Now, you will always have your daddy with you. As long as you have that on you, you will never be alone or be afraid of anything because your father would wreak Havoc on the world for you."

# Chapter Twenty-Three

**CASSANDRA**

I have nothing to pack and I'm bored of sitting in this fucking room every single day so I decide to head downstairs, Erika said I was welcome to roam the house and help myself so I'm going to take her up on that offer. I grab a quick bite to eat in the kitchen before I make my way out to the back patio, the sun is shining and the sky is clear of clouds. A smile spreads across my face, even in a shitty situation a beautiful day can make anyone smile.

"You're not that pretty." I snap my gaze toward the table chairs in the center where London sits, I've never spoken to her but I have heard about her from conversations I have overheard when the others were talking about her.

"Uh, thanks?"

She rolls her eyes and turns her gaze back to her iPad. "Wasn't a compliment," she sasses, my jaw unhinges.

"Wow, you really are blunt, aren't you?" I say, utterly surprised how someone so innocent and cute could be so curt.

"Beats lying to people."

I snort. "Amen to that, sister," I mutter as I walk over to her and drop into one of the seats opposite her. She flicks her gaze to me and frowns.

"What are you doing?"

"Sitting?" I don't know why that came out sounding like a question.

"I can see that, why?"

I'm honestly stumped and it takes me back a second before I answer. "I just thought you might like some company."

"The last friend I had died, you should just go back inside and hide in Uncle Chaos's room until he kills you." My jaw practically hits the floor, this ten year old child speaks and behaves as if she is a grown woman. Sadness shines in her eyes and that breaks my heart.

"Your uncle isn't going to kill—" She pins me with a deadpan look that has me cringing. "Okay, maybe he might." She quirks a mocking brow, earning a groan from me. "Fine, he does have plans to kill me but you shouldn't be worried about that."

"Why not?"

I frown. "Because children shouldn't worry about such things."

"If he kills you it might make him hate me less." I balk at the little girl.

"He doesn't hate you," I say, wanting to ease some of the sadness from her, she is way too young to worry about shit like this.

"You're a terrible liar and clearly you don't know my uncle."

I purse my lips and slouch back in my seat. "I know him well enough," I mutter.

"Dad says he only tolerates you because you keep blowing him." I choke on my own spit.

"*What?*" I screech.

She shrugs. "I don't know what that means but Dad says it's disgusting. I asked Aunt Nelly what it meant and she said it means that your desperate and have no self-worth." I'm floundering like a fish out of fucking water, trying to wrap my mind around the fact that this is a child I am speaking to and learning the adults around her are lying... well exaggerating the truth at my expense.

"Your dad's full of shit and so is your aunt." I huff and slouch further into my chair.

"See, no self-worth." I jerk upright in my chair at the sound of Chanel's voice. She pins me with a blank stare as she claims the seat beside London. She peeks at the iPad then looks at me and laughs, my brows pinch knowing that she is only laughing because London has done something on there that involves me.

"Can I see?" I ask, she huffs and turns the iPad to me, I stare at the screen in equal parts horror and outrage. It's a picture of me from my Facebook with illustrations of blood, devil horns and other deathly shit with the caption *dead woman walking*.

"She's talented, right?" I scowl at Chanel.

"That isn't funny," I scold the woman.

"It is, considering she isn't wrong, Chaos learned from mine and Royal's mistakes so we are inclined to believe him when he says he is going to kill you."

I throw my hands up in the air. "How can you talk about murder like it's nothing?"

"Because it isn't to us. You will pay the price for your families crimes, simple as that."

"You are a real bitch," I bite back, Chanel's eyes harden and her jaw locks.

"You get a free pass once, call me that again and I'll kill you."

"Oh, I thought I was Chaos's to kill," I mock.

"He never marked you, so that means you're free game."

"What?"

She rolls her eyes. "I marked Kacey, Royal marked Erika, none of us can touch someone else's mark."

"And?" I prod.

London answers for her. "Uncle Chaos doesn't care about you or what happens to you so he didn't mark you, that means you're not safe." I snap my mouth closed and stare at the both of them, trying to decipher how I feel about that declaration. So, if Chaos had given me his card, that means I had his protection or some shit but without it... I'm a sitting fucking duck!

"Now, you can see that he isn't the prince charming you are trying to make him out to be in your head. He isn't your savior, he is your demise. Come to terms with that fast because the final move is in motion now and then you're next. But, before you die I owe you a thanks."

"Huh?" I'm too caught up in my thoughts to say more.

"Your article managed to get Kacey off the most wanted list and freed of all charges against him, he's a free man now."

"Whatever," I mutter as I head back inside only to come to a stop at the sight of Chaos standing just inside the threshold of the backdoor. We stare at each other for a long time without uttering a single word. He looks... different.

"Go to my room, I'll be there when I finish this shit." Too emotionally drained from my conversation with London and Chanel, I just nod and do as I'm told. The moment I'm inside the room I flop onto the bed and groan. My phone begins to vibrate in my pocket. I pull it out and answer it without checking, knowing it will only be Tabby checking in.

"Hey," I answer dejectedly.

"You sound sad, Momma Tot."

"Shut up!" I hiss.

"Geez, someone is snappy today."

"It's been a... shit day."

"Well, I am here to make it better." I scramble to sit up as hope blooms inside me.

"You did it?"

"Sure did, everything is out of your apartment and locked up in a storage unit and the keys have been handed back to the land-lord." I could fucking cry, Tabby has been my rock through this. We have a plan and the sooner I can execute it the better off I will be, we both will be. "How long, Cass?"

I sigh. "I'm working on it, Tabby, I just need an opening and then I'm taking it."

"Are you sure about this?"

"Yes. If I don't, he will kill me, Tabby, and I can't let that happen, not now."

"I'm here for you, Cass, always." Tears prick my eyes.

"I love you, Tabby."

"Love you too, baby." I end the call and flop back against the pillows, staring up at the ceiling wondering how the fuck I ended up here. Could I have done something differently to change how things have turned out?

I startle awake to the sound of the door slamming closed. I bolt upright in bed and turn the side lamp on. The sight of Chaos standing there at the foot of the bed with blood covering his face, hands and clothes has bile rushing up my throat. I leap off the bed and rush to the bathroom to empty the contents of my stomach and the small bowl of fruit I ate this morning. I can feel him behind me. I can't stop myself from heaving, I don't even care that he can see me hurling my guts up. I hope the sight puts him off and disgusts him.

"You good?" he asks when I close the lid and stand to flush. I ignore him as I move to the sink to brush my teeth and splash some water on my face. I can't stop my gaze from straying to him in the mirror as I watch him undress. When he turns and the tattoo on his back becomes visible guilt churns inside me. His brother's name with angel wings takes up the top half of his back, it's a tribute to the love he has for him. I drop my gaze when he steps into the shower not wanting him to know that even though I hate him, the sight of him sets me a blaze and has a want so powerful roaring to life inside me.

I step over his bloodied clothes as I exit the bathroom, I know without him needing to say it that the blood he is covered in is Ricardo Dominico's. With him now dead that means my time has come, I need to put my plan into action or soon enough it will be my blood he is washing off. I take a seat on the edge of the bed and wait for him to be done, this is my last-ditch effort to walk away amicably, not look over my shoulder for the rest of my life. If he refuses, then I have no choice but to run.

I lift my gaze at the sound of his footfalls, then gasp at the sight of him naked stalking toward me. His cock is hard slapping against his stomach, the predatory look in his green eyes robs me of air. I attempt to shift back on the bed to keep space between us but he clamps his hand around my throat hauling me to my feet and into him. No words are exchanged as he crashes his lips against mine, forcing my mouth open with his tongue. All rational thought flees me as I get lost in the taste of him. His free hand slips beneath his shirt that I'm wearing, cupping my bare pussy and growling into my mouth.

Chaos never asks permission, he takes what he wants without apology. Call me crazy but I just know if I was to tell him to stop he would, he may take what he wants but he would never hurt me like that to get what he wants. He's shown me that each time he's fucked me. He always makes sure I'm wet and ready before claiming me, if I'm not, then he has no issue eating me out until I'm screaming and begging him to fuck me senseless.

He pushes two fingers inside me, forcing me to my tiptoes. I wrap my arms around his neck and draw him in closer, allowing myself to have this final moment with him. I cement everything about him to memory—the way he tastes, the way he feels pressed against me and the way he can play my body like a fiddle without effort. His pace is systematic, he knows I need him to finger me harder in order to orgasm but he refuses to allow me to come without his say so, it's become a game to him lately. He yanks his fingers out of me and grips my hips in his hands lifting me. Locking my legs around his waist, I keep my arms around his neck as he moves us across the room to the far wall.

He uses his body to keep me in place as he lifts my shirt to expose my tits, latching onto one of my nipples, drawing a sharp cry from me. He tweaks the other between his fingers as I try to grind down against his shaft, needing the friction but I can't fucking move. He's too strong and the fucker loves the fact he can throw me around and keep me from doing what I want because of my size.

"Chaos, I need you to fuck me," I gasp out.

He releases my nipple with a wet pop, staring up at me with bright green eyes. I can see it now why he looked so different earlier, he isn't haunted by the severe pain like always, it's still there but not as prominent.

"You want me to bury my cock inside you and make you come?" he taunts me by gliding his cock through my slick folds.

"Yes," I cry out when presses against my clit.

"Admit you don't hate me and then I'll fuck you so hard you forget where I begin and you end." His words have my brain short circuiting, never before has he ever asked something like this of me. I want to tell him to fuck off but if this is the last time I get this with him then I want there to be no secrets. I cup his cheeks between my hands and place a soft kiss to his lips. Pulling back, I rest my head against his, holding his gaze as I tell him the truth I've been to scared to even allow myself to think.

"I don't hate you," I whisper against his lips. His eyes blaze as he slams his lips against mine, and true to his word, he slides his cock inside me, torturing the both of us going this fucking slow. Relief washes over me when he finally slams the remainder of the way inside me, my legs already beginning to tremble in anticipation of the orgasm I know he is about to give me. I gasp breaking the kiss when he pulls almost all the way out and slams back inside me.

"You're my whore, no one else's," he grits out between thrusts. I'm too dazed by the pleasure he's inflicting on my body to take notice of what he is saying until he stops moving inside me and glares at me. "Tell me you want me."

"I want you," I shout as I grind down against him chasing my release. "Fuck me."

"You're a dirty little whore, aren't you, my rotten apple?"

"Only for you." I moan as he slams inside me, his pace is ruthless and punishing but I don't care. I need this. I need to feel him inside me for days to come, the reminder of him being in me is all that I'll have and I need it more than I need my next breath, because running is going to destroy more than my life and he and I both know it. I can lie to myself all I want but he can see through it, he knows when I tell him that I hate him I really mean three other words that I'm not willing to say aloud or even think.

# Chapter Twenty-Four

## CHAOS

I wake feeling thoroughly satisfied, I couldn't keep my fucking hands off Cassandra all night. I finally gave her a break when the sun started to rise. Sitting up I peer down at her naked body beside me and smirk, my marks are all over her—bruises from where I gripped her hips as I fucked her over the back of the chair can be seen, the hand print on the back of her neck is from when I gripped her as I fucked her against the counter in the bathroom. I was unstable last night, I needed to get lost inside her after finally ending Ricardo.

Torturing that bastard was anticlimactic—he was piss weak and started crying before we even began, we barely got his fingernails off before he passed out from the pain. Even when Royal hit him with a shot of adrenaline he still fucking passed out! I've never seen anyone pass out after receiving one of those. So, to save time and make sure I inflicted the most amount of pain I could before he passed out, I took a drill to his kneecaps, and Sin used her expertise with knives to remove the cunts eyelids so he saw everything even if he was passed out.

Royal took a turn slicing him up and using the nail gun to mark out an *A* across his torso. The final blow was delivered by me, I used Havoc's knife to carve his calling card into his forehead. Last night was the final time the Ace of Diamonds will ever be used, that card will now lay in rest with its owner, it hurt to know that never again will we deliver a royal flush. Last night marked an end to an era and as much as it hurt, I felt a sense of... closure, like now my brother was finally at peace. Ricardo's body is now sitting at the bottom of the ocean with some nice concrete shoes on his feet.

With him now dealt with and his territory ours, the next stage of our plan is in action. We need to take over the surrounding states from the other families before the meeting with the head five families in four weeks. Uncle Bishop tried to hold them off but wasn't successful. Being deemed one of the head families of the US by the Murdoch mafia means we now have to play by the same rules as Uncle B and the other five families. We have already set up a meeting with Constance and Albert to discuss the terms of the Albanians surrender, the two of them know they cannot win a war against us. We now outman them and outgun them. We will now control the Columbians, Albanians, Miami and the surrounding states. Royal wants all of this sorted so he can marry Erika by the end of next fall. Kacey even plans to propose to Chanel, watching him ask Uncle V for his daughters hand in marriage was fucking hilarious.

I slip out of bed, not wanting to wake Cass knowing she will be exhausted, I pause beside the bed as I look down at her and wonder when the fuck I started caring about how she felt. I push the thought away as I take a quick shower and change before heading downstairs to meet Royal and Sin in his office, except when I enter it isn't him sitting behind the desk, it's London.

Her eyes harden at the sight of me, she isn't like most kids who would cower and hide. This little demon feeds on the thrill of a fight. I clench my hands into fists at my sides, my good mood from a minute ago evaporating. Yesterday was surreal, meeting my nephew and finally settling things between me and Lani, I even made an effort with my parents and promised to keep in contact with them more. Yesterday when I left, I handed Lani the keys to my house and told her she and Ryat were welcome to live there. She wanted to refuse but I told her I needed to know Ryat was close so we could protect him.

She has four men stationed there round the clock, she will never be unprotected. She is raising the heir to our family and we will never allow any harm to come to him.

"I'm sorry." Her voice pulls me from my thoughts. Dealing with all the shit from yesterday and killing Ricardo has me feeling like a weight was lifted but now, facing the reason my brother died brings that weighed down feeling back. "If I could take it back I would."

"You can't," I bite out. She blinks rapidly as if trying to fight back tears.

"I know," she whispers. "I hate myself, I never should have did what I did, but I won't keep saying sorry."

"You are the reason my brother is dead!" I shout, she flinches back.

"Chaos!" I spin around to find Royal storming toward me with a nasty look on his face. I crack my neck from side to side, ready to throw down if that's what he wants. He shoves me back a step and gets right in my face. I push back into him.

"Come on, Royal, show me what you're made of," I taunt him.

"You ever speak to my kid like that again and I'll—"

"Send me to hell so I can join my brother?" He tries to hide the cringe but I see it.

"You need to stop blaming us."

"I'm not blaming you!"

"But you're blaming her and by doing that you blame me! Deal with this shit now, Chaos, because you will not keep hurting my kid."

"Dad—"

"Stay out of it, London." Royal silences the demon as he keeps glaring at me. He snaps a hand out and grips the back of my neck pulling me in until our heads touch. "It's time to let yourself heal, brother. Let us help you move forward. You will never move on from him, nor will we, but we can honor him by living *for* him and executing the plans we all made years ago." His words hit me right in the chest, cracking it open and forcing me to feel something other the constant state of pain I am in.

"I don't want to heal. The pain reminds me of him," I admit bitterly.

"No, the pain doesn't remind you of him. You use the pain to mask the love and happiness you refuse to allow yourself to feel. The pain will always be inside you but you can choose to not allow it to control you and live a life he would want for you, because you aren't living, Chaos, you're existing and that isn't what he would want."

"I-I don't know how to do that." It's true, I don't know how to not be angry anymore, it's like it's my default setting and I don't know how to switch the fucker off.

"We'll figure it out together like we always do," he promises. I nod accepting his offer to help me. I pull free of his hold and turn back to the demon who is now standing in front of her father's desk with a letter opener.

"The fuck are you doing with that, Satan?" Royal growls behind me but says nothing when he steps up beside me and sees what she is holding.

"London," he scolds mildly, "you cannot stab people, I told you that." The little demon just rolls her eyes and drops the blade atop his desk and shrugs.

"I guess Uncle Chaos isn't the only one who needs to work on their anger issues." The little shit strolls out of the room, smiling.

"She was going to fucking shank me in the back?" I accuse as I turn and scowl at my cousin. He sighs and runs a hand through his hair tiredly.

"Kids are fucking hard work," he mumbles as he moves toward his desk to claim his seat.

"That isn't a fucking kid, she was going to shank me, Royal!" He throws his hands in the air and pins me with an accusing look.

"You all thought it was fucking funny when she was doing that shit to me and when I did try to punish her Havoc fucking protected her and said it was normal for children to lash out." I scrunch my face, he isn't wrong, we all did laugh at his expense.

"If *Emily Rose* shanks me I am coming for your fucking throat," I snarl.

"Blame your fucking brother for spoiling her. He taught her to embrace her urges and clearly maiming is one of said urges."

*Fucking Havoc!*

Shock ripples through me, that's the first time I have thought of my brother without pain exploding in my chest.

"I will talk to her," Royal says, trying to appease me as Sin walks into the office.

"You need to fucking sprinkle holy water on her," I grumble as I claim the seat next to Sin in front of Royal's desk.

We spend the day locked in meetings with the Albanians and formulating a plan with our men to encroach of the surrounding states to claim their territory as our own. Constance and Albert agree to our terms and will now operate under the *Memento Mori*. South and North Carolina will be easy to take, they don't have the manpower we do and from what we have learned, if we push on them hard enough they will surrender without fighting. Tennessee will be harder, Callum Salinski is a power hungry fucker and will fight to keep his turf. We'll save him for last so he knows we are coming, the thrill of what's to come has my cock twitching.

Fighting and the prospect of death always gets me hard.

"We move on North and South Carolina next week then we hit Callum, that'll leave us three weeks to sort out the operations and get shit running as smoothly as we can before we fly to Switzerland." Sin and I nod our agreement.

"I can't wait to get that shit done," Chanel says, I grunt my agreement.

"We'll send Kacey to scout out the family in the north tomorrow and then Terry can go to the south, I'll have Marco head to Callum's turf and get eyes on them," I say. They both agree with my plan. I move to stand but Royal speaks, keeping me in place.

"Erika and London are coming with me to Switzerland, what are you planning to do with Cassandra?" I've been waiting for one of them to bring her up, they hate not being in the know.

"I'll deal with her."

"What does that mean, Chaos?" Sin pushes.

"Why the fuck do you care?" I snap.

"Because we need to know if she is going to be a liability or not. She's a fucking reporter, Chaos. The shit she has seen and heard is damming for all of us."

I cut off Royal's tirade. "If you're so worried, why don't you kill her?"

He shakes his head, Sin scoffs beside me earning a scathing look from me. "You think because you haven't marked her that you outsmarted us?"

"What?"

She rolls her eyes before continuing. "You don't need a card to mark her as yours, Chaos. We can see it in the way you jump to her defense and how you keep her around constantly. Maybe at the start you did plan to kill her but now, even I am doubting that you will be able to deal that final blow."

Tired of their shit, I stand and shoot them both the bird. "She won't be a problem, I'll deal with her now." I can see the surprise on their faces as I storm out of the room and head straight upstairs to put an end to this shit. I'll show them that she means nothing to me and killing her will be an easy task. I kick the bedroom door open, marching into the room ready to prove she is nothing, but it's empty. I stalk into the bathroom and find that empty as well.

*Where the fuck is she?*

I head out for the door but pause at the sight of her phone and a note on the edge of the bed. I snatch up the note and her phone, clutching the phone so tight in my hand as I read over the fucking note.

*Before you go on a murdering spree and accuse people of helping me run, no one helped me. I just had to pay close enough attention to the times the guards changed shifts, the gate at the back of the property was handy. I'm only telling you this so you can know for sure I was not helped and don't hurt anyone.*

*Last night meant more than you will ever know, I can still feel the ghost of you between my legs. You awoke something inside me that I thought had died a long time ago and I can't thank you enough for that, but I also can't stick around and run the risk of you actually following through on your threat to kill me.*

*I know I am the last piece of the puzzle for you to finally get closure and move on but I can't allow you to hurt us. I'm so so sorry for what my brother did, Chaos, I really am but I'm not Quintin and I will not allow you to harm the child I carry inside me because you* thirst that deeply for revenge. I wish you could see yourself the way I see you and realize that you are more than your demons but you can't and I won't allow you to harm our child by hurting me.

Please, let me go...

All my hate and so much more,

Your Cass.

# Chapter Twenty-Five

**CASSANDRA**

"Just keep driving, Tabby, we can't stop anywhere unless it's for gas, we need to keep moving until we hit the Canadian border," I say in a panic, we have at least a five hour head start, but I can't bank on that in case he returned from the meetings Erika said they would be in all day. I have never been so scared in my life as I was today running through the backyard and escaping through the back gate toward the golf course where Tabby was waiting for me. We burned rubber getting the fuck away from there as fast as we could.

"I know!" she snaps and cringes. "Sorry, I'm just freaking out here, I've never been on the run from the mafia before!" Guilt eats away at me for dragging her into this mess.

"I am so sorry, Tabby."

"Don't be, I wouldn't want to be anywhere else." She shoots me a smile before focusing back on the road. "So, I hate to be the one to ask but are you sure you're pregnant?"

"I haven't had my period since the week before I slept with him, I'm two weeks late, Tab." I've never been late a day in my life and mix that with the fact I have been nauseous and throwing up daily, I know without needing the proof that I am pregnant.

"Well, I brought a couple tests just to be sure." I would be lost without her. I promise to take them the next time we stop for gas. In hindsight, I probably should never have mentioned a baby in my note to him but I also didn't want to do to him what his brother's baby momma did and hide his kid. My stomach is all in knots, we still have at least twenty hours to go before we reach Canada. We agreed that we wouldn't stop for the night and each take turns napping while the other drives, we can't afford to take that risk.

Tabby has gone above and beyond for me, securing passports from some shady guy so we could cross the border, packing up my apartment and being there for me when I needed her most. I knew that my messages would be tracked so I kept it simple but the phone calls are where we spoke about our plan. Erika unknowingly told me that the rooms didn't have cameras so I knew I was safe to speak freely. We drive a few more hours before pulling into a gas station. My body is aching from being stuck in the car for so long but I don't dwell on it as I snag the tests from Tabby and rush into the restroom while she pumps and pays. I pee on both sticks deciding it's better to be double sure. I can feel it, I know without a shadow of a doubt that I am carrying Chaos's child.

Exiting the stall, I place both sticks face down on the counter as I wash my hands, knowing and thinking I'm pregnant are two totally different things. I stand there for so long just staring at the tests too scared to have solid proof of what I already know. I'm snapped out of my stunned state when a worried Tabby enters the restroom, she takes one look at me and pity shines in her eyes.

"Did you check them?" she asks as she follows my gaze to the tests, unable to speak I just shake my head. "Want me to do it for you?" My only answer is a nod, she steps toward them and I break.

"Wait!" She spins around so fast I think she may have whiplash.

"What?"

"Tabby, if they say what I think they do..." A lump begins to form in my throat, she rushes to me and wraps me in a hug as tears slowly cascade down my cheeks.

"I'll be by your side the entire time, babe. I will be the best non-bio baby daddy that kid could ever have." Trust her to get me to laugh at a time like this. She releases me and gives my arms a gentle squeeze. "We got this, Cass."

I shake my head. "It's not that."

"What is it then?"

"He will never let me go, even if I didn't tell him about the baby he would still hunt me down."

"Then, we best get ourselves a house in the mountains where we only go into town once a month and no one knows our names or faces."

"Tab, he is going to find me, it's not a matter of if, but *when*. I am running away from one of the leaders of the mafia and I'm taking his kid with me. I am going to die when he gets his hands on me." Her eyes harden and her nose gets all scrunched like it always does when she's mad.

"You listen to me, Cassandra Blake, I may not be big or tough but I will shove my curling iron up that man's asshole if he tries to harm a single hair on your beautiful head." Gratitude swells inside me.

"I love you, Tabby."

"I know, now let me check these freaking tests before the bio-crazy-daddy finds us." I nod and start to wring my hands in front of me as I wait with bated breath for her to confirm what I already know. She flips the tests and stills, gathering them both in her hand she slowly turns back to me with tears in her eyes. "Congratulations, I'm gonna be an aunt."

I continue to drive the remaining five or so hours while Tabby gets some sleep in the seat beside me. Between the both of us we don't have much, not even enough money to be off work for a month, but what we do have is each other and that's all I need. I place my hand over my flat stomach and smile, this child may never know their father but I'll make sure that my baby never feels unloved or unwanted because no matter the situation of how he or she came to be, I will always cherish this gift Chaos gave me.

"I love you already, Chilly Bean," I whisper. Tabby stirs beside me and stretches as best she can, yawning. It's pitch black out now and the roads don't have much scenery but at least there is no traffic.

"How long do we have left?" she asks while yawning, how she manages to talk and yawn at the same time has always baffled me.

"GPS says five and a half hours, try to get some more sleep." She shakes her head.

"Nah, you know I only need a power nap to recharge. I'm good to drive if you want me to."

"I'm okay, I'll swap with ya soon though," I tell her. Tabby brings up her playlist on her phone and syncs it to the car's stereo and before long we're both belting out the lyrics to Adele's song. Neither of us can sing a note to save ourselves but we don't give a shit, I need this and so does she. We haven't been able to hang out like this in weeks. We used to do it all the time but since things with Chaos started, I took a step back from her not wanting to involve her in my fucked up life.

"Do you remember Charles Oliver from senior year?" I cringe and scrunch my face in disgust.

"The jock who used to fart in a can and then throw it at people?" She throws her head back and laughs.

"Yes!"

"Why the hell did you bring him up?" I ask, bewildered by her trip down memory lane.

"He added me on Snapchat this morning." I turn to her in a panic.

"Tabby, you need to delete all of those apps now, he can track you through them."

"No, he can't, he's the mafia, not some tech guru," she defends.

"He is one of the best trackers in the world, his uncle—Chanel's father is renowned for his tracking abilities, all of those kids can track a fucking needle in a hay stack. Tracking an IP address is child's play for them. Please just delete them." I feel like an asshole, she is giving everything up to help me and now that I have a second to think about it I'm starting to regret dragging her into this.

"Fine, I'll delete them now," she grumbles as she scrolls through her phone, the Adele song long forgotten.

"I'm sorry, Tabby," I say softly.

"I know, this is just going to take... some time to get used to," she admits.

A whoosh of air escapes me. "I know," I say just as her phone begins to ring. Worry surges inside me. "Who is it?" I snap.

"Calm down, it's my mom," she says, shaking her head as she answers the call. It connects through the car's Bluetooth system. "Hey, Mom, I told you I would call when we got there," she says.

"Tabitha Connelly, I wish I could say it was a pleasure to speak to you but I'm not a fucking liar." The sound of his voice has fear strangling me. Tabby looks at me with wide eyes. I mouth for her to hang up but then he speaks again, halting her. "I know she is with you, I bet she can hear me right now." A cold sweat begins to trickle down my spine. "Hello, my *Rotten Apple.*" The husky tone of his voice can't mask the rage I hear in it. "Run, run, as fast you can because I'm coming for you and I'm taking back what's *mine.*"

"Fuck you!" I blurt.

"Sure thing, tell me where you are and I'll come to you so you can fulfill that promise." I cringe, he's acting calm and sarcastic but I know it's just a ploy.

"No. Leave me alone."

"Never. I'm coming for you, Cass, and when I find you, be ready to fucking scream, baby. Hide for as long as you can because I *will* find you. I have nothing left to lose except the child you carry inside you. That is my fucking baby!" he roars, I flinch in fright.

"Just let me go, please."

"Never." Tabby ends the call and rolls her window down, chucking her phone out.

"Tabby!" I scold.

"What? You said he could track us and clearly he did because the fucker called me from... Oh my God, Cass, he called me from my mom's phone!" The hysteria in her voice rises as she continues to ramble for a minute before I finally get her attention.

"He doesn't have your mom's phone, he tracked your records and hacked into her number. I've seen it done before. When we get there, we'll call her straight away."

"Yeah, okay," she says but I can tell she isn't buying what I'm saying. I probably wouldn't believe me either if that was my mom, but my parents died when I was eighteen so I wouldn't know. We're both silent, lost in our thoughts. He meant what he said, he won't stop until he finds me. I shift in my seat, feeling the ghost of his cock inside me and I still have the marks he left on me. Even after everything he has done and said, a part of me does hope one day he will find us but instead of wanting to kill me, he would be rejoiced at the sight of me and finally admit that he *loves me*. I saw it in his eyes last night, his mask slipped for a split second and I saw it, the love he feels for me. God, sometimes I wish love was enough for people to change but Chaos Murdoch isn't like normal people.

*I'll love you enough for the both of us, Chilly Bean.*

# Chapter Twenty-Six

## CHAOS

"What's the plan, brother?" Royal asks me as I continue to pace the length of his office, the moment I found that fucking letter I ordered every one of our men to scour the area and find her. I know her messages about Texas were full of shit, she is smarter than that. Royal offered to send some guys down there to check but I refused, Cassandra is a lot of things but stupid isn't one of them.

"The phone call was too short to trace but Sin is working on tracking her phone through the *find my phone* app now. Once we have that, we'll have a general idea of where the fuck she is going," I grit out through clenched teeth.

"We'll find her." I turn to him and smile, he stills at the look on my face.

"Oh, I have no doubt about that. When we do find her, she's mine."

"Chaos, she's pregnant with *your* kid," he rushes to say.

"I know!" I roar then throw my phone across the room, smashing it to pieces against the wall. I drop down into one of the couches in his office and bury my face in my hands. "She's pregnant," I mutter more to myself than anyone, how the fuck did that happen? She was on birth control so how could this have happened?

I don't realize I've said that shit out loud until Royal answers me. "No birth control is a hundred percent, sometimes these things just happen, brother."

"This isn't just a thing!" I growl. "This is a fucking kid, Royal. Jesus, how the fuck did I fuck up this badly? I can't have a fucking kid!" His gaze hardens as he drops down onto the sofa opposite me.

"You didn't fuck up, this type of thing happens when you don't wrap your dick up. There is always a possibility of getting someone pregnant each time you have sex."

"I turn twenty-one next week, I'm not ready for a fucking kid. I don't even like the bitch carrying my kid."

Royal scoffs. "Yeah, right, you just keep fucking the same chick you claim to hate for over two months, right?" I glare at the fucker.

"I had a plan."

"Was that plan to fall in love with the woman you claim to hate?"

"Fuck you," I snap, the bastard laughs.

"Well, that wasn't a denial so I'll take it." His pale blue eyes dance with humor.

"I'm not in love with her!" I shout.

"And I remember a time when I said the same thing about Erika and yet, I'm going to marry her." I stand glaring down at the son of a bitch.

"You're a real fucking prick, you know that?"

He shrugs his shoulders. "I've heard that once or twice." I turn ready to flee the fuckers office, ready to go search for this fucking little shit by myself but Chanel and Kacey enter the room giving me pause.

"Did you find her?" I rush to ask.

"I located the phone. They must have ditched it on the side of the road," she says as she hands me a print out of a map. I scan it, frowning.

"Where the fuck are they going?" I mutter to myself.

"My guess is Canada," Kacey says.

"We have to stop her before she gets there, if she crosses that border we can't enter there without permission or we start a war with one of the families," I say as I look at Kacey and my cousins, each of them have somber looks on their faces. "What?" I snap.

Royal rubs the back of his neck anxiously as he looks to Sin, she rolls her eyes and answers for him. "We won't reach her in time. You're going to have to let her go until the meeting and ask permission to enter Canada to find her."

"Motherfucker!" I roar. "I'm going to strangle the shit out of her."

"Not while she's pregnant you won't be!" Erika scolds me as she enters the room with a disapproving look on her face.

"She won't be pregnant forever," I sneer.

"You would kill the mother of your child?" Erika counters as she slides up beside Royal.

"You think I won't?"

Her eyes narrow in response. "I don't think you will because you care about her." I throw my hands in the air, cutting her off.

"I'm real fucking sick of people telling me how I fucking feel. She doesn't mean shit to me, never has," I say in a cold tone, the plans I have for her when I finally get my hands on her again are fucking depraved, I'm going to make her wish she was never born.

"You're full of shit," Erika snaps.

"Babe–" She turns to Royal, silencing him with a look.

"No. We have all tiptoed around him and I get why but not this time, I will not stand by and watch him harm a child, *his* child or its mother." She turns her gaze back to me, this time when she looks at me, the warmth you can normally find in her gaze is gone, replaced by the look of a fierce badass. "If you can look me in the eye right now and tell me that you feel nothing whatsoever for Cass, then I will help you with the baby after you murder its mother."

I smile darkly as I take a step forward, Royal grunts in warning not to overstep my bounds where his girl is concerned. "I don't need your help. That's my kid and I have a family that will help me raise it without its mother's toxic ass around."

**One week later...**

I've been dreading this day. I used to live for our birthday and the celebrations that marked our arrival into this world but now, I wish I could just skip the fucking day and never have to celebrate again. Do I have plans for the day? Yes, I am going to get lit by myself and drink until I black out and can't fucking think or *feel*. That was my plan until I made my way downstairs only to find my cousins, Erika, Kacey, London, my parents and the most shocking thing to see was Lani and Ryat standing there. Lani looked so out of place and uncomfortable, no doubt her being here had everything to do with my mom forcing her to attend the celebration.

It wasn't until that moment that I realized this day would be just as hard for my mom and dad as it would be for me. Taking a deep breath, I move further into the room and stand here awkwardly as they all sing me "Happy Birthday". When it comes to the part where they say my name, I tense, all my life it has always been mine and Havoc's name together and the fear of them changing that has me wanting to flee.

"Happy Birthday to Chaos *and* Havoc..." Air rushes out of me hearing them say our names together, this day is already hard enough without them cutting him out of this small thing. My mom has tears in her eyes and I know it isn't because her baby is growing up, it's because one of her babies isn't here to celebrate this day with me. Before the song has even finished, I cross the room and pull my mom to me. She clings to me like I am her lifeline as she weeps for the son she lost.

I don't allow my emotions to show, knowing she needs me to be strong while she breaks down. I'm slowly learning to take the advice I was given to not allow my anger to control me, it's fucking hard but I am trying. When the song ends no one says anything as they give my mom this moment. She pulls back and sniffs, wiping her eyes. Dad moves in beside me, reaching out to cup her cheek, she melts into his touch. It's always astounded me how they could still be so into each other after so many years together, wouldn't you get sick of the same person?

"I'm okay, playboy," she says softly, trying to ease my dad. The old man just ignores her as he wraps an arm around her shoulders and pulls her into his side, placing a kiss to the top of her head.

"I know you are, I also know you're full of shit but I won't call you on it," he says, trying to lighten the mood but it doesn't work, like me, my mom fakes a smile daily and forces herself out of bed. I once thought me not being around would ease their pain but I see that I was wrong. Mom continues to live for *me*. She loves my dad so fucking much but he wouldn't be enough to keep her here if she lost both of us. I can see a glimmer of happiness in her eyes these days and that, I owe to Ryat.

She is not so shrouded in her hole of despair now thanks to the grandson she is helping raise. I haven't told my parents about Cassandra being pregnant or that she ran from me. I don't want to add to their shit they have going on but now that they are here, I know I will have to come clean. I leave my dad to contend with my mom as the others come and wish me a happy birthday. London doesn't hug me, she just stays by her mother's side and wags her brows. *Slowly*, I am starting to warm back up to the demon—baby steps!

"Happy birthday," Lani says awkwardly as she comes to stand

in front of me with Ryat on her hip, resting his cheek against her shoulder trying to hide away. Warmth fills me at the sight of the necklace I gave him around his neck, I can see she had some links taken out of it so it fits him properly.

"Uh, thanks," I mutter. She looks over her shoulder to make sure my mom and dad aren't paying attention before she speaks low enough for only me to hear.

"I didn't want to come but your mom wouldn't listen to me and said we had to be here. She wanted you to be able to spend the day with Ryat. But, if it's too much I can go and—" I reach out and place a hand on the opposite shoulder to Ryat, silencing her.

"You're a Murdoch now, Lailani, this is your family as well." Her eyes widen. "Regardless of how I feel, you have every right to be here and so does he, this is his family and his birthright."

"I don't know what to say," she mumbles.

"Me either, this is awkward enough." She chuckles.

"Yeah, can't say you're wrong. I never thought I would be here and talking to you without threats being hurled at each other."

I snort. "One day, we may even be friends." Both of us stare at each other for a second before laughing, garnering the attention of the others.

"Yeah, no. That will never happen but I can respect you as my son's... uncle."

All laughter flees me as I stare her in the eyes. "And I you, as his mother but also as the woman my brother loved." The last part has her swallowing a couple times and nodding, unable to speak.

Erika ushers us all out the back. The back patio has balloons and streamers set up, the table filled with food. I pause watching everyone claim their seats as I just stand here and try to take it all in. "You deserve this." I turn to see Erika standing there smiling up at me.

"You did this?" She shrugs.

"London and Royal helped, so did Kacey. It took us strong arming Chanel into helping but she did blow a couple balloons up so that has to count." I fight back the laughter that wants to come out of me at the thought of Chanel blowing up balloons, she would have hated that.

"Thank you." I surprise myself by how much I mean that, I never expected this.

"You're welcome, I didn't want to see you spending the day getting blind drunk."

"I would never have done that," I mock.

She shoots me a deadpan look. "And I didn't blow Royal while waiting for your muffins to bake." I balk at her as she walks away, laughing at my expense. I twist the ring on my finger and look up at the clear blue sky.

"Happy Birthday, brother," I whisper as I make my way over to join the others. This feels different sitting out here, seeing everyone smile and watching my mom cut up food for Ryat. Conversation around the table continues as I take it all in, Havoc may not be here in person but I feel his presence with me.

"Where's your girl?" my dad asks. All conversation halts, my cousins, Kacey and Erika stare down at their plates and continue to shovel food into their mouths leaving me hanging out here on my own. Dad frowns at the four of them before looking at me with a raised brow.

"She went away."

"Where?" he pushes.

"Just away," I growl.

"Cassandra ran away because Uncle Chaos wanted to kill her." I glare at the little fucking she-devil that sits between Royal and Erika. She smirks and shoots me a wink before resuming eating.

"Away, huh?" I groan tiredly, I haven't been getting much sleep between trying to hunt Cassandra down and pushing the families out of North and South Carolina, it has all taken up my fucking time, not to mention we have started buying up properties here in Miami and plan to open a couple night clubs.

"I'm handling it," I reply.

"He's having a baby."

"Shut the hell up, London!" I snap.

"You shut the fuck up, don't ever speak to her like that!" Royal shouts at me.

"Enough!" Mom says, putting an end to our almost fight. "What the hell does she mean you are having a baby?" I flinch under the pressure of my mom's gaze, the woman can still make me sweat at the age I am.

"Turns out when Cass ran, she took something of mine with her and I am going to get it back, mark my fucking words, her days of freedom are numbered," I sneer.

"You get her the fuck back here with that baby safely or I am sending your father and uncles after her. She will not take another person from me!" The threat is clear, *my* days are numbered on getting her ass back here or my mother is going on a hunt and somehow, I think Mom getting to her before me would be worse.

# Chapter Twenty-Seven

## CHAOS

### *Three weeks later...*

"Are we all set?" Royal asks as he walks into the new night club we just purchased. I've been here all morning meeting with contractors, I got stuck with this bullshit job because I got trigger happy when we went to take over Callum's territory. I shot him before he had a chance to surrender, so Sin and Royal are punishing me for not sticking to the plan. Fuck the plan, I could see it in his eyes, there is no way that prick was going to surrender, so I took him out.

"Yes," I snarl, fucking pissed off from dealing with people all fucking day.

"Good, now go see your nephew before we fly to New York tonight."

"Fuck you, don't tell me what to do." I shoulder check the asshole on my way past, he laughs which just serves to piss me off further.

"Don't be salty," he calls out.

"Coming from the fucker who owns a club he can't legally enter," I clap back, enjoying the sound of him cursing me out as I push through the doors. Royal and Sin don't turn twenty-one until December, which means since this is one of our legal businesses to funnel cash I'm stuck running it for the next six months. Ever since my mom put a clock on me to find Cassandra, I've been wound tighter than normal. It's been a fucking month since she fled and surprisingly, we can't find her. I even reached out to Uncle Vin to help me, but he was away in Paris on a job so I'll speak to him when I get there tonight since he got back from his job yesterday. Aunt Anya and Uncle Gage have offered to help me behind my parents back—Uncle G still loves to fuck with his siblings any way he can, so I accepted his offer.

I get in my car and drive to Lani's house, my mom and dad have her convinced that moving to New York is a great idea so Ryat can grow up in the same house his father did. I rebuked the idea at first but now, I'm starting to think it might be best. Our childhood bedrooms are back there, he would be able to see pictures of his father growing up and Mom and Dad would be able to return home so my dad could stop fucking trying to micro manage me. I've been spending time with Ryat every other day. I'm trying to do better and change, with my own kid on the way I know I have to do this and shockingly, Lani has been helping me. We aren't friends, but we do have a mutual respect and that's about as good as her and I will ever get given our past and what I did to her.

I think about my kid daily. The fear is still there knowing that there will be a mini me in the world in a matter of months and I honestly don't know if anyone is ready for that. I'm not, that's for fucking sure. Seeing how Lani is with Ryat and how much he clings to his mother and the way he will run to her for validation or if he's hurt has been fucking with my head—if I did kill Cass would my kid survive that?

*Would I survive that?*

I shut that stupid fucking voice in my head up, the fucker has been saying shit like that for a couple weeks, trying to deter me from my plan to take out the last remaining Blake and finish my plan, but for some reason I can never picture it. I've tried to close my eyes and envision killing her, but all that plays out is the times I have spent inside her and the way she bent to my will, called to the monster inside me and refused to give up on me. I didn't see it until recently, Cass has been trying to fix me since the first moment we met. She saw something in me I didn't and I need to know why!

I spend my afternoon hanging out with my nephew and fielding off questions from my mom, that woman is driving me fucking crazy! Dad left her here with Lani and flew back home this morning so he could be brought up to speed about the meeting in two days time.

"Why aren't you looking for her?"

"Jesus Christ, Mom," I finally snap, having had enough. Ryat jolts in front of me at my loud shout and I immediately feel like a dick for scaring him. Lani sits across from us, she shoots me a look of warning not to start shit while her son is present.

"Well, answer my question," Mom claps back.

"You don't think I want to find her?" I fire back. "I have been searching for her day and night as well as trying to run an empire with my cousins and claim territories so we can build something for ourselves. When this meeting is over, the gloves are coming off and I am hunting her ass down myself. It's my kid she's carrying, not yours, not Dad's, mine! I've got this, let me handle it." She crosses her arms and pins me with a look only a mother can master.

"I just don't want to see you miss out on anything with your child." Lani flinches but remains silent, Mom didn't mean it as a dig at her and she knows it.

"I know, Mom, I won't miss out, I swear. Just let me handle it, okay?" When she finally relents, I want to fucking praise Jesus. I love my mom, I do, but fuck me dead, she can get on every one of my nerves. Twenty minutes later, Mom tells me to say bye to my nephew so he can go down for a nap. I hold the little guy close and relish in the feeling of having him in my life.

"Love ewww." My heart melts at his words.

"Love you too, little man," I say as my mom leads him out of the room, leaving Lani and I sitting here on the floor. I didn't realize how much spending time with that kid would help me in ways I didn't know was possible.

"You ready for what's to come?" she asks me.

"Ready for what?" I say confused.

"To live out of control and never know if or when you will ever get that control back?"

"The fuck does that mean?"

She laughs and shakes her head. "When you see her, give in, Chaos, and don't fight. It is the most exhilarating feeling, but at the same time so scary, because you are surrendering control of your happiness and life to someone else."

"You high or something?" She glares at me.

"No, you asshole. I'm telling you to give into loving her."

I groan and roll my eyes. "Not you too," I grumble.

"You forget I have been on the receiving end of your anger." I scrunch my face, I still feel bad about that but I can't change it. "I also know what it looks like when you love someone."

"No, the fuck you don't."

"You are an identical twin, Chaos. Havoc looked at me the way you look at Cass. I know the look of love when it comes from those green eyes, they may not have been *your* eyes but I saw it in your brother's. When you were angry with me you meant it, but with her, you were forcing yourself to feel anger to mask the other feelings you were feeling toward her. Take my advice, time is too fucking short. Me and my son were robbed of the time we could have had with your brother, don't live with ghosts, live with memories. Love her, let yourself feel, it's okay to move forward."

"Her brother killed mine," I grit out through clenched teeth.

"She is innocent, don't forget that. If she wasn't and she was the reason why my son will never know his father, I would have slit her fucking throat myself." My eyes widen at her declaration.

"You've been hanging out with my mom too much."

Being back in my childhood home in New York has me feeling fucked up. I left Royal and Sin to meet with Uncle B and the others while I came back to my parents. I head upstairs and bypass my room, heading for Havoc's. I step inside and look around at all his things—his bed is still unmade and his clothes are still scattered across his floor, I smile at the sight.

He was a messy fucker.

"I miss you, brother," I say to the empty room that is now a shrine. I don't touch any of his things. I just stand here letting memories play out in my mind of all the times we had snuck out his window and met up with Royal and Sin. Fuck, we were terrible kids and always got into trouble. I smile at the memories. Fuck, maybe Lani was right, being able to live with memories I do have with my brother is better than living with his ghost.

"I knew I'd find you in here." I turn around to find Uncle Bishop standing in the doorway, he still wears a suit and I've never been able to understand why he would choose to wear those monkey suits daily.

"Yeah, I just wanted to... I don't know what I wanted," I admit.

"I came to talk to you about something, mind if we do that downstairs or you need more time?" I shake my head, stuffing my hands in my pockets.

"Nah, I'm good," I say, surprised that I actually mean it and follow him downstairs. He heads into the kitchen, I claim one of the stools at the counter while he reaches inside the fridge to grab two beers. He pops the caps on both of them before handing me one. We clink bottles and each take a sip. He leans against the wall staring at me, it's fucking unnerving to say the least.

"Knox Bronson granted you permission to enter his turf to find your girl." My brows raise.

"I thought I had to wait till the meeting to ask him?" He shakes his head.

"You did until he needed access to New York to track down his wayward fiancée, I granted him entry on the condition you could enter his."

"Thank you."

"He's only allowing you, Sin and Royal to enter... Kacey, Erika and London will not be granted entry, nor will any of your men. You three will be on your own."

"I understand."

"I have a hunch though."

"What is it?" I ask genuinely curious.

"I don't think she is in Canada."

I reel back. "Why?"

"Being a reporter means she is smart and knows to never stay the course, I think she wanted everyone to believe that's where she was heading."

"We tracked her friend's phone."

"Exactly. The girl knew you would call and ping her signal, she heard enough while being with you all that you wouldn't be able to enter Canada to get to her, forcing you all to focus your attention on gaining entry into there, when in reality she was never there."

I mull over his words and find that he makes perfect sense and that fucks with me. How did I not think of that?

"Because you're too close to her to see clearly, she used your blind spot for her against you." Fuck, I need to stop saying shit out loud.

"Where the fuck did she go?" I mutter.

"That, my nephew, I don't know."

"Fuck me," I growl as I scrub a hand down my face. "She played us like fools."

He smirks, tilting his beer toward me in a salute. "She played you at your own game, one might even say that she is worthy of something other than a hole in her head."

I scoff. "*You* said that." He laughs.

"Yeah, I did, but it doesn't change the fact I am right. She is a smart girl, Chaos. Finish this meeting and then dedicate your time to hunting her because the chase is the thrilling part, but the greatest reward is finding the prize that you never knew you wanted until it stood in front of you."

"Yeah, I never saw this coming when I walked through the door," Dad says as he enters the kitchen snatching the beer right out of Uncle B's hand. "Buy your own fucking beer."

"The fuck? You just drank my eight-hundred dollar whiskey!" Uncle B snaps.

"*You* offered me the fucking drink, dick."

"You were never my favorite twin." I cough to mask my laughter when Dad pins me with a glare.

"Rook doesn't even like you, he always favored King, so fuck off and go annoy your own son." Laughter bursts out of me, this time it's my uncle that pins me with a glare.

"You were never my favorite twin either," he mumbles as he leaves the house. Dad and I both laugh at his expense.

"You set for the meeting?"

I nod as I twirl the bottle between my hands on the counter. "Yeah."

"Talk to me, Son."

I lift my gaze to his, I can see he wants to help so I tell him what's on my mind. "I'm going to find her."

"Of course you are, I taught you everything you know about hacking and your Uncle V trained you all to track."

"I know."

"Then what are you worried about?"

"When I get her back, it's not just her, Dad."

"You're worried about the baby?"

"No," I say before changing my mind. "Yes, sort of... fuck, I don't know."

"Chaos, just take a second and explain to me what has you so wound up?"

"What if I'm no good at being a dad and fuck it up or worse, what if I fuck the kid up because let's be real here, it's not like I'm a saint and I tend to be trigger happy ninety percent of the time." Dad rolls his lips over his teeth to keep from smiling, I throw my hands in the air. "See, this is why I didn't want to fucking tell you."

"Shut the hell up for a second and listen, you dipshit." I scowl at him but close my mouth. "I'm only smiling because the same thoughts went through my mind when I found out your mother was pregnant—add the fact we learned we were having twins, nearly fucking sent me into a mental breakdown."

"How did you manage then?"

Sadness clouds his eyes. "My brothers helped me and so did your aunts, but the person who gave me the courage I needed was your mother. She never doubted me and my abilities to be a father, she believed in me before I could believe in myself."

I drop my gaze to the counter. "He would have been the better father," I say quietly. Dad comes around the counter and places a hand on my shoulder.

"He would have been amazing at a lot of things, but so will you. I think you should also know something that your mother and I haven't told you." I turn and look up at him, his brown eyes darken with bloodlust.

"What?" I'm slightly worried because of the way he's looking at me.

"The survivors that escaped that day—the agents, Albanians and Dominico's men."

"Yeah..."

"There are no survivors," he says in a cold tone. "We couldn't let them live after what they took from us. You may be the bringers of death but we are the Murdoch mafia and I couldn't allow those cunts to continue breathing when my son... They all paid the price, your brother was avenged, Chaos."

"That was you *and* Mom?" I balk.

"Fucking right it was! I needed that and so did your mother, but even after all of that, it didn't change anything. My son still remains in pieces of jewelry and a jar that your mother has with her. No matter how many lives I took, it didn't bring my boy back."

I can hear the watery tone in his voice and see the unshed tears in his eyes, fucking hell. I have been drowning in my own grief over the loss of my brother. I didn't even stop to think how my parents were handling it. Looking into my dad's eyes, I can see he isn't handling it all. He puts on a brave face for my mom and remains strong for her, but now I can see it clear as day, my dad is fucking broken inside.

"Dad, I'm sorry—"

"Sometimes, I just like staring at you because I can trick my mind into seeing Havoc through you for a split second." I drop my gaze, I know they can't help it but it hurts that my mom would call me Havoc or look at me only to know she wasn't seeing me but him for the first couple of weeks. "But I know that isn't fair to you. Don't ever for a second think that we would trade your life for his, if there was a choice to be made I would trade my life for the both of yours every single fucking time, because that is my job as your father. I should have been there to protect my son. I failed him, Chaos, not you."

"No, Dad," I rush to say. "You didn't–"

"When your child is born you will understand what I'm saying, until then, Son, let me have this." I nod, accepting his answer.

"I'm gonna make sure my kid knows everything there is to know about their uncle."

He smiles lovingly. "I know you will, Son. You will be an amazing dad and if you fuck up, I'll be there to help you."

*I respect the fuck out of my dad and I know with him by my side, I will be able to pull off this whole dad thing.*

# Chapter Twenty-Eight

### CHAOS

I feel like King fucking Arthur and the Knights of the Round Table, this is some medieval shit right here. We're all sitting around a massive round fucking table, we were all frisked and made to leave our guns or any other weapons outside of this room. Most of us only had a gun or two, maybe even a blade, but not fucking Chanel. That crazy bitch had three guns, six blades and a pair of knuckle busters! The four members from the English sit with six men behind them, Andreas and three of his men sit while four stand behind them representing the Russian's, the Irish have five men seated with three behind them. Knox Bronson is a surprise, I expected him to be old and gray but the guy must be near our age, he has two men and a woman sitting with him but no one behind him, the Greeks, they only have one man seated with two behind him.

Us on the other hand, my five uncles and my dad sit with Luka behind them, the three of us sit with Kacey behind Sin. Erika and London were left with eight guards and sent out for a girl's day, much to the demon's displeasure. Switzerland puts all of us on equal ground, this is the one country no one runs. It's not through lack of trying, anyone who has tried to take over this country has been pushed out by all of the families currently claiming a seat at this table.

Knox Bronson looks to the three of us, the curiosity is clear in his gaze as he stares intently but when his gaze lingers on Chanel too long, Uncle Vin and Kacey both grunt out their displeasure. Knox raises his hands and smiles.

"I meant no disrespect, Murelo," he says to Uncle Vin quickly dismissing Kacey. "I'm just honored to be alive to see a woman claim a seat at our table for the first time as a leader." Sin being the bad bitch she is just smirks and winks at the Don of the Canadian mafia.

"Now you've seen it you can look elsewhere," Kacey grits out, earning a disapproving look from all the others.

"You allow your men to speak out of turn?" Karl, the head of the Irish syndicate asks us.

Royal shakes his head. "He isn't *my* man, he's *hers* and if you try to silence him you will learn why we call her Sin." All the men around the table seem to eye Sin with a certain level of respect now. I know most of them here view women as a hole to sink their cock into but not us, Chanel is just as good, if not better than Royal and me at shooting, fighting, killing and everything else.

"Noted, young Murdoch," Karl says. Royal bristles but says nothing.

"We're here and kept our word to introduce all the families to the *Memento Mori*, is there anything else?" Uncle Bishop clips out.

"Yes," comes from Ian, the leader of the English family. "The war between you and the Albanians has caused setbacks for us. Our shipments have stopped and with them out we no longer have a supplier."

We knew this was coming, which is why we had a plan in place to take over all their dealings. "Your shipments will continue." All eyes turn to Royal. "Constance will now be running the arms shipments under our guidance. The price for the firearms will remain the same but the contract you had with Halil will be changing."

"You do not dictate the terms, boy, the Albanians weren't yours to take out–"

I cut Ian off speaking for the first time. "Yes, the fuck they were. Those cunts took the life of my brother, they're fucking lucky we stopped at killing just them and didn't go after their fucking families!"

"And the feds that were killed, that brought a lot of heat on your family," Andreas says.

"My son had nothing to do with that," Dad interjects, drawing their attention to him. "I will not apologize—my wife and I took the lives of the survivors from that day. You want to argue over heat from the feds and the loss of Halil, come at me, I'm right fucking here and ready to go to war with any of you if you so much as show me an ounce of disrespect over avenging my fucking son!" I watch as each of them slowly lower their heads in a show of respect.

"No one will take action against your family, you were within your rights to avenge the death of your son, Knight," Knox says.

"I say you should have taken the families out," Costa says. I look toward the leader of the Greeks and study him, this is my first encounter with them. I know they do shit differently than all of us, they have never disclosed how they do things and no one has ever gotten close enough to find out how their operations work. We know they run a society that you're only allowed to be entered into if you are blood or part of their founding families, but that's it.

"If you are here to argue or try to come after my family for the backlash over the death of my cousin, then I am telling you now, you will have the entirety of the *Memento Mori* and the Murdoch mafia coming after each of you," Chanel says, each of the men smirk at her.

"I just said, no one will come for any of you. We voted earlier about that, Knight was within his rights to do what he did. Any of us here would have done the same thing." Knox pulls his gaze from Sin to look at my dad for a second before settling his gaze on me. "You have my condolences; my twin sister was murdered six years ago and she is the reason I currently sit where I am. The bloodlust will pass over time, but the hunger for revenge will never stop." He reclines in his chair and shrugs. "Well, for me it hasn't stopped, it may be different for you but just know, the Canadians will never seek repercussions against you for avenging the loss of your brother. If you ever need to cross my border to find a fucker involved in his slaying, you need only ask."

I bow my head in thanks. "Appreciate it," I say, respecting Knox a bit more in this moment, he grew up with nothing and rose to the top. I can respect any man who earned what he has.

"As new members to this table there are rules to be followed," Andreas says.

Royal scoffs. "Coming from the guy who only has his seat at this table because my aunt gave it to him?" The Russians behind him begin to start firing off in their language.

"Zakroy svoy chertov rot, poka ya ne zakryl yego dlya tebya!" (*Close your fucking mouth before I close it for you!*) Uncle Gage shouts, silencing the Russians.

"Your nephew disrespects us, we will not stand for that," Andreas claps back, glaring at Uncle G.

"And I will not stand for your men hurling insults at my family, pull them the fuck in line now. Do not forget who you are speaking to, Andreas. My wife may not be present but remember who the fuck she is and it is by her mercy you have Russia. Push me again and see what happens." Uncle Gage is a fucking savage, I've never seen him like this before.

"Enough, I did not come here for petty squabbles between families," Ian snaps, putting an end to the disagreement.

"I move to petition the *Memento Mori* as a head family in the US alongside the Murdochs, all in favor?" Uncle Bishop asks.

"Before we vote," Costa says cutting in, "what guarantee do

we have that they will not disturb the peace we have built? It has taken generations for us to get to this point where we are able to meet. I will not vote *yes* just because they are your kin."

"They will be under our guidance and we will vouch for them," Uncle King says.

"That is not enough, they are young and seek power," the bastard says, running his gaze over us. "Rumors have reached us that they operate without your consent, they have a man who is on the FBI's most wanted list in this room with us." Costa is going to be the one that is fucking hard to win over by the looks of it. If they don't agree to allow us to operate, it means that they can attack any territory we claim. We would cause a war with these families if we didn't quit and fall in line under our parents, meaning this would be the end of everything we have built under the *Memento Mori*.

"Those charges were overturned," Chanel snaps.

"Forgive me, but that means nothing to me, I want assurances, Bishop."

"What assurances, Costa?" Uncle Bishop's tone is hard and it's clear he's fucking pissed that this fucker is putting up a resistance, but his hands are tied here.

"I want the peace to remain amongst our families. If they are coming for the Albanians and from what I hear, they also possess Columbia through a union of your son and his wife to be, what is to stop them from trying to wage war against us? Can you stop that and personally guarantee me that if I was to offend your son he wouldn't retaliate?"

Uncle Bishop shoots Royal a look but before either of them can answer, an image of Ryat pops into my head. Given the life we live and who we are, a target will be painted on his back for his life, not only his but also my kid. We need this to work, the only way we can do that is to unify the families and get them to agree to allow us to operate under our name and not our parents. They are old school and we want to move in a different direction to them.

"A school." All eyes turn to me.

"What?" Karl asks.

"We can guarantee peace through a school," I say.

"How?" Knox hedges.

I scan my gaze around the table as I speak. "We open a school here on neutral territory, where all future heirs attend. It will be a school for kids like ours, if we can raise our children in a setting like that, then peace will be achievable for all future generations."

"A school?" Andreas says in wonder.

"Yes. Hatred and bias is taught, no child is born with hatred in their heart, they learn it from us." I can feel Royal's gaze burning a hole into the side of my head, but I ignore it. I know he is thinking of London and not wanting her away from them, but I also have to think of my kid and my nephew. If I can broker peace and make sure no harm ever comes to them, then I'll fucking do it because I cannot lose either of them.

"Who would run this school?" Knox asks.

"We would all be able to vet any potential staff members, as this wouldn't be a normal school, it would be a school that teaches our children how to run our empires—fighting, shooting, self-defense—we would be raising our children in a unified setting." I'm talking out of my ass here but I can't stop it.

"We do not operate like you, my children are raised and taught–"

I cut Costa off. "We make the school a maximum of four years, from the ages of sixteen to nineteen so if they should so choose, they can still attend college but this is mandatory. This way none of us are there to influence them and they are able to mingle and meet others, brokering their own form of peace without us interfering."

"You will send your children to this school?" Ian asks.

"Yes," I say without hesitation.

"I don't have children so therefore my vote is null and void for this," Andreas says.

"Who covers the cost for the school?" Karl asks me. I open my mouth but Uncle Rook cuts in before I can.

"We all do." I snap my gaze to him in surprise. "I have two young daughters as you know, if this school is a way for me to protect my daughters, then I say we all fucking fund it." Discussions continue on about the school for the next hour or so until we come to an agreement. I can feel the anger vibrating off Royal but he isn't the only one with a kid to worry about now, I have to worry about my own and my brother's son. Karl and Ian agree easily, so does Knox. Andreas has agreed to go with the majority given the fact he isn't planning on having children and the fact he doesn't fancy women, his words not mine. Costa tried to vote against the school but lost to the majority. The construction on the school will begin immediately, they will board at the school for four years and need to integrate with other kids from different families. We have also agreed to open the school to politician's kids, princes and princesses and so on, as long as they understand how the school is run, they may attend.

"Now, all in favor in offering the *Memento Mori* a seat at this table with the notion of peace in the works?" Everyone nods and a chorus of yeses sounds out, we are on a trial basis here, provided the school works out.

"Don't fuck this up, kids, see you for the opening," the Irish leader says, nodding in our direction as he stands. The others follow suit so we do the same, but before I can follow after the others, Knox calls out to me. I turn to face him.

"Yeah?"

"Your uncle asked for permission for you to cross my border," he says.

"He did, but turns out, she isn't there." His brows raise.

"Really?"

I narrow my eyes. "The fuck does that mean?" He smiles and shakes his head before shooting a glance over his shoulder to the woman that is still seated next to his chair.

"It means, I know what it's like to be led on a woman hunt,

only for them to outsmart us." He tries to sound annoyed but I can see in his eyes that the guy is fucking head over heels in love with the woman who looks like she ate a lemon and would rather stab someone than be sitting where she is.

"Oh, this bitch thinks she is smart but she isn't that good. I'll get her ass back and show her what the fuck happens when she runs from me."

He nods. "If you manage to keep her ass by your side, send me instructions on how you did it, I think I may need it." His girl pops her head up then and shoots him a glare. I snort. "Looks like you just need to cuff her ass to your side."

He scoffs. "I tried that, she picked the lock and then stabbed me before jumping out of my second-story window and running." My brows raise in surprise, she's a tiny little thing so the thought of her surviving the fall stuns me.

"Yeah, good luck with that one," I say.

"Thanks, I'm gonna need it." We shake hands before I head out to find the others. Knox Bronson isn't a bad guy like I thought he would be, he and I could actually get along.

I find the others gathered around the side of the cathedral we were just in. At my approach Royal breaks away from our family and storms toward me, gripping the front of my shirt in his clutches. I keep my arms at my sides, ignoring the others' protests for him to let me go. I knew this was about the moment I mentioned the school.

"You son of a bitch, you just sentenced my kid to that fucking school!" he shouts.

"Royal, let him go!" Uncle B says, but he ignores his father. I press my head against his.

"My kid will have to go there as well, I did what I had to do in order to secure our families fucking future, you dumb ass. You adopted London and plan to make her a Murdoch, she is going to have a target on her fucking back. I just made sure that your kid would live to see her twenty-first birthday, unlike my brother, you fucker!" He recoils as if I slapped him and drops his hold on me, shaking his head.

"Destiny, Unique and Nytress will also attend this school, and I for one will be glad to know my daughters and niece will have a chance at not having to fight for their lives like you three or us. Don't deny that this wasn't a great idea, Royal. Chaos just gave us all a solution to ensure the safety of our children," Uncle Rook says. I nod my thanks, which he returns before looking back at Royal.

"Nothing is guaranteed. We are sending our kids away without protection, she could be killed, Chaos," he shouts as part of the terms were that no security or weapons would be able to enter the school. I get why Royal is pissed but this had to be done.

"Knowing your kid, she would just blow the fucking school up anyway," Kacey says, my uncles laugh while Royal groans and Sin shakes her head.

"If I didn't think this was the way to go or that this school wouldn't help *our* kids, then I would never have said it, but I believe this will work, Royal. I just need you to trust me."

He stares up at the sky for a beat before looking back at me. "I do trust you, that's the fucking problem." I smirk. "If anything happens to London–"

I cut him off. "Dude, we should be fucking worried that *your* fucking kid doesn't ruin the peace we have just made and kills all the heirs starting a fucking war we can't win!" A normal person would rebuke my claim but not Royal, he genuinely looks worried.

"Fuck, I need to get back and talk to her because that is a real fucking possibility," he grumbles, all of us laugh at his expense.

"Fucking karma. God, I love that bitch," Uncle Bishop says, earning a glare from his son before he stomps away, muttering about how much of a dick his father is. Uncle B turns to me all traces of laughter void from his face. "Did you find her?"

At the mention of Cassandra, I stiffen. "Not yet, but I will.

We managed to track the car down they fled in, it was ditched at the border."

He nods. "You need anything, you ask." I thank him before he stalks off to his car as my dad comes to me.

"You okay?" he asks.

"I will be when I find her," I answer.

"You need me, call me. I'll help you hunt her ass down. Find her soon, Son, before your mother leads your aunts on a mission."

"Just stop her," I snap, he pins me with a deadpan look.

"Have you fucking met your mother and aunts?" I roll my eyes.

"What a pussy," I mutter as I walk away.

"You little shit, one day you will understand the power a woman wields and I am going to fucking laugh!" he calls out to me, I flip him the bird over my shoulder.

*Now that we are settled with the other families, it's time for me to hunt down my Rotten Apple.*

# Chapter Twenty-Nine

## CASSANDRA

### *Five months later...*

The humidity in Bali is killer, Tabby and I haven't been able to adjust to it but the beauty of this country makes putting up with it easier. We have been on the move for months, never staying in one place too long or we risk *him* being able to find us. We knew we had to get the fuck out of the US. We had planned to head to Canada but Tabby and I both agreed if we crossed the border and hid it wouldn't be smart, because he would search there, he would search the whole fucking country. So, we ditched her car and purchased a pickup truck near the border before turning around and heading south. We have been working to get enough cash so we could fly from country to country using our fake passports.

We got here about two months ago thanks to the help of Tabby's parents, they wired her some money through some crypto app thing that I don't understand. Tabby assured me it couldn't be traced. Bali is amazing and we have been here ever since we escaped the States, living in a little hut near the beach in

Kuta. Tabby and I had enough money between us to buy into a local restaurant and make enough money from the revenue of that to live, we don't exactly have a lot but we have what we need and that's all that matters.

I walk along the beach heading back toward our house, being nearly six months pregnant I feel like a whale and can't even see my feet. I'm a swollen mess and constantly sick. The doctor we saw in Chile said the morning sickness should pass after the three month mark, but it hasn't stopped. We sought another doctor here when we landed and she said some women suffer the whole way through pregnancy with sickness, looks like I'm one of those women.

"Hey, Mama Tot." I look to see Tabby sitting on our little back patio in one of the old cane chairs we nabbed from the side of the curb. I smile as I make my way toward her, I have to use the rail to climb the two steps it takes. I plop down into the chair beside her, exhaling loudly. God, being pregnant is not what I thought it would be, it's fucking rough and my back and feet always ache. "You look like shit."

I scowl at my best friend who just smiles. "You try carrying this fucking watermelon around daily and see how you look!"

She scrunches her face. "God, I can't wait for you to not be pregnant, you are so moody." I sigh and slouch back into my seat.

"I'm sorry, I'm just so tired and sore," I say as I rub my hand over my rounded stomach. Okay, maybe I'm not as big as a watermelon but given that I have always had a flat stomach my whole life, this shit is hard.

"Just wait, soon I will have to help you put your shoes on." I lift my feet and manage to see the tips of my toes.

"I'm gonna be as big as a house." My bottom lip begins to tremble.

"Babe," Tabby whines as she reaches over and claps my hand in hers. "You look beautiful and you're glowing."

"How the hell am I going to do this, Tabby? We can't afford–"

"Stop!" she snaps, I clamp my mouth closed and drop my gaze. "We'll make it work. I have a meeting tonight to discuss options for us expanding our restaurant to another location here, that will bring in more income. We'll make this work, Cass." Tears well in my eyes, I don't deserve this woman.

"Tabby, I love you and I couldn't have done any of this without you." Her eyes soften.

"Yes, you could have. You are a strong ass woman and you are going to be an amazing mom, don't ever forget that." Every time I think about it, I get emotional. I should be doing this with the father of my children, not on my own with my best friend.

"They should know their father, Tabby," I say as tears begin to fall down my cheeks.

"I know, babe, but we can't take that risk," she says quietly. I know she's right but the guilt is eating at me daily. Ever since I found out I was pregnant with twins, I felt this deep resentment toward myself for keeping them hidden from him. Being pregnant with one baby was hard but knowing that there are two, and after what he went through, I feel like a fucking bitch. I mean what are the fucking chances, right? It feels so fucking cliché to be having twins, like how can his family have four fucking sets of twins? Isn't it supposed to skip a generation?

"I just wish shit wasn't so fucked up. He should be here–"

"Stop that," she scolds, every time I mention Chaos she gets all up in arms about it, telling me how much of a piece of shit he is and me missing him and pining after him is just PTSD or something like that, but it isn't and she knows that. She tried to push me to go on a blind date with her, she's been dating Chris for a month, he's the other owner of our restaurant, but I refused. Chaos and I may have been toxic and explosive but I fell for him and I can't just turn those feelings off. "He hurt you."

"He didn't mean to," I defend him even though I know it's going to piss her off.

"Yes, he did, he wanted to kill you Cassandra. Is us being on the run from your crazy ass baby daddy not enough of a wakeup call for you to see how fucking crazy he is?" I recoil into my seat. "He is the fucking mafia, you need to move on and get over him, because he *will* kill you if he finds us, you ran with his kids, Cass."

"I know!" I shout as tears continue to fall. "I know you're right and hear what you're saying but it's not that simple, Tabby. I fucking love him!" Her eyes widen, I've never said that out loud before. I slap my hand over my own mouth and stare at her in fright.

"Holy shit," she breathes out. "You need to get the hell over him fast, you have a max of ten weeks before the twins are here and you can't be worried about that shit." Technically I'm due in three months' time, but Tabby says twins never make it to their due date and always come early.

"How the hell can I do that? He's the father to my kids."

"And where the fuck is he, Cass, huh?" I drop my gaze to my lap and cry quietly. "Shit, I didn't mean that–"

"Yeah, you did," I whisper.

"Cass—"

"It's fine, Tabby. Just go to your meeting and I'll see you when you get back." She sits there for a minute before sighing and climbing to her feet.

"I'm sorry, Cass. I love you and you know I will always support you and whatever decision you make."

"I know." She places a kiss to the top of my head before heading inside, leaving me alone with my thoughts.

There have been many times I have debated calling him or sending him pictures of my scans but I never follow through with it out of fear. I have no doubt he's still searching for me now and turning over every stone to track me, but with the twins so close to being born we had no choice but to settle down and prepare for their arrival. Every day that passes by has guilt weighing heavier on me, I am robbing him of the chance to watch his children grow inside me. During the day I can push those thoughts away but at night, when I'm lying in bed alone, I can't push away thoughts of him. He's in my dreams every night. I picture him finding us and being so happy to see me and the size of my belly that contains our babies. I know he may never have said it but I could see it in his eyes that night we spent together, he feels something for me but he just can't allow himself to embrace it.

Loving someone who doesn't feel the same as you is hard, but loving someone and knowing they feel the same but won't admit they feel anything is fucking torture.

I startle awake in my chair when one of the babies kicks my ribs, I groan as I push forward and stand stretching my back, fuck. Pain explodes in my lower back, that was stupid falling asleep in that chair, now I'm going to pay for that for the next day or two. I take a step toward the back door but pause, my heart thumps inside my chest as I slowly turn back toward the beach where I saw a shadow in the corner of my eye. My breathing kicks up a notch as I turn fully and face the beach in front of me. There, shrouded in the darkness, stands a lone figure with their back to me.

*It's him!*

I know it with every fiber of my being that it's him standing out there alone. I dart my gaze to the back door, debating if I could make a break for it without him catching me. I nix the idea almost as quickly as I thought it, there is no way he is here alone, he would have every exit covered making sure I have no way out.

*What if it isn't him?*

The thought flees my mind the second his head turns and he peers over his shoulder toward me—I may not be able to see thanks to it being dark out, but I can feel his gaze boring into me.

"He can't kill you while you're still pregnant," I say softly to myself as I grip the rail and slowly descend the stairs. My legs are shaky and my hands are clammy as I walk toward him. Fear claws its way up my spine, if he was going to hurt me he could have done it while I was passed out in the chair but... he didn't, that has to mean something, right? As I get closer to him I drink in the sight of him standing there in a pair of denim shorts, a fitted white T-shirt and a baseball cap turned backward on his head. I take a breath and manage to force my legs to carry me to his side. I keep my gaze ahead and focus on the waves as they crash against the shore, the moon the only source of light out here.

Nerves are warring inside me as we stand here not saying a word just staring out at the ocean, in my dreams about him there was none of this awkwardness or tension but given the circumstances between us, I can't blame him. I should be running for the hills and trying to escape not standing beside the man who vowed to end my life every time we were together. I want to blame the pregnancy hormones but, this stupidity is all me. He's like a magnet, I can't fight the pull against him and honestly, I think I stopped fighting the pull a long time ago.

"Bali, huh?" The sound of his husky voice jolts me out of my thoughts. I close my eyes savoring the sound. I wish I could say I didn't miss the sound but I would be lying.

"I was running out of places to hide," I answer honestly. He turns toward me then and I do the same slowly lifting my gaze to his. Jesus, is it possible he got hotter? His green eyes bore into mine, but I can't get a read on his emotions until he drops his gaze to my stomach.

*Fear.*

Joy.

*Fear.*

Wonder.

*Fear.*

Love.

I see all those emotions play out across his face as he stares down at my rounded stomach. "You took something from me." There it is, the cold angry tone that I'm used to—I need to remember he isn't my white knight, he is my executioner.

"You promised to kill me," I say in a firm tone, his gaze lifts to mine. Fire swims in the depths of those green eyes that I've come to love. I wish I could switch my feelings for him off, it would make this whole situation so much easier if I hated him.

"Tell me something, Cassandra." I stiffen at the sound of my name coming from him. "Did I ever hurt you?"

I splutter. "Are you fucking serious?"

"You loved it when my cock hurt you," he snaps, I scoff and turn to leave.

His eyes harden then he snaps his hand out gripping the back of my neck and pulling me in close—well, as close he can given my size. At the feeling of my bump pressed against him he stills and drops his hold on me. I tense in anticipation. The longer he stares at the bump, the more I worry he's gone into shock or something until he hesitantly reaches out with his hands and cups my stomach on either side, drawing a gasp from me. I can feel the heat of his hands through my sundress, I'm too big for my pants so dresses have been my go to.

"You took *them* from me." I gasp and step back, forcing him to drop his hands to his sides, his gaze meets mine and I see it in his eyes.

"You know?" I whisper.

His brows raise as an angry glint enters his eyes. "I told him." I spin around and come face to face with my best friend who looks like a deer caught in headlights, Chanel and Royal stand behind her.

"What?" I ask her utterly confused at what the fuck is happening right now. Earlier she was against him and him being anywhere near me and now here she stands with his cousins at her back and admitting she told the man she claimed to hate information about me. She comes forward and reaches for my hands but I step back only to smack into Chaos. I try to escape him but the moment his hands reach around me and grip my stomach, I still in fear.

"I did this for you," she says quietly.

"For me?" I screech. "How is this for me?" I shout at her, she hangs her head in shame.

"You refused to let him go, so I had to do something to ensure you survived *him*." Chaos scoffs behind me but I ignore him, taken aback by my best friend's treachery.

"What did you do, Tabby?" She lifts her gaze to mine, the glassy look in her eyes has me wanting to soften toward her but I can't, she just killed me!

"I reached out to him a while ago."

"Why?" I snap when she refuses to continue.

"Because I hear you crying every fucking night!" she shouts, I press back against Chaos. "You don't think I know you cry for him or the fact you are fucking terrified to bring these kids into this world and never be able to tell them who their father is out of fear they will look for him?" She doesn't allow me to answer. "I fucking love you, Cass, you know I do but I couldn't sit by and watch you fall further into that dark hole you live in because *he* isn't with you." Now, I hang my head in shame. "I thought we could do this, I wanted to do this with you but let's be real, Cass, you don't want to do this with just me, you *need* him too." I lift my gaze to hers fighting back tears.

"I do," I say brokenly, she smiles sadly and steps toward me. This time when she reaches for my hands I don't pull away, not that I could thanks to the giant standing behind me who is currently massaging my stomach and distracting me from how good it feels to have his hands on me after so long.

"Nah, babe, today when you said what you did, I knew I made the right call in keeping him in the loop."

"Tabby–"

"Just... talk to him." She cuts her gaze to Chaos and scowls up at the beast of a man. "I have his cousin's assurances that he will listen to what you have to say and will not harm you." I cut a glance to Royal and Chanel, each of them nod their head, confirming what she says.

"You never had a meeting did you?" I ask, she smiles and shakes her head.

"No, this was planned already, it just happened to fall on the day we had a revealing conversation." I feel the blush coat my cheeks, she squeezes my hands once more before turning and leading Royal and Chanel away leaving me alone with *him*. My mind is reeling, Tabby has been feeding him intel on me and I didn't fucking know—I'm not sure how I feel about that. A part of me feels betrayed but another part is grateful for her doing this for me, giving me the chance to see him again.

Time seems to quit existing as we stand here with my back to his chest and his hands roaming my bump. When the babies kick, he gasps and jerks his hands away in fright. I slowly turn to face him and crane my neck to meet his gaze.

"How long have you and my best friend been talking behind my back?"

He doesn't hesitate to answer. "Since your first scan when you found out you were having twins." My eyes widen, that was months ago! "I've known about them from the beginning and everything about your pregnancy. They're my kids," he says with such conviction.

"They are *mine*!" I snarl. "You're not taking them from me."

"You took something from me!"

"I had no choice, they are growing inside me, it's not like I could have left them behind," I shout.

"I was talking about you!" he shouts back.

"W-what?"

"You. Are. Mine." My jaw unhinges.

*Holy fuck, are my dreams coming true?*

# Chapter Thirty

## CHAOS

Her mouth opens and closes a few times as my words sink in, I say nothing giving her a chance to process what I said. Don't get me wrong, the thought of wrapping my hands around her neck and strangling the life out of her is strong but I can't do that and it isn't because she's carrying my kids.

"What does that mean?" she whispers.

"It's about who stands in the rain with you, when they can be dry if they wanted to."

"What?"

I scrub a hand down my face and pray for fucking patience. "No one aside from my brother has ever believed in me or seen beyond what I allow people to see. You saw *me*."

"You can't just say things like that!" she says, throwing her hands in the air.

"Why the fuck not?" I snap.

"Because, you told me time and time again that you wanted to kill me. I ran because of that reason. What the fuck has changed,

Chaos? I won't allow you to hurt me or the babies, they deserve better than that and so do I."

"Oh, and how do you think you should be treated? You want me to buy roses, massage you, paint your fucking nails while I'm at it?"

"Yes!"

"I'm not that guy!" I roar whilst pounding a fist against my chest.

"I know," she screams at me.

My eyes narrow as I step into her and grab the back of her neck, forcing her gaze to mine. "I dare you to go try to find that guy and see what the fuck I do to the cunt. Your pussy being punished will be the least of your worries." A shiver works its way down her spine, she tries to mask her reaction but fails. She fucking loves it when I get all handsy and controlling over her ass, I bet her pussy is wet for me right now.

"Oh, there you go again, you gonna kill me if I try to find Mr. Right?"

"Nah, I'll just keep fucking you until you come to your senses and realize *I am Mr. Right*!" Her eyes widen to the size of dinner plates.

"Say what?"

"I've known for months where you were and what you've been doing. You didn't think you escaped me, did you, my little Rotten Apple?" Her jaw slackens and she pales slightly.

"You knew where I was?" she asks quietly.

I smirk. "Of course I fucking did, I found you months ago."

"Why did you let me keep running?" There it is, the question I have been trying to answer myself and avoiding what it meant whenever the feeling inside arose. Like now, it's surging inside me and I want to fight it, but Lani is right, I don't want to keep chasing ghosts.

"I knew you wanted freedom," I answer honestly as I take a step backward.

"There's more, I know there is so tell me, Chaos, please," she begs. I run a hand through my hair and debate if I should give in or keep everything inside me. "I need to know."

"I didn't want to keep forcing you, okay," I shout.

"Forcing me to what?" she shouts back.

"To be with me!" There, I said it.

"You were giving me a choice?" she asks, the uncertainty in her tone is clear.

"Yes."

"Why? You never cared about how I felt before when I begged you to let me go, what changed?"

"Everything," I mutter. She growls and moves to stand in front of me, claiming my attention.

"You need to give me more."

"Or what?" I sneer.

Anger swirls in her gaze, fuck she looks like a wet dream with her blonde hair blowing around her, her tits have grown and so has her ass. I want to mark her and sink my teeth into her soft flesh as I fuck her senseless.

"I'll walk away from you." I laugh and shake my head, she huffs and places her hands on her hips trying to look angry but the sight of her in the yellow sundress with her hard nipples poking through and that bump just makes me hard.

"You can try, you got away once but you won't escape me a second time, my little Rotten Apple. You carry the lives of my children inside you, you had your chance at freedom but you blew that today."

She frowns and cocks her head to the side. "How?"

"Tabatha called and told me about your little conversation."

Her nostrils flare. "What else did she tell you?" she grits out through clenched teeth.

"She sent me photos of your scans, updates on your pregnancy and everything to do with the twins."

"Why did she do that? I know her and you had to have promised her something for the information." I grind my teeth, the little bitch was hard to convince that's for sure.

"She made me swear to leave you be. I mean, come on, Cass, you really didn't think ten grand was enough to buy half a five star restaurant, did you?"

She gasps. "*You* paid for it?"

I nod. "She said you were worried about money. Chris isn't part owner of the restaurant, he is one of my men and was sent here to keep tabs on you. You own the whole restaurant with your best friend."

"Oh my God," she breathes out as she turns away from me. I step into her back and relish in the shiver that flows through her.

"You were never far from my sight, I have been watching you from a distance for months."

"Was there ever a blind date?" The sarcasm is thick in her tone.

"Yes." She turns and peers up at me over her shoulder.

"You were going to let me go on a date?" I grind my teeth.

"Fuck no, I was going to be your date if you accepted, but you declined. Your friend agreed with me then that you weren't going to get over me and what we shared, she began to become more open and forthcoming with information. She agreed when I called yesterday that it was time I came for you. I didn't expect her to call again today and tell me that *you* needed me. When I got here and saw you sleeping, I..." I take a deep breath and push on knowing I need to let go of this grudge I hold against her because of her brother. "I realized, I... don't hate you." She turns slowly to face me, tears well in her eyes.

"What if I hate you?" The husky lilt in her voice gives her away.

"I told you once before, when you say it, you mean something else. Now tell me, my little Rotten Apple, am I going to have to chain the mother of my children to my bed and fuck you into submission until you admit that you love me or will you be a good girl and admit it now so I can take you inside and give us both the release we have been craving for months?"

Her pupils dilate as her breathing notches up a speed, lust

clings to her like perfume as she stares up at me with need. I watch the rise and fall of her chest as my need begins to claw its way inside me, begging me to claim what is mine, the sight of her pregnant with my kids inside her, panting and needy for me has my cock twitching in my shorts. If I'm what she wants, what she *really* wants, then she needs to be the one to come to me and show me that she is prepared for this life and what it entails and most importantly, she needs to show me that she can handle being with *me*.

"You say I need to admit that I don't hate you and I have, yet here you stand refusing to reciprocate and give me the same courtesy of telling me that you love me too."

*Those three fucking words!*

"If that's what you need from me to prove to you that I am not going to hurt you, then you are a fucking fool. I'm standing right here on this fucking beach with you, telling you that I want you by my side, I want to raise those babies with *you*," I say, pointing toward her bump. "I don't want to do that shit on my own. I won't be an every other weekend parent, that isn't how shit works in my world, Cassandra. Those kids will be with me, that isn't a threat, it's a fact. You have a choice to make and you need to make it now."

"Fuck you."

"Right now?"

She throws her hands in the air frustrated by me. "I don't want those options!" she shouts.

"What fucking option do you want?" I shout back.

"I want the option where I get *you*!" A tear trails down her cheek as she stares up at me.

"I gave you that option," I growl.

"No, you gave me the option where you fuck me into admitting that I love you but you never gave me the option where I get you. Can't you fucking see that all I want is you, Chaos—your tender side, the part of you that hates yourself for loving me, the part of you that fucks me and claims my body as his own—I want all of it, but you aren't ready to give me that which is why my answer is no." I clench my fists at my sides as I grind my teeth, trying to control the urge to lash out at her. "I can't love someone who won't admit they love me too, it's too fucking hard. I won't raise my children in a home where their father is too scared to admit he loves their mother... I can't do it." She's crying and clutching at her chest like she is trying to hold the pieces of her heart together that are breaking away. She sniffs and bats away her tears with the back of her hand, trying to appear strong but I can see inside she is dying, and that fucking kills me.

When she meets my gaze I see it, the resolution. She is going to walk away and leave me, when she turns her back pain explodes inside me. Breathing becomes hard. Watching her walk away with my future inside the palm of her hand and inside her belly feels like I'm losing Havoc all over again. I can't bring my brother back, I can't change what happened to him, but I can change what happens right now.

"Cassandra!" I roar, she pauses but doesn't look back. She seems so far away, out of reach almost, fear wants me to shut down my emotions and latch onto the anger I have been feeling for months but if I do that, I lose her and my twins.

*I can't fucking lose her.*

I race over to her and cut in front when she tries to stalk off, she glares up at me and shakes her head.

"Let me go," she begs. I cup her face between my hands and bend until my forehead rests against hers and close my eyes, I breathe her in for a minute needing this contact from her. "Chaos, please, just let me go," she whispers. I open my eyes and shake my head, she tries to pull back but I tighten my hold.

"I can't let you go," I say quietly. "I have treated you like shit and God fucking knows I don't deserve you or those kids, but I want them and I want you, I want it all with you, Cass. I'll fuck up more times than I want to admit but I'll learn from my mistakes if you teach me. I don't want to be angry anymore, I don't want to hide away from life and drown in my grief over losing my twin. I want a life with you and our kids. I'm so sorry for everything I have done and put you through, baby. I was a fucking cunt for blaming you for what your brother did."

"Chaos–"

"Shut up and let me finish." Her eyes narrow but she does as she's told. "The old saying is true, *you don't know what you got until it's gone.* I learned that harsh lesson when you left me. I may not deserve it but I am asking you not to give up on me. I can't let you walk away, Cassandra, it's not in my DNA and, baby, if you don't agree to being with me then I promise you, you will never feel the touch of a man again because I will have no qualms about chaining your ass to a wall so you can watch me torture and kill your bitch ass wannabe lover."

"Seriously?"

"Yes, seriously."

"No–" I slam my lips to her, silencing her argument, I'm all talked out and right now I just need to hold her and feel her against me.

# Chapter Thirty-One

**CASSANDRA**

I want to give in and get lost in the feeling of his lips against mine and the way his kiss breathes life back into me after so long, but I can't allow him to distract me with his body. I need to be strong for my babies—I know my worth and I will stand my ground. I push against his chest and I pull away, his hold on my face remains but I turn away before he can kiss me again.

"Jesus fucking Christ!"

"Fuck you!" I shout as I turn to meet his heated stare, our breaths intermingle at our close proximity.

"Please do, baby, because my cock is aching to slam inside that tight little cunt."

"Never."

He smirks as he slowly glides his hands down my body, cupping my breast in one hand and grabbing my ass with the other, drawing a gasp from me. "I love you, my little Rotten Apple, and I am never allowing you to walk away from me again." My jaw unhinges as warmth explodes inside me, forcing the anguish I was feeling a moment ago out. "Now, that you got those three little words you better be over playing hard to get because I'm three seconds away from fucking you right here on the beach." I clench my thighs together to try to dull the ache between my thighs, but it's no use, my panties have been wet since the moment he looked at me.

"What about Tabby and your cousins?" He recoils in disgust.

"Why the fuck are you asking about them?" he growls.

"Our house is tiny and there is no way they won't hear us fucking, you don't do quiet sex, Chaos!" I scold, the cocky fucker just shoots me his famous panty-melting smirk as he grips my hand and drags me back toward the house. "Chaos–"

"Shut the fuck up, Cassandra, you got what you wanted and now I'm getting what I want. They aren't here, now quit stalling, get the fuck inside that house and lose that fucking dress," he growls at the base of the stairs. Need tears through me at the lustful look in his eyes. I grip the railing and carefully climb the stairs, he grips my waist offering me extra support. He keeps his hands on me as I lead us into the house and come to a stop in the tiny living room. He doesn't look around, just keeps his eyes on me. "Lose the dress."

I grip the hem ready to pull it over my head but hesitate. "I..." Doubt begins to swirl inside me. "My body..."

He closes the space between us and grips the hem of my dress, yanking it over my head. "Your body is fucking perfection, you have never looked more beautiful to me." I feel tears prick the backs of my eyes, but I refuse to let them fall. He has never spoken to me like this before and I'll admit, it's a shock to hear such things come from him. His hands roam all over my naked stomach, my tits are out and he doesn't even seem to notice them, too distracted by the sight of my bump. When he drops to his knees in front of me, I gasp. He rests his cheek against my stomach and butterflies in the form of baby kicks begin to war inside me. He pulls back and smiles up at me, this is the first time I have seen him smile like this and fuck me my heart does a flip inside my chest.

"They know their daddy's here," I say.

He swallows and frowns, I begin to worry that I said the wrong thing until he drops his gaze back to my stomach.

"I promise I'll be the best fucking dad, I'll never let anyone hurt our kids, Cassandra. I made sure that their futures would be protected. No one will ever harm our children. I know I'll be an over the top fucker and want them by my side all the time, but you have to bear with me because it is going to take me time to allow them out of my sight."

"Why?"

He takes a shuddering breath. "Because the moment my parents let me and Havoc out of their sight, my brother died." My heart melts, there is so much more to this man than he lets anyone see, I knew he had a heart buried beneath all that anger. I rest my hands on his shoulders and lower to my knees in front of him with the grace of a baby elephant.

"I'll be with you every step of the way, we will do this together."

"Promise me you will never leave and take my kids. I can't lose another person I love, promise me."

"I promise you," I say, meaning it with every beat of my heart. He closes the space between us and claims my lips, then kisses me with such passion I forget to breathe. I wrap my arms around his neck and hold him close, loving the fact there is no barrier between us anymore, our feelings for each other are out now.

Breaking the kiss, he climbs to his feet and offers me his hands, helping me to stand. "I can't imagine fucking you on the hardwood floor would be comfortable right now." I laugh and nod my head, grab his hand and lead him to my tiny bedroom. I release his hand as we enter and walk over to my modest double bed. I crawl up the bed, giving him an eyeful of my thong-covered ass, relishing in the pained groan that tears from him. I rest back against the pillows and spread my legs for him. "You going to be a good little whore and let me fuck you how I want?" A moan escapes me, I worried that he would stop calling me his little whore or telling me I'm his slut after professing his love, but it seems I had nothing to worry about.

"Yes."

He tosses his cap to the side and grips the back of his shirt, yanking it off and dropping it to the floor. Fuck, the sight of him shirtless has me growing wetter by the second. Stalking toward me, he stops at the edge of the bed, grips my ankles and pulls me down, until my ass balances on the edge. He forces my legs wider and dips his head, running his nose on the front of my panties, groaning.

"Fuck, you're soaked through."

"Hmmm."

"I can smell it," he growls as he licks me through the lace, making me arch off the bed.

"Fuck," I cry out when he does it again.

"This greedy little cunt wants my cock."

"Yes, I need it," I plead.

"Shut the fuck up, you get what I give you." I groan loving how he commands dominance in the bedroom and bends me to his will. He grips the sides of my thong and peels it down my legs. I hear him inhale and know without a doubt he's sniffing my soaked panties. He wastes no time, burying his face in my pussy, my back is arches off the bed as my legs clamp around his head and I cry out.

"Oh, fuck, yes," I scream when he pushes his tongue inside my tight, wet hole.

"Fuck, this rotten little pussy tastes so good," he rasps out before sucking my clit into his mouth. It's been so long since I've been touched, I know I'll only last a minute before I'm coming all over his face. The instant he pushes two fingers inside me, stretching me open and laps at my clit, I detonate.

"Chaos!" I scream his name so fucking loud I bet our neighbors can hear and I don't give a fuck. He doesn't bring me down gently, he stands and rids himself of his pants and boxers. He stands there and grips his cock in his hand, pumping it twice as I watch transfixed.

"Get on your knees like a good whore and suck my dick." I scramble to do as he says. Normally he would shove me to the ground and ram his cock down my throat, but this time, he waits for me to position myself comfortably on my knees before slapping his dick against my mouth. I open and try to shift my head so I can get him in my mouth but he keeps moving, drawing a growl from me. "Look at you being a greedy little slut."

I flick my gaze up to his. "Only for you." His eyes blaze at my words and he doesn't shift away from me when I open my mouth for him, then gag when he rams his cock down my throat. His hand tangles in my hair, holding me in place as he fucks my face, spit dripping down my chin in sync with the tears that fall from constantly gagging, but fuck I love this. I missed him using me and fucking me like a little whore.

"Fuck, yes, swallow me like that." I swallow around him and groan at the taste of his pre-cum coating the back of my throat. Before I can enjoy the taste of him any more, he yanks his cock out of my mouth and grips my arms, hauling me to my feet. He pushes me backward, using just enough force that I land on the bed. He looms over me, careful to keep his weight off my stomach as he stares into my eyes for a second, before claiming my mouth, the taste of both of us mingles and I moan. He pushes back so he rests on his knees between my legs, grips his cock and lines it up with my entrance. I wait for him to slam inside me as he always does but this time, he eases in slowly forcing me to feel every glorious inch of him as he pushes inside me. A fine sheen of sweat beads his brow as he stills inside me giving me a chance to adjust to his size. "I need to move," he grits out through clenched teeth.

"Move, please," I beg.

"I don't want to hurt the babies." The unease in his gaze astounds me, it clicks now. He didn't slam inside me because he was worried he would hurt them. I melt further into the mattress as my heart warms at his concern.

"You won't hurt them unless you push against my belly. I promise, they will be fine but I won't be if you don't start moving right this second!" His eyes narrow in warning, sending a delicious shiver down my spine. He swiftly reaches out and slaps my right breast, drawing a sharp cry from me.

"You better fucking mean it, if they get hurt your pussy won't see my cock until after they are born." I gape up at him.

"What the fuck?"

"Your pussy won't see any action but your ass will." The thought should have me disgusted and protesting but... "You want me to fuck your ass, don't you?" The breathy tone tells me he is pleased.

"I'm not opposed to the idea."

"You dirty little slut." He pulls almost all the way out, before slamming back inside me. I cry out at the feeling of him stretching my pussy wide open. "You gonna let me fuck your ass and come inside it like a whore?" He repeats the same movement but this time groans when my pussy clamps down on him, trying to keep him inside me.

"Yes, I'll let you come wherever the fuck you want, if you just keep fucking me." He slaps my other breast this time.

"You don't call the shots here, I do!" he growls before fucking me so hard and so deep I can't tell where he begins and I start. My orgasm crests and I can tell this one is going to be intense and without a doubt rip me apart. He lifts my legs and rests them against his shoulders giving him a deeper angle. I feel him stroking that sweet spot inside and without warning my orgasm slams into me. I scream his name as I come all over his dick. Aftershocks wrack my body as I claw at his arms, begging him to stop and telling him I can't handle another orgasm but he ignores me.

"I can't, too much," I cry I out as he continues to fuck me like a starved man.

"You can and you will," he forces past clenched teeth, then presses the pad of his thumb against my clit, applying the right amount of pressure to have another orgasm building inside me.

"Chaos!"

"Come with me, I need to feel your pussy strangling my cock." I moan in response, powerless to stop the impending orgasm cresting within me. "Come on my cock like a good little slut." His crass words are my destruction, I come so fucking hard I nearly pass out until I hear him roaring my name for the first time as he comes deep inside me. Both of us are breathless and panting, covered in sweat—we don't have an air con in the hut, only ceiling fans, which don't do shit to keep you cool.

"Fuck," I rasp out, panic flares to life in his eyes as he quickly pulls out of me and stands at the edge of the bed.

"Did I hurt them?" I press up to rest on my elbows and frown.

"What?"

"You said *fuck*."

I roll my eyes. "Yeah but it wasn't because you hurt me, I meant it as a good thing." The tension drains from his shoulders, now that he isn't inside me and some of the sexual tension has eased between us I begin to wonder, *did he mean everything he said*?

"I'm not staying here." His words are like a bucket of ice water being tipped on me. I shuffle into a sitting position suddenly feeling exposed and vulnerable.

"Oh, okay," I say quietly as I drop my gaze to the floor and try to shield my nakedness with my arms.

"The fuck are you doing?" he asks. I shake my head not trusting my voice. He grunts his displeasure and grips my chin, forcing my gaze to meet his. I bat his hand away and push to my feet, ready to escape him but he grips my wrist and hauls me back until I'm facing him. "Use your fucking words, woman."

*This motherfucker!*

"Just leave already," I shout.

He frowns clearly confused. "What?"

"You said you weren't staying, so just leave." The frown disappears and is replaced by an angry glint in his eyes. He shifts his hold and grips the back of my neck, forcing me to my tiptoes as he gets right in my face.

"Let me rephrase that then, when I said *I'm* not staying here, I meant you and I are both leaving." I feel my cheeks flame. "I am not going to spend the night fucking you while I sweat my ass off, so pack a bag. We'll spend the night at my hotel and then we're flying home tomorrow." I open my mouth but he pins me with a stern look. "I dare you to try to fucking argue with me and tell me your ass is staying here, go on, try it," he taunts.

"I really like it here," I tease, then squeal when he uses his free hand to slap my bare ass.

"And I really love being balls deep inside your little cunt. You have five minutes to pack... Keep me waiting and I'll fuck you in the cab on the way back to the hotel." And just like that, my pussy is fluttering and clenching on air at the thought of him fucking me again. I snatch my robe off the back of the door and turn to leave so I can get a bag from Tabby's room.

"Cass?" I pause in the doorway and peer back over shoulder at him, watching him stand there with just his shorts on and his cap clasped between his hands.

"Yeah?"

"I meant it, you know."

"Meant what?"

The left side of his mouth hitches in a half smile. "I meant it when I told you that I love you." Jesus Christ, my heart pounds against my rib cage as the love I feel for him bursts inside me.

"I hate you too." He laughs, the sound is so rich and additive I just know I will do anything to keep that sound coming from him.

"I hate you more, my rotten little apple, and I plan to show you just how much I hate you all night long."

"Promise?" I tease, his eyes darken as he takes a step toward me. I laugh as I dash into the next room.

"Start massaging your jaw, baby, it's a twenty minute ride back to the hotel and for that comment you'll spend the drive with my cock in your mouth."

# Epilogue

## CHAOS

### *Two months later...*

I smile at the sight of Cass trying to stand from her spot on the sofa. I remain where I am, leaning against the doorway watching her on struggle street. I would go help her but every time I try to help her stand or walk she loses her shit and yells at me, saying I'm only helping because I think she's fat! That is far fucking from it, the woman is blind if she can't see how fucking stunning she is. Every day I wake up and see her lying next to me with her big belly and I can't help but rub and kiss it. She tries to act annoyed that I greet the babies first in the morning before kissing her, but the look in her eyes tells me otherwise, she loves it.

"Chaos!" she shouts, I fight my smirk from breaking free and stroll into our living room. After we got back to the US we stayed with Royal and Erika for a couple weeks until we bought this place. She refused to move back into my other house that is now vacant since Lani chose to move to New York with my parents and raise Ryat there. That shit stung but I understood why she did it. She wants to raise Ryat in the city his father grew up in. Cass wants me to sell my *haunted house* as she calls it but I refuse, that place has the perfect set up in the basement for interrogation.

"You called?" I tease as I come to stand in front of her. She glares up at me and I roll my lips over my teeth to keep from smiling.

"I swear to fucking God I am going invent my own card and mark you with it so I can kill you once these two get the hell out of me." My laughter bursts out of me. Last week I came home to find hundreds of my calling card scattered throughout the house, when I eventually found Cass on the floor in the kitchen with a tub of ice cream and tears rolling down her cheeks and no idea what the fuck was going on, she screamed that I was marked and she was going to kill me because she can't even sneeze now without peeing herself. When I laughed, she threw the tub of ice cream at me and started explaining how she planned to kill me between sobs.

"I know, baby, I'm a bastard for putting my vile sperm inside you."

"I hate you," she snaps.

"I hate you too, now how about I help you up, then get you upstairs in the bath I just ran for you?" The anger evaporates from her eyes and tears begin to well inside them—fuck, she cries all the time now and I never know if they are good tears or bad. These pregnancy hormones are no fucking joke and keep me on edge all the fucking time. Sin even refuses to come over now, saying Cass scares the shit out of her, nothing scares that heartless bitch so you gotta know it's bad if Sin refuses to be near her.

"I want a shoulder rub while I'm in there," she demands.

I fight back the eye roll and smile. "Yes, dear."

"Don't fucking patronize me!" I drop my head back and stare up at the ceiling praying for calm.

"Fucking hell, woman, I'll rub your fucking shoulders and feet while you sit in the tub and when you're out, I'll bring the fucking tub of ice cream so you can sit in bed and watch reruns of

*Outlander*," I snap, then cringe and want to punch myself in the dick when she begins to cry. "Fuck." I grab her hands and haul her to her feet, pulling her against me as best I can thanks to her large bump.

"I'm sorry," she cries as she clutches my shirt in her hands and buries her face in my chest. "I don't mean to be a bitch but I can't help it."

"Apple, this is my karma for being a prick to you when we first met. You put up with my shit and now it's my turn to put up with yours." She sniffs and pulls back, looking up at me.

"Yeah, you were a dick to me." I smile and nod, choosing to keep my mouth shut while silently reminding myself that I love this woman and it would be wrong to strangle her! "I want my bath now."

"Yes, dear," I answer like the good little bitch boy I have become. The one bonus is that every night she takes out her anger on my cock and I make sure to wear her ass out until she is boneless and sated, so she passes out within minutes.

Now that Cass is set up in bed and happy with her ice cream, I FaceTime Royal and Sin from my office, unlike my last house this one is furnished. Erika and Cass had a blast taking my black card and buying everything they wanted for the house and nursery that is set up next to our room for the twins. Royal answers first, grinning from ear to ear, pulling a groan from me.

"Don't fucking say a word!" I warn him, making the bastard laugh just as Sin answers, she and Kacey now have their own house as well. Did I mention we bought houses on the same street as Royal?

"Oh, are you giving him shit about the twins being girls?" I groan and stare up at the ceiling.

"No, but since you brought it up," Royal says through his

laughter. "He finally got better and now he is going to go backward killing every fucker that looks at his daughters." The both of them laugh at my expense. I grit my teeth and count to ten. The parent books I've been reading say that you should count in your mind to give yourself a chance to calm down before approaching the situation.

"Can you two fucking focus?" I snarl, they both ignore me as they continue to laugh. Today is the last day I have free to go over the plans of the school before construction starts in the morning, so we need to get this shit done, but these fuckers don't seem to care.

"Bet you he wraps his dick from now on!" Royal wheezes out between fits of laughter. Cass didn't want to find out the sex of the babies until they were born but yesterday, when we went to her scan, I managed to bribe the woman to tell me and I made the mistake of telling these fucking idiots.

"Clearly his pull out game isn't strong," Chanel says before bursting out laughing again.

"Fuck you both. Royal has to deal with London getting a boyfriend before I have to worry about my girls." His laughter dies off immediately.

"Way to kill the fucking mood, asshole."

"Oh, so it's okay for you and Sin to make fun of me but not when I do it to you?"

"Exactly, it's only funny when it's at your expense, not mine!"

"Fuck off, Royal. Now, help me with this shit so I can send it to Costa, the fucker has been up my ass for the plans for over a week." We spend the next hour going over everything and all the details for the school. Each family was sent a list of names for staff for the school, but no one has been able to agree on a headmaster or headmistress as of yet, but Costa did put his eldest son forward for the role. The dorms will be coed, much to Royal and Uncle Rook's dismay. Uncle G didn't seem too worried about it, saying his daughter hates boys and he hopes to keep it that way, but Knox argued that keeping the dorms separate would come across as segregation as most families only choose to allow the boys to lead and not the girls.

"How long before it will be open and running?" Sin asks.

"Even with the amount of contractors we have hired, it will still be at least two years, three max," I answer. Royal sighs and scrubs a hand down his face looking tired. With Cass being so close to giving birth, I have taken to hacking and tracking for Sin and Royal while they do the hands on shit with cunts that are trying to test us. We knew many would try to come for us, given how new we are, and each time we show them that we are ready and end each of the bastards.

"London will be thirteen, let's hope by then she has changed her mind and given up on the idea of blowing up the school." I snort out a laugh, earning a glare. "If she blows up that school with Costa's kids in there, the Greeks will be coming for us!"

"I know, let's just hope she doesn't kill the *white rabbit* and get initiated into their secret society," I joke but Royal pales.

"Not funny. If that shit was to happen, I wouldn't be able to help her. She would have to face the trials alone and I couldn't handle that shit." We have learned recently that the Greeks initiate their members by sending them on a hunt. They don't kill their snitches, they lock them up until it's initiation time and implant a chip into one of them then set them free. The one that finds the *white rabbit* is the one that is initiated to lead the Greeks—the last person to find and kill the *white rabbit* was Costa's son at the age of eighteen, he is the youngest in the Greek history to ever kill the rabbit. Artemis is the apple of his father's eye and so are his four brothers.

"Chaos!" At the sound of the panicked scream from Cass, I'm on my feet and racing out of my office. I barge into our room with my gun drawn looking for whoever the fuck scared her, but when my gaze lands on her, I begin to hyperventilate at the sight of her pants soaking wet. "I think my water just broke."

# LONDON...

I refuse to go back to that godforsaken school; he can't make me!

All those pussies do is moan and drone on and on about how much money they fucking have. I have spent three fucking years there, I'm eighteen, I should be able to make my own choices now, but my father won't let me. If I drop out, the rules of the families state I can never take over for my dad. I am his only heir—he and Mom have been trying for a child for years. She has suffered many losses and Dad refuses to keep putting her through the pain of more miscarriages. I know my birth will be a factor in other families protesting me taking over the *Memento Mori and the Murdoch mafia*, but I am a Murdoch and have been since I was ten years old.

Royal and Erika Murdoch are my parents, maybe not by blood but in every way that counts they are.

"London!" I cringe and turn away from the TV in the in the living room to see my dad standing in the doorway, looking pissed the fuck off. At nearly twenty-nine years old, the guy still looks good, but I would never tell him that. He likes to fuck with my grandpa and call him old, so I help my grandpa out by giving his son shit about looking old.

"Yeah?"

His pale blue eyes burn with rage. "Why the fuck did another headmaster just hand in their resignation?"

I balk and place my hand over my heart batting my lashes. "Daddy, how could you think I had anything to do with Mrs. Thompson quitting–"

"Cut the shit, she said she refused to continue working at Blackwood Academy as long as you were a student there."

I manage to catch myself before I roll my eyes. The old hag was too uptight and constantly had me in detention after school, so I may or may not have played a little prank on her.

"Well, simple then, I quit and she can have her job back."

"You are not dropping out!" he shouts, now I do roll my eyes. He should know by now that him yelling at me never gets him anywhere. All it does is piss me the fuck off and force me to fuck with him, like right now. As soon as he leaves to go find Mom so she can *talk sense* into me, I plan to take his new G-Wagon for a joy ride.

"Why the hell not? Who are those old bastards to tell me that I have to attend a fucking school I hate?" I never went to a normal school growing up, I refused so my mom homeschooled me and I passed with flying colors.

"They are the heads of each fucking country, your grandfather happens to be one of the people who voted yes for the school. Why don't you call him and scream at him while I go find your bloody mother to talk some damn sense into you." I smirk when he turns his back and mumbles how much he hates that I'm exactly like him. The second the coast is clear, I dash out of the living room and snag his keys off the counter, then run out the front door. Climbing behind the wheel of his car, I don't fuck around, starting the beast and burning rubber as I floor it out of the driveaway.

*Two minutes.*

I count the time in my head as I race down the street passing by Aunt Nelly's and Uncle Chaos's houses. I make it half a block away before my phone rings. I answer on the second ring and place it on speaker.

"Hey, Dad."

"You little shit! Bring my fucking car back here now."

"What? You're cutting out, Dad, it's really bad service," I lie.

"London, I am–"

"*Warning you*," I say, mocking him.

"Erika!" he screams for my mom as I fight back laughter. I round the corner and jerk the wheel to the right when someone runs out in front of me. I'm too late, screaming when I feel the person hit the front of the truck. That isn't the worst part. When I feel the tire roll of the guy's body, I know without a doubt I just killed him. I slam the car in park and jump out, racing around the back of the truck—the sight of the guy's mangled body has bile rushing up my throat. This is so fucking inconvenient and is going to delay my plans from going to pay that bitch Mrs Thompson a visit for ratting on me.

"Fuck!" I shout. I look around, trying to find someone to help but the dark street is empty, the only lighting from the street lamps. I hedge toward the guy and stop a couple steps away, leaning forward to get a better look. Eww, the vacant look in his eyes is gross.

"Who the fuck are you?" I spin around to find three guys around my age standing behind me, they each hold a Glock and immediately I'm on high alert—fuck, I left my phone in the car!

"Who the hell are you?" I snap, making sure to stomp my foot like a petulant child, I feel my knife in my boot and relax. Dad says never bring a knife to a gun fight but believe me, these fuckers have no idea who I am and how good I am at wielding a blade.

The boy on the left peers around me at the body on the ground. "Ares, she killed the rabbit." I frown and look back to make sure it was a person I hit and not a fucking bunny.

"No fucking way." The one on the right says as he steps forward to get a better look.

"Ares, he's right, she did kill the rabbit." The one in the middle says. Ares (the guy just called him that) eyes me warily.

"Apollo, get back here," Ares snaps. The three of them stand there eyeing me with accusation in their gazes. "I'm Ares, these are my brothers Apollo and Adonis."

"Cool, how the hell do you know him?" I ask, jabbing a finger over my shoulder toward the body. I play this whole thing cool trying to gauge their reactions, we already have one dead body here, I would fucking hate to have three more to clean up if they felt they need to strike out.

"He was ours to capture, we were supposed to be initiated but you claimed that right."

"What?" When headlights shine toward us, the three of them turn ready to flee. Fuck, I have no doubt that's my dad and his men and I am so going to be in shit for this.

"See you soon, goddess," Apollo says before he races after his brothers. Three cars come to a screeching halt and within seconds my dad is in front of me checking me for injury.

"Are you okay?"

"Yeah, I'm okay," I answer.

"What the fuck happened, London? Marco, check him for a pulse and ID," Dad barks.

"Dad, he came out of nowhere and ran in front of the car, I didn't see him! You can't blame me for his stupidity, the dude ran in front of my car, like come on it's not my fault he wanted to die!"

"Boss." Dad darts his gaze over my head.

"What is it Marco?" Dad snaps.

"No ID but he has a brand on his neck." At the somber tone of Marco's voice, I turn around and find him looking panicked.

"Show me," Dad growls as he steps around me to inspect the body. Marco tilts the guy's head to show my dad the brand on his neck. I can't see it clearly from where I stand and I don't want to get closer and risk my dad focusing on me. "Get rid of the body and clean the scene now," Dad barks, all the men rush to do as their told.

"Dad?" I ask, suddenly feeling the shift in his mood from anger to worry.

"Get rid of the car and scrub any video evidence. I want no witnesses—"

"Too late," I mutter drawing their attention to me.

"What do you mean?" Dad clips out.

"Three guys, their names were Apollo, Ares and Adonis were here, they took off when they saw your lights."

"Fuck!" he roars.

"Dad, what the hell is going on?" I shout, getting pissed off that they all know something I don't!

"The guy you just killed was marked by the Greeks. I allowed Costa to host his hunt here as a show of goodwill because of all the trouble you are causing at Blackwood."

I shake my head not following what he is saying. "What does that mean?" I shout.

"It means you just killed the fucking *white rabbit*! The Greeks are beholden to their laws, London, they will come for you!"

"So fucking let them come for me, I'll run their asses down too!" I rush to say.

He shakes his head and pins me with a stern look. "You don't understand what the fuck you have just done!" He roars.

"Don't understand what?" I scream.

"A new headmaster has been appointed, Artemis Argyros."

"I don't know him," I say.

"You're about to. He's the son of Costa Argyros, the leader of the Greeks. We need to meet with them now before Artemis comes for you. The school is the first place he will look for you and if he can't find you, he'll send the fucking triplets you just met after you. I'd kill them all if I could, but I can't."

"Dad, what's going to happen to me?" I whisper, the fear in his eyes has me suddenly feeling like this is a huge deal and this wasn't just some random guy I ran down.

"If I can't work something with Costa, you will be forced to go through a series of trials to be initiated into the *God Father's Of The Night*, it's a secret society led by Costa's son, Artemis."

I shake my head. "No, I'll kill them all," I say with conviction.

"London, Artemis was trained from birth the same way me and your aunts and uncles were. To hunt, track, kill—you name it, he can do it. There is no escaping him if he comes and we'll

wage a war against them if we have to, because I won't allow them
to take my daughter from me."

"But, if you go to war with the Greeks, that means the end of
the peace treaty you worked so hard for."

"Then let's hope I can con my dad into backing me when I
meet with Costa to try to right this wrong."

*I have a sinking feeling it's already too late. They know what I
did and they will come for me... Well, guess what motherfuckers, I'll
be ready and waiting for you to try take me out.*

***Pre Order London's book now...***
https://mybook.to/Londonhasfallen

## THANK YOU!

Where the fuck do I begin?
I guess I have to thank the OG. Bishop Murdoch started this entire journey and it's because of him we now have this next generation.
Aside from him, I have to thank YOU!
Without you reading this series and loving it, I wouldn't be able to do what I do and bring these characters to life. This *Memento Mori* series means the fucking world to me and I am shattered that it has come to an end. I was so upset over having to say goodbye to them and the OG's that I had to create a spin off series, *The Godfather's Of The Night*!
You guessed it, the FMC will be none other than our crazy ass London Murdoch!

From the bottom of my heart I just want to say thank you for taking a chance on this unknown author from South Auckland, New Zealand.

# ALSO BY SAMANTHA BARRETT

## PARANORMAL ROMANCE

### **The Dream Series**

A Beautiful Dream

A Twisted Fate

A Beautiful Nightmare

Redemption

Anarchy

### **Brutal Savages**

Savage Lies

Brutal Truth

Savage Beast

Brutal Beauty

## MAFIA ROMANCE

### **Murdoch Mafia Series**

Played By The Bishop

Tormented By The King

Tortured By The Knight

Tempted By The Queen

Turned By The Pawn

Ruined By The Rook

**<u>Murdoch Mafia Novella</u>**

Stalemate

**<u>Memento Mori Series</u>**

Reign Of Royal

Broken By Sin

In Havoc Lays Chaos

**<u>Godfather's Of The Night</u>**

<u>London Has Fallen</u>

**<u>Fairytales With A Twist</u>**

Condemned Beast

# Sports Romance

**<u>Playing For Keeps</u>**

Offside

Touchdown

End Game

Hail Mary

Blindside

# RH Sports

Hate Us Like You Mean It

Love Me Like You Mean It

# ACKNOWLEDGMENTS

Marcus, my dirty little toy, my bed warmer, my gangster that fucks me like a starved man. I can't thank you enough for allowing me to treat you like my little whore as I wrote these books so I could get in the head space for Chaos, you're the real MVP my man!

Leah-*motherfucking*-Maree, WE DID IT! We fucking made it, babe—15 books were written in a year, 15 covers were made and graphics. You, my dark little angel, are everything, I couldn't have done any of this without you, babe. From the bottom of my dead heart, I thank you!

Jaye-*fucking*-Pratt, bitch I love ya! You held my hand through all of this and swear to God, I don't think I could have finished this series without you. Thank you will never be enough for all that you have done for me.

My demons, fuck, I love you both more than I ever thought would be possible. You two inspire my inner gangster and give me the courage to write these torture scenes when you two fight and scream at each other. Never change who you are to fit in, the world can change to fit with you. I love you to the fucking moon and back.

My alpha's, Debbie, Clare and Sarah, you ladies have no idea how much I love you, these books would not be what they are without you. Each of you plays a role in keeping me on track and pushing forward, without my Three Musketeers none of these books would be here, thank you my loves.

My Army & my beta girls, you ladies are the core of this whole book journey, without your hype, love and constant support I don't think I would be where I am today. I love each of you so fucking much for all you have done and continue to do for me.

Lizz, my dear friend, you are amazing, not only do you edit each of these books but you also help me with each story and constantly hype me and push me to continue on the path I am. I know for a fucking fact I would not have reached my goal of publishing a book a month for a full calendar year without you. This one is for you my friend, it seemed only fitting as we started the OG's together and now, we end it with Chaos together.

My darling dark delicious readers, you are the most amazing bunch of humans I have ever had the chance to interact with and also be able to meet some of you has been the highlight of my year. Thank you so much for taking a chance, reading these crazy motherfuckers and loving them as much as I do.

Sam xxx

# About the Author

Samantha Barrett is a dark romance, PNR author who loves to write out-of-the-box stories. She is originally from the land of the long white cloud, New Zealand. She is totally fluking her way through this whole author gig, if she isn't writing you can find her kicking back with her kids and husband with a bag of chips and a glass of wine in her hand.

Sam loves Twilight and is a TWIHARD proudly.